Shadows
in the Grass

Shadows
in the Grass

Rose Senehi

Writer's Showcase
San Jose New York Lincoln Shanghai

Shadows in the Grass

Writer's Showcase
an imprint of iUniverse.com, Inc.

For information address:
iUniverse.com, Inc.
5220 S 16th, Ste. 200
Lincoln, NE 68512
www.iuniverse.com

ISBN: 0-595-18224-0

Printed in the United States of America

For Jessica and David

ACKNOWLEDGEMENTS

Joanne Goldy, for hours of reading and rereading my manuscript and all her astute suggestions. To Helen Beale, Liz Grabosky, Helen Tuck and Sean Byrne, loyal friends who let me bounce ideas off them. To my agent, Howard Pelham and his associate, Jim Meals, who took the time and effort to guide me during the two years it took to write *Shadows in the Grass*. And to all my friends at the Dieter Company in Pawleys Island, S.C. who have read, and continue to read, my manuscripts.

PROLOGUE

Marylou Cramer pedaled joyously, the crisp spring breeze rushing through her hair. She threw her head back, closed her eyes and stood motionless on the pedals as she sailed around the bend in the road, breathing in the rich perfume of the Norway spruce forest.

This part of the trip was cooler with little light making its way through the thick woods on either side of the road.

She had promised her mother, busy in her father's country church, that she'd call her grandmother before she left, but the line had been busy. After two tries, the ten-year-old had put her *A* paper in the envelope she'd dug out of her father's wastepaper basket and taken off on her bike.

Now sitting comfortably, she leisurely looked around as she pedaled to an easy rhythm and looked forward to seeing her grandmother's house at the end of the dark stretch.

A beat-up white van appeared from around the curve and crept up behind her. Marylou quickly glanced over her shoulder and the queer expression on the face of the man behind the wheel made her uneasy. Why would this stranger smile at her that way? She pedaled faster.

The van pulled up alongside, and another quick glance caused the girl to lose her balance. Barely able to keep the bike on the asphalt, when the van edged closer she swerved and the wheels bounced onto the gravel shoulder.

Pedaling feverishly on the washboard of a surface, she fought desperately to steady the bike, the envelope flaying in the wind. When the van came close enough to touch the pink streamers trailing from the handle grips, she panicked and in one horrible split-second was slammed into the culvert below.

Marylou froze with her eyes fixed on the underside of the motionless van. Not breathing, she watched in terror as two feet dropped to the ground and ran toward the front. She sprang up and raced along the culvert, clutching the envelope with an iron grip. Heavy footsteps splashed in the wet ditch behind her. Franticly pawing her way out of the steep culvert, a brutish arm grabbed her around the waist. Kicking wildly, her arms hopelessly tried to scratch him as he ran with her to the van.

The man held her tight to his body while he opened the door, sending the sound of rusty hinges echoing through the wooded cavern. As she was being thrown inside, the sight of the manila envelope being blown along the road made her burst into tears.

Cowering against a wall, she watched a chain being taken from a bucket. Mercifully, the door slammed shut and the strange look on Gary Snyder's face disappeared.

The van jerked forward and Marylou skidded to the back, knocking against trash and tools. Her raw, burning hands franticly searched for a door handle. But when she tried to throw open the two doors all she saw was the chain strung between them with the asphalt road zooming by below.

The sight of her grandmother's house through the gap sent an ugly message to her brain, like she would never see it again. She yanked violently at the doors, and then with her face pressed between the gap, cried heart-brokenly as the house faded from view.

Gary Snyder's eyes nervously scanned both sides of the road looking for a deserted driveway he could pull onto. Any minute somebody was going to be coming up behind them and the little bitch's screams would be heard. Through squinted eyes, he spotted a clearing in the woods ahead and slowed down.

The overgrown roadway could barely be made out but it was high and dry. In moments, the van was swallowed up in the dense forest.

When the van stopped, Marylou's heart thumped in her parched throat. First, she heard the sound of the door opening on the driver's side, then the clanking of chain against metal. She forced herself to breathe as she spread her arms against the walls of the van. Her ears rang.

When the door opened, the pungent smell of his sweat pierced her nostrils as he crawled toward her. Her muscles were tense and stiff as he pulled her down.

She could hear the strange sound of an owl fluttering and hooting in the distance, then the more peaceful songs of sparrows. She floated from the dark cavern up among the trees and listened to the birds' sweet songs. She thought of her beloved parents and felt deep sorrow that she would never see the delight on her grandmother's face at the sight of the big red A.

She felt the tightening around her throat. Grasping for air, she began to struggle, then slowly relaxed until her breathing stopped and there was only the sound of the birds.

CHAPTER 1

With her typical long strides, Lynn Richardson traversed the hundred yards or so from the mailbox to the front porch of the old farmhouse with her dog Lucky trailing behind. When she hit the top step she stopped and eyed the patchwork of newly plowed fields surrounding the farm. A warm breeze ruffled her cropped hair.

Lynn glanced at the clock as she entered the kitchen. Not even noon. Her nine-year-old son, Jess, wouldn't be getting off the school bus until three. She sat down at the kitchen table and continued inserting seeds into packets. Twenty-five seeds in each envelope, then a label carefully folded over the top and stapled twice. She was careful to make sure each and every one looked crisp.

She lovingly smoothed out the image of a cottage garden imprinted on the subtle brown paper, and could still hear her husband's soft, confident chuckle when she had announced the name of her business: Richardson's Herbs & Seeds.

"That'll get 'em," he had said. "They'll all say we couldn't make any money farming so we turned to selling weeds and their seeds."

But Lynn knew it had made him proud by the way he'd leaned way back in the kitchen chair with arms folded behind his head, legs crossed at the ankles, and the usual thick shock of blond hair lying across his forehead.

Then her body yearned for the man she fell in love with the instant he walked into the noisy, smoke-filled college hang-out, a thirty-year-old hunk of a farmer come to town to find himself a girl.

A scream started to race upward from the pit of her stomach, but she took a deep breath and gulped it back. Tears streamed down her cheeks as she pictured Ken after the tractor was lifted from his still body.

Everyone figured she'd sell the farm and leave, but she was still there.

As Lynn stared out the picture-window thinking of those painful days, she noticed Shelly Ferguson, her old college roommate, coming over the hill in her new car. Suppressing a strong impulse to run upstairs and hide, Lynn quickly rinsed her tear-streaked face, patted it dry, then managed to flash her broad grin and wave as Shelly pulled in and got out a basket from the trunk of her Porche.

"We're going to have lunch," Shelly breezily announced as she flounced through the kitchen doorway.

"I love your car," Lynn said as she helped unpack the basket.

"Marry a dentist and you *too* can have one."

In an effort to skirt the marriage issue, Lynn squealed "My favorite!" as she discovered the paté. Ever since the one-year anniversary of the accident, the importance of finding another mate was the object lesson of every one of Shelly's visits. Lynn had even caught her trying to peddle the concept to Jess.

The two women were total opposites. Food. That was the one thing they had in common since their popcorn and pizza bingeing days at school. But their bond was final. A simple fact they both accepted. None of Shelly's frank statements ever hurt Lynn. In fact, she generally liked to examine viewpoints different from her own. As for Shelly, Lynn was the only person she felt truly comfortable with. She could be outspoken, her natural character, without fear of repercussions.

The women voraciously dug into the lunch and were a picture of compatible contrasts with one in plaid shirt and jeans and the other in a Channel-styled suit.

"So what are you going to do?" Shelly asked as she tossed her long hair back.

"Do?"

"Come on. You know what I'm talking about. You can't hide out here forever. You've got to be running out of money."

Lynn sat with her elbows on the table chewing on a celery stick. "The farmers' markets will be starting up strong in a few weeks."

"Give me a break! How much do you make at those things? Fifty bucks?"

"Don't knock it. Weeks I do three markets I can take in five hundred dollars." Lynn reached for a napkin and wiped her hands as if that sum made a big dent in her bills. Casually, she added, "I should sell a lot of perennials right here at the farm this coming season. Last year I sold over five thousand dollars worth."

Shelly rolled her eyes toward the ceiling. "Good Lord, Lynn, what are you thinking? You can't live on that kind of money." Exasperated, she dropped her fork on her plate.

Shelly pushed her chair back, then went over and started washing her hands in the sink, taking care not to let the water splash on her silk blouse. "Look around you. I know you've done a lot, Lynn, but this place is a dump." Wiping her hands on a towel, she said, "If you sell the farm, you can get a nice little house in Eastlake. Pete said he'd give you a job as his receptionist. You'd get insurance, retirement. You'd be set."

Shelly was obviously just getting rolling, so Lynn absent-mindedly reached for another piece of celery. She almost sighed with relief that she hadn't told Shelly about the calls from a realtor whose client was interested in buying the farm.

"God, Lynn. You're thirty-one. Your whole life's ahead of you. You'll rot in this place. Besides, you and Jess living out here all alone just isn't safe. You heard about that little girl in Cortland." She shuddered, "I can just imagine what might have happened to her." Shelly walked over to Lynn and put an arm around her shoulder. "Honey, I know you want to keep the farm because of Ken. But he's gone. His parents are gone. What's the point?"

Lynn felt frustrated because there was no way she could ever explain to Shelly why she was determined to hang on, and the enormity of her emotions made her feel like she was tied in knots.

"Shelly, this farm's been in the Richardson family for four generation. You know how Ken felt about passing it on to Jess."

"For Christ's sake, Lynn, you can't spend the rest of your life living someone else's dream!"

"Keeping this place is my dream too. I never really belonged anywhere until I came here."

Lynn got up and topped off her coffee. "You got to know what my mother was like before she died. She lived from one alimony check to the next, then in a matter of days blew the money on clothes we couldn't afford. We got kicked out of every apartment we ever lived in."

Lynn wanted to change the subject. She had determined years ago to put her unhappy youth as an only child of a loving, but otherwise totally unreliable mother behind her.

"Shelly, don't be so damn negative. Why so much doom and gloom for Pete's sake. I've got fourteen shops selling my seeds now and my mail-order business is taking off." Lynn proudly tossed her four-page spring price list toward Shelly. "The Smith girl will be home from college in a few weeks and she's promised to work for me again. Cal Wilkinson's a big help too, and so is Jess."

Lynn went over to the window and pulled her collar tight around her neck and looked out at the hay meadow that was just starting to turn green. "Next week I've got an appointment to talk with a buyer at Farmway. If I can only land some shelf space in their Central New York farm stores…" She bit her lower lip and gazed out on the field without really seeing it. "…I'd be all set then."

After a moment, Lynn turned around, slid down onto the sill and hugged herself. The confidence was gone, replaced with a vulnerability she would only reveal to her old friend. She pleaded, "Please don't sell me short, Shelly. I need *somebody* on my side."

Lynn leaned forward, rested her forearms on her legs and stared at the floor. Finally, she looked up, and with one eyebrow raised, said thoughtfully, "I've got something going here, Shelly... and if I let it go, I don't think I'll ever get it back."

Shelly crossed her arms and looked hard into Lynn's eyes for a moment. The intensity of Lynn's gaze, like someone who was desperately searching for something, had been there ever since she walked into their freshman dorm room clutching two shopping bags and a beat-up suitcase. Shelly knew Lynn had caught a glimpse of what she'd been looking for all her life when she married Ken and ran headlong into a world she knew nothing of. Shelly also knew that there was something indomitable about Lynn's spirit and it frightened her. This intensity made Lynn vulnerable.

Shelly stood up, gathered her utensils and tossed them into the basket. "You're too much," she said, shaking her head. Then, her voice softening, she walked over to Lynn and ran her velvety, manicured hand down her friend's face. "I can't help myself, Lynn. I've got so much. When I think of you out here in the middle of nowhere with that little boy of yours, burning wood and living from hand to mouth, my heart breaks."

Lynn, not wanting their visit to end on such a down note, let out a warm, rippling laugh. "You're so dramatic, Shelly." She stood upright and threw her arms open. "Look at me. I'm not withering away." Then she took a deep breath, threw out her chest, and with her hand on her hip, whispered suggestively, "And lifting all that firewood hasn't done my figure any harm either."

"You're hopeless. I'm going."

As Lynn watched the Porche pull out of the driveway with Lucky barking after it, her confidence evaporated. She turned and looked around the kitchen that had somehow suddenly turned shabby. The teakettle got swiftly filled with water and slapped on the burner; then she sat down at the desk and pulled out her worksheet.

Shelly was right. No matter how many times she went over the figures, fifteen thousand was all she could come up with. If she sold every last mature perennial in the cold frames and garden as well as every seed packet, maybe she'd make around seventeen. But not one dime more. Her eyes skipped down the columns. There was no way Robin Smith would work for less than she could make at the grocery store.

Then there were the "what ifs." What if she *did* get the shelf space at the Farmway stores and for some unknown reason her packets went like hotcakes and she couldn't supply them? What if something happened to her next year's crop of perennials, now small seedlings in the greenhouse? Her heart started to beat in her throat. What if the truck needed an expensive repair? Don't panic. Take one step at a time, she told herself as she got up and made a cup of her own chamomile tea.

As was her habit, she strolled with cup in hand through the downstairs rooms, darkened now that the sun was on the other side of the house. She groaned when she looked at the massive dining room table she now used as the headquarters for her mail-order business. Her cat, Queenie, stiffly rose from the settee in the parlor and stretched.

There was so much Lynn wanted to do. For the umpteenth time she leaned back against the wall and went through her dreams for restoring the huge rooms filled with antiques. Would she in her lifetime be able to complete the task, she wondered as the cat rubbed against her jeans.

She went over to the fireplace and straightened the framed 1826 document from the Holland Land Company that deeded the farm to the Richardsons. As her eyes traced the elaborate handwriting, she recalled old Cale and Emma Richardson welcoming her into their home after she and Ken got married, convinced that she was the one who would eventually bear them a grandson and the Richardson farm would pass into the hands of a fifth generation.

Lynn was now the guardian of this piece of earth and the only one left to make sure it went to her son, Jess. She had bought into this dream with her whole heart and wasn't about to let it go.

Back at her desk, she made up her mind she would just *have* to make it through to next spring, and abruptly shoved her worksheets back under the blotter. All her life she'd run away from her fears with work. And ever since Ken's accident she'd worked so hard she sometimes couldn't remember why she was working. This was a habit since childhood. A way to escape to a safe, thoughtless place in her mind.

The mail was quickly skimmed over and separated. Then as she started to toss the newspaper into the kindling box, the picture on the front page jumped out at her. Slowly, she sank into her chair and read. Two days ago little Marylou Cramer disappeared while bicycling to her grandmother's house on a sparsely populated country road. Hundreds were searching the countryside and creeks. Her parents were imploring anyone who might have seen anything or might know anything to contact the State Troopers.

That was two counties over, an hour's drive at the least, Lynn thought as she put the paper down and hugged herself, a shiver suddenly racing through her.

CHAPTER 2

Instinctively, Gary Snyder rolled down the window to let in some of the sweet spring air that lingers in open country like Oneida County, New York. But all he got was a lung-full of exhaust as the rust-bucket of a van chugged up the winding ribbon of road.

Oily tools clinked against the empty cans rolling around in the back, and months of ignored mail lay on the seat and spilled onto the floor. The man reached over and pawed through the papers on the front seat for his pack of Marlboros. He shifted his eyes off the road to quickly scan the cluttered seat, when the picture of the missing little girl with long chestnut-brown hair caught his eye as she solemnly stared from the front page of the Cortland *Democrat*.

The van swerved as it started down Richardson Hill, but he pulled it out before he reached Lynn Richardson standing on the side of the road. Lynn didn't notice this event as she intently shuffled through her mail, however unhealthy looking beads of sweat started to pour off the man's face.

A feeling that he was about to be grabbed from behind crept over him. Time was running out. He was going to have to move on.

Just over the next hill, the van took a left onto Swamp School Road and got a pounding from the gravel roadway for a mile until it hit the Mile Strip and took another left. A few hundred yards beyond, the van turned into a narrow dirt driveway spilling out from a bramble-entangled row of huge old maples.

After rolling to a stop, Gary Snyder sat there for a moment listening to the crackling sounds of contracting metal on the van's underbelly. Montana would be too dangerous, he thought, even though he knew the ropes. Maybe he should find a place somewhere in the South.

The grim sight of rusted auto parts scattered among the abandoned farm equipment made him angry. These relics of his and his parents' past efforts at trying to make some kind of a life for themselves brought back too many humiliating defeats. Suddenly he pounded on the steering wheel, causing the pack of Marlboros to bounce around on the dashboard.

When he finally lifted his head, his eyes traced the lush rolling hills beyond that backed up to the Richardson's two-hundred-acre spread. Then he glanced over at the house he was born in, something in its day, two or three generations back, but now bare of paint with missing shutters and nothing but torn shades at the windows.

The bag of groceries was grudgingly retrieved from the back and he made his way to the house with the paper under his arm.

Gary Snyder, at forty-three, looked sixty. A sallow spent sixty at that. The doughy flesh hanging on his six-foot-five frame was the obvious result of years of just existing with no order to his life.

No one knew where he'd been since he ran off in the seventies, leaving his mother to slug it out alone with his drunk of a father. But now that both parents were dead he was back on the farm. When short on cash he worked at planking lumber in the family's small saw mill that neighboring farmers sarcastically referred to as the Thick and Thin Lumber Company.

Gary was used to much worse than sarcasm. Painfully, he remembered his mother's hopeful eyes as she dressed him in his best T-shirt and jeans for his first day at school, and how she tugged at her worn clothes in embarrassment when the kids stared down at both of them from the school bus windows. Before that day was over he understood he was one of the "dirts" the kids from prosperous farms and the village of Eastlake called someone like him.

Eastlake would never have existed at all if not for its alpine lake, which the wealthy from Syracuse surrounded with summer estates at the turn of the century. Eventually these homes, with their long sweeping lawns for croquet and promenading, became permanent. Eastlake's shops and businesses prospered, catering to the rich as well as the comfortable middle-class that settled in the village proper.

However, in the sixties when the schools were centralized and the district started busing in kids from all the farms around, it was like Oliver Twist meets Little Lord Fauntleroy. The daily impact of the "have nots" rubbing elbows with the "haves" only served to deepen any wounds these children already suffered at home.

Gary Snyder had been such a child. He had loved his mother and hated her at the same time. The only comfort he ever knew was when she wrapped her work-worn arms around him and held him next to her warm body. But when the strange men came to the house with a bottle of rye whiskey for his father and took Gary to the shed out back, he hated her for just cowering in the corner, afraid of getting another pounding.

Every time the ugly memories of what happened to him in that dark shed exploded in his head, he seethed with hate for his mother, remembering with bitterness the throbbing soreness, and how she'd promise never to let that happen to him again.

The screen door slammed shut as he started for the barn. Birds were trilling and a warm breeze carried the scent from the field of daffodils in the woods beyond. The rusted hinges screeched as he opened the side door. Darkness and musty-smelling air enveloped him as he went inside. The ancient workbench stood in the center and the long, narrow bundle lay on top.

CHAPTER 3

The thumping in Lynn's chest woke her. She crept out of bed, pulled back the curtain and pointed the flashlight at the thermometer just outside the window. Just as she feared: below freezing. She pressed her forehead against the icy glass, looked out into the freezing night and worried about the seedlings. In minutes she was in the kitchen slipping on her boots and barn-jacket while Lucky stood at attention in the dark.

"Come on, boy. Let's check out the greenhouse."

The two moved stealthily across the frost-laden lawn with the full moon casting their shadows in the grass, like silent messengers in the dark. The minute the greenhouse door opened, Lynn breathed more freely as she felt the heat on her face. Then the overhead space heater kicked on, reassuring her that the plants would be all right for the night. She didn't bother to turn on the light, just reached down and ran her hand over the dog's furry forehead. "Everything's okay, boy. Let's go back."

Several hours later, she pulled her knees up close to her chest, careful not to shift from the warm spot underneath, and slipped down under the blankets. Finally, she peeked out and glanced up. The red glow of the clock confirmed it was past five. The wood stove needed to be tended before she woke Jess.

As her sock-clad feet hit the cold wood floor, she reached for a quilt and quickly ran down the back staircase into the kitchen. Lucky was standing next to the door whimpering, so she let him out and waited for Queenie to jump from the porch railing and come in. The cat ran to its dish in the corner as Lynn went over to the wood-burning stove, flipped the lever on the chimney flue, and opened the door.

Crackling sparks shot up the minute the air rushed past the huge chunks of red-hot cherry wood in the stove's belly. Shivering, Lynn pulled a stool in front of the fire, wrapped the quilt around herself Indian-style, and sat down. Soon the lingering odor of age that took over the house in the night would start to dissipate. When she placed two maple logs on the fire, they instantly exploded into flames, causing her shadow to dance eerily around the room.

Outside, the horizon was nothing more than a thin pink line. Lynn figured it was now six. Since moving to the farm, she had learned to tell time by the sun and predict the weather by the signs in the sky. Today would be cloudless, and from the sounds and feel of the morning, sunny and warm by noon.

The sudden sharp trilling of a bird startled her. Then, for no apparent reason she felt hopeful, as if the day would bring something good. Possibly the nature all around her gave the assurance that life goes on. Then, as she started to look down at the cat that was nudging her to be petted, she noticed Jess standing in the doorway half-awake. Lynn opened her arms. A broad smile flashed across the boy's face as he sprinted and jumped into his mother's lap. She lovingly caressed him with the blanket, and buried her nose in his soft blond hair, recalling that it smelled just like Ken's.

After the school bus pulled away, Lynn walked with her coffee to the greenhouse with Lucky following behind. When the door slammed behind her, she stood carefully scanning the rows of plants, not missing a detail. She could almost hear them growing. She hugged herself and a soft laugh trickled out as she realized the irony of her situation. Not only did she belong, but also the whole Richardson legacy was depending on her and her seedlings, all five thousand of them.

This mood didn't last long as the possibility of letting everyone down edged into her brain. But she quickly shook off the feeling of impending doom that perpetually dogged her and got busy.

She turned the sprinkler on the first four rows, then went over to the Shasta Daisies. Their dark green jagged leaves looked strong. What a glorious plant she thought, perfect for the first-time gardener since it would survive just about any abuse and then forgivingly put on a big show.

As she made her way down a row picking off vagrant shoots, Lucky feverishly nosed the door open and headed straight for the road, barking non-stop. A pick-up had turned into the driveway and two county trucks had pulled to the side. Deciding to see what was going on, as she approached, one man was uprooting her mailbox across the road and another boring into a big old maple with a chainsaw.

A man, climbing down from the cab of a truck, spotted Lynn. "Sorry we've got to move your mailbox, Mrs. Richardson, but we're putting in culverts for the driveway your new neighbor's going to have constructed." He turned and pointed to the hilltop across from the farm. "He's building up there, and his road's going in right here."

Lynn's mind raced. Mrs. Reichert passed away in Florida. She must have sold her property.

"Can't you put his driveway down the road fifty or sixty yards, across from my nursery entrance? Where he comes in from won't matter much to him, but all I'm gonna see is this scar running straight up the hill."

"Mrs. Richardson, the county engineers selected this location for ingress and egress to this parcel of land. I'm just following orders."

As the men went about their work, Lynn paced angrily across her driveway, every once in a while kicking a stone. Then she started to resent the fact that everyone on the crew probably knew everything about her. Betsy Smith, Robin's mother, certainly did. Mrs. Smith's sister worked at the bank and Betsy slipped a couple of times when she and Lynn were talking. Obviously she knew more about Lynn's finances than she should. That was the way things were in the country. Lynn felt it unfair she would never be a member of this club since she didn't go back far enough.

Finally, the foreman came toward her looking like he had just made a decision. He slowly took off his gloves, carefully folded them, and tucked them into his hip pocket. With his eyes cast downward, he said, "I'm sorry we've upset you, Mrs. Richardson."

He looked around like he was searching for words. "Sure was a shame what happened to Ken." He hesitated for a moment. "Call the county engineering office. Ask for Bill Tolson. We're just here to put in the culvert and compact a couple of tons of gravel for the entrance. This guy's contractor isn't scheduled to start on his road until tomorrow."

Once back in the house, the county engineer's secretary informed Lynn her boss was out in the field until four. He'd get back to her the minute he got in.

Lynn couldn't afford to let this change her plans for the day. Four stores had to be checked and she had to send off some seeds and pick up a package at the post office. Hopefully, her order of paper seed envelopes had come. There'd be no problem getting back before the school bus came if she got started by eleven.

She pulled a clean white T-shirt over her head then slipped on a denim shift, after which she took a quick look in the mirror and ran a comb through her hair. Her cheeks got a quick pinch as she ran down the stairs.

By two-thirty all the stores were stocked and she headed for the post office where she couldn't help noticing the man opening the door for her had an unusually appealing appearance, something one didn't see every day in Eastlake. When she thanked him, he politely reached for the mailing bin she was carrying and said, "Can I help you with that?"

She was uncharacteristically shy as she told him, "No, thanks. It's not heavy."

Lynn was uncomfortably aware of the man in line behind her, when the person ahead of her spun around and sent the mail bin balanced on her hip flying across the room. Flustered, Lynn rapidly picked up the dozens of small parcels with everyone pitching in. When she stood up, the man standing behind her looked her straight in the eyes and ceremoniously dropped a packet into her bin.

Lynn turned quickly and set everything on the counter. Addressing the postal clerk, she said, "They're all stamped, Mike." She reached into her pocket and retrieved a slip. "You've got a package here for me too."

After a few minutes the clerk came back scratching his head. "When was this in your box?"

"Yesterday."

"I don't know what's happened. I couldn't find it."

She was almost out of the small envelopes she put her seeds into.

"Mike, can you please try again? It's got to be here."

He shrugged and said, "Okay. I'll look again."

Lynn could hear the door of the post office open and close several times and knew the line was getting longer. Finally, she turned around, and with an apologetic expression scanned the faces in the room, her eyes finally resting on the man in line behind her.

Standing with his arms leisurely crossed, he flashed a big grin. His perfect white teeth contrasted with his rugged good looks and stood out from his reddish beard. The crisp white shirt, open at the collar, blended nicely with his comfortably worn suede jacket. The graying sideburns told her he had to be in his forties. Realizing she was staring at him, embarrassed, Lynn quickly turned and faced the counter.

She self-consciously ran her finger under the rim of her shirt at the neck while listening to Ben Browning, who being retired for years, just floated around town passing the time of day. He was standing two down in line, and presumably, talking to the man behind her.

"Gardening's the thing now, don't ya know."

Even with her back to them, Lynn could tell the talkative retiree was stroking his jaw while he unhurriedly addressed his captive audience.

"She sells seeds, don't ya know. Yep. She's got quite a little business going there. See her in here all the time. Heard a lot about her too."

Lynn closed her eyes and rocked back on her heels. She could feel her cheeks getting warm. Mercifully, the clerk appeared from the sorting room.

"Here you go. Just sign there."

Lynn needed an empty mail bin but couldn't get out soon enough. As she rushed through the door, she involuntarily glanced back at the man waiting at the counter and caught him looking at her.

There was just enough time to get home before the school bus dropped Jess off. Why had she been so flustered in the post office? She noticed her hand on the steering wheel. She hadn't worn her wedding rings since the time they were almost knocked down the drain after she had placed them on the edge of the greenhouse sink.

She glanced at herself in the mirror and brushed her bangs back as she gave herself a quick appraisal. She could still get away with going without makeup, and her dark brown hair was glossier than ever.

What was she thinking? She had no time for this kind of thing. How could this stranger in the post office set her off like this? She decided to get her mind off this man she'd probably never lay eyes on again and concentrate on her business instead.

As she headed down the road leading directly from town to the farm, Richardson Road, no less, the school bus turned off a side road ahead and Lynn followed it home. A smile spread across her face as her Ford rolled over the crest of Richardson Hill and she caught sight of Lucky dutifully waiting at the end of the driveway wagging his tail as the school bus approached. Obediently, he didn't step one foot on the road as he watched Jess cross in front of the bus. When the boy knelt down and hugged the dog, Lynn's throat tightened as she batted back tears.

Something was terribly wrong with this picture. Ken had always made a point of being there to greet his son and carry him joyfully into the house. Lynn wondered if this was the saddest part of the boy's day.

Lynn spent the rest of the afternoon filling out the seed orders that had arrived in the mail while Jess glued a small model airplane together.

The phone rang.

"Hello, Mrs. Richardson?"

"Yes."

"This is Bill Tolson. My secretary told me how you feel about Mr. Reynold's driveway. I looked at the report and see no problem with moving it east eighty yards. But that's on paper. We'd have to come down and take another look."

"That's wonderful!"

"Don't get all excited now. I've put in a few calls and understand Reynolds has contracted the road out and they're scheduled to start tomorrow morning."

"Can't you ask them to wait?"

"Mrs. Richardson, you don't understand. Reynolds has all his permits. I don't have the authority to tell his contractor to stop. I don't mind tellin' you Reynolds has really put the pressure on Conway Construction to get that road built since he's got materials coming in next week and is looking to have the house built by July."

"I wish I had known about this sooner."

"Sorry about that."

There was a pause.

"Normally, we would have stopped by to talk to Ken." Another pause. "I tried to get hold of Mr. Reynolds, but he's out of town. I gave his answering service my home number along with a message for him to call me if he comes in tonight." In a voice that didn't sound too hopeful, he said, "I'm afraid that's about all I can do."

"Thanks, Mr. Tolson."

The next morning right after the school bus pulled away, the trucks arrived. Lynn disappointedly watched for a few minutes as they unloaded the bulldozer and grader, but when they tore the first dark gouge out of the earth, she turned away and started for the greenhouse.

How was this happening? If Ken were here, the old country boys' thing would have kicked in a long time ago. Before a permit was granted, the county engineer would have come over and talked with him. After passing the time of day a bit, Ken would have asked them to put the road across from the nursery entrance. Just as simple as that.

No matter how hard Lynn tried she couldn't get into the rhythm of potting the seedlings. She went over and slapped the first cassette she found into the tape player, but the next time she passed by, snapped it off. Bruce Springstein was too depressing for her this morning.

Maybe a fresh cup of coffee would make her feel better. She went to the house and as she rinsed the pot couldn't keep her eyes off the road crew. Then she got an idea. She put in eight cups of water and four heaping tablespoons of fresh grounds.

When the foreman saw Lynn coming with a tray, he shouted for a break. Once the dozers were turned off, the sounds of the country returned but the icy air was blue with exhaust. The men appeared grateful as they climbed down from the equipment and reached for a mug, but then stood around self-consciously waiting for someone to break the silence.

"Sure is nice country," one of them finally threw out.

Lynn decided a smile would be too insincere and just nodded.

"That sure is a nice, big farmhouse you've got. You don't see many like that around any more," the man continued as he scratched the back of his neck.

Lynn nodded again, and trying hard to suppress the edge on her voice, said, "Where exactly is this road going?"

The foreman, motioning with his coffee cup, said, "Straight up until it hits that grove of trees. Then, it's going to swing left along that ridge and turn up the hill again."

After placing his coffee on the running board, he leaned back against the dozer and took out a cigarette. Lynn could tell by the way he slowly lit up, he was getting ready to tell her all he knew. The minute he had spotted her coming across the road with the steaming tray of coffee he must have figured she wanted something.

"He was in to see the boss with his builder yesterday. Evidently, this guy wants this road done *pronto*. His house is supposed to go up inside of three months. Kincaid's coming with his rig this afternoon to start drilling the well and we're supposed to have the road finished and the foundation and septic field dug by next Tuesday."

He paused as they all watched a State Trooper car speed by.

"My boss said this place is going to cost over a million before it's done."

He took a deep drag and then put the cigarette out on the heel of his boot.

"Well, thank you, madam. I guess we better get back to work if we're going to finish in time."

Everyone's eyes were drawn toward the road again as three more State Trooper cars sped by, each with four men inside. Lynn was used to seeing an occasional squad car use this back road as a shortcut out of the county, but was puzzled.

"Where are they going?" she asked.

He shook his head. "They're sending every trooper they can spare over to Cortland County to look for that missing little girl."

"This is one of the biggest searches they've ever launched," added one of men. "I'm going up myself with Eastlake's volunteer firemen this weekend." He paused. "That is, if they don't find her *before* then."

CHAPTER 4

As Sam Reynold's Blazer moved down the streets of Manhattan at 3 a.m., the eerie stillness enveloping the monolithic buildings struck him. He felt a surge of love for the great city that was getting some rest for the night; the only place he'd ever lived. Then doubt about his move upstate started to creep up on him. Did he need New York's vitality to feed his creative drive? Was he running headlong to a place that would nurture him, or just running away from Lillian and a life void of the kind of warmth he longed for? Hell, maybe he was just getting old.

Then, for the first time in years, the piercing sound of sirens registered on his consciousness. He laughed out loud as he slapped the dash and pulled into the parking garage under his building. I'll be damned, he said to himself. I'm already getting used to the quiet of the country. How many times had he told himself not to think when he was tired. That's when all the fears grab you from behind.

The next morning as Sam came out of the shower, the clock on his desk read noon. He was beginning to regret his decision to drive back from Eastlake after dinner instead of staying overnight. He hit the button on his answering machine and vigorously dried his hair with a towel.

"Hi, Sweetheart."

The familiar voice made him smile.

"I couldn't get you on your cell phone all day. Star Place Productions is looking for you. I told them you'd be back Friday afternoon. Ralph's looking for you too. Can you please do me a favor and tell that guy to call just *once*. There was a call from a Mr. Tolson in Eastlake. He wants you to call him at work, or if you get in late, at his home tonight. His numbers are..."

Sam grabbed a pen and jotted them down.

"That wraps up your messages for today, Sunshine. By the way, you're never going to find anyone upstate to lie for you the way I do." The voice took on a professional tone. "As always, if I don't hear from you, I'll put your messages on your phone tomorrow at five."

Sam went back into the bathroom and caught sight of his reflection in the mirror. There was still some definition in his abs and his stomach was flat, but the river of hair running down his chest was starting to streak with gray. He massaged his beard and moved closer to the mirror to get a better look at the gray in his sideburns, and then his brain reminded him about the woman in the post office. Early thirties, no ring.

A little thin, but she had something: a mixture of self-confidence and spunk. He laughed out loud at himself and got into a pair of jeans and a sweatshirt.

He decided to call Mr. Tolson at the business number.

"The widow who owns the land across from you wanted your entrance moved so it wouldn't be directly in front of her house," Tolson told him.

"Sure, that'll be okay with me if Conway hasn't started already."

"I'm afraid he has. After the fire you lit under him yesterday, he sent out two crews at seven this morning. They're probably well into the grading by now."

As he put the phone into the cradle, Sam hoped this wasn't going to be a big issue with his new neighbor. From what his realtor had told him, she wasn't anyone to mess with and had been out-and-out rude when the realtor tried to list her farm. Sam had felt badly when he heard that. He hadn't meant to offend.

He thought for a moment, then went into the bedroom and pulled out the Conway Construction business card from the breast pocket of his suede jacket. He ran it back and forth on his beard as he reflected, then decided to call. He'd had enough trouble with women in his life.

"Hello, Mr. Conway. It's Sam Reynolds."

"I reckon Tolson's finally caught up with you."

"Yeah."

As Sam walked over to his sound system and popped in his favorite disk, he wished he'd stopped and called his service when he discovered his cellular was on the blink.

"I was between a rock and a hard place, Sam. There's no way I was going to meet your deadline unless we got started this morning.... And....since I didn't hear from you, we went ahead gangbusters."

"What if you move the road?"

"We'll have to stop until Tolson's people come out and take another look." He paused. "I rescheduled all kinds of work to get the boys out there. They've been dumping gravel right behind the dozers all morning."

Sam thought for a minute. He'd sold the loft and had to be out by the first of July. More importantly, Joey was all set to start installing his studio June fifteenth so everything would be ready to go the minute he moved in. With the big contract Joey was getting from the record company, Sam doubted his sound engineer could change his schedule even one day.

"That's okay, George. Let it rip."

As Bach's double violin concerto sent up competing rivulets of dark emotion, Sam started to second-guess himself. Maybe there was a way? No. If his neighbor was still bent out of shape about the road once the house was finished, he'd move it. He didn't want anything to mar the setting in the hollow they both shared either.

Sam didn't know why, but there was something about that place that called out to him. He'd fallen in love with it the minute the realtor drove over the hill while showing him the frontage on the property across the road. The Richardson's farmhouse was like a delicate pearl brooch lying on a green velvet pillow. The gingerbread on the eaves, the sweeping porches and the way it was comfortably nestled in the hollow surrounded by hills appealed to him. He guessed restoring the charming old place would be fun, and was confident a good architect could add on a sound studio without disturbing the look. But once the realtor told him the widow who owned it didn't want to sell, he gave up the idea and bought the property across the road instead.

The doorbell rang. Ralph was downstairs. Sam buzzed him in.

The tall lanky man waltzed over to the large antique cherry table and took some papers from his briefcase. He had the look of someone who was hungry for success but too easy-going to put up with all the crap you have to take to get it. They'd been friends since Julliard. These days, Ralph hustled independent television productions.

"Here's the script I told you about, hot shot," Ralph sang out. "Work your magic for me. I need the tape by next Friday."

Sam was leaning against a pillar in the expansive former loft holding a mug. "You want a cup of coffee?"

"Not that decaf you drink. It's hi-test for me, baby."

Sam casually walked over to the table, picked up the script with one hand and walked around holding his coffee in the other. As Sam studied it, Ralph talked, not expecting to be heard.

"Boy, I wish I'd had the dough to buy this place from you."

Ralph sat on the edge of the leather couch looking aimlessly at the endless open space. The heart pine floors created a lustrous carpet that led his eyes to the clusters of Early American furnishings and objects d'art that Sam had found at auctions and antique stores all over Manhattan.

Ralph finally fixed on the huge Jackson Pollock hanging on the brick wall in front of him. "How much of this stuff is Lillian getting, anyway?"

Sam didn't look up from the script. "She doesn't want a thing."

Ralph let out a cynical laugh. "She's so fuckin' rich she can probably buy and sell everyone on this block."

Sam ignored the comment and continued to read. References to his wife's wealth stopped making an impact years ago.

Right after graduating from Julliard, Sam had met Lillian at a New York Symphony Ladies Guild reception honoring the orchestra's major benefactors. As one of the symphony's youngest musicians, he made a splash; and as one of the guild's richest heiresses she confidently targeted the handsome prodigy as a marriage candidate.

This kid from the Bronx took a while to figure out he didn't fit into Lillian's society world and never would, almost ten years after they married. But he had to give her credit; Lillian tried. As blue as her blood was, she was every bit as tenacious as the street-wise mothers he'd known in the Bronx. She was hell-bent on making him someone she and her stockbroker father, scion of one of the largest brokerage firms in New York, could be proud of.

Through most of marriage, Sam kept loving her and wished they'd had a child. There was a spot in his heart for one that never got filled.

Sam went along with Lil's demands as far as he could, but music was his soul. In fact, music never left his consciousness. He was either composing, arranging, or had other artist's music playing in his head. As the marriage failed, he fell completely into that world which delivered the sublime satisfaction of creating something wholly new and beautiful to share with other people.

In the end he blamed himself for everything that went wrong with the union. For the past couple of years, the only time they got together was when she was in need of a partner for one of her charitable or political events. They both fell into relationships from time to time; except for Lillian it was more frequent. Sam looked for casual affairs that would never lead to anything. His nature was to be a gentleman and stay in the marriage.

Lil finally threw in the towel. Turning forty scared her. If she was ever going to make the leap, she had to do it while she still had her youthful looks. The long nightmare finally ended one day when Sam answered the door and was handed the divorce papers.

For years Sam had fantasized about building a studio somewhere in the country. He earned his bread and butter, or should he say crackers and caviar, from composing and producing sound tracks for major television network productions. Once the theme was developed, he only had to weave the same score around the action in each weekly episode. He did everything in his state-of-the-art studio in the loft using synthesizers, multiple sound tracks, and either playing some of the instruments himself or pulling together some musicians or a whole orchestra for a taping session.

But his real love was composing for independent filmmakers. The money wasn't the greatest, but he could soar. Even conduct. Since leaving the symphony and parking his cello in the corner, he ran after this kind of work. He finally had a reputation on the East Coast that garnered him constant work. In fact, he was in the middle of discussing the possibility of doing the score for a major foreign film. Once he left the distractions of the New York rat race, he hoped to do more of this.

Sam sat down across from Ralph, placed the script on the coffee table and studied the face of the biggest distraction he had.

He and Ralph went way back. Ralph was always there when Sam needed to get out and listen to other artists' music. They'd do the clubs, shows, opera, Julliard. Ralph was the first person he tried his compositions out on, a lot of times over the phone.

But their relationship was a two-way street. Ralph made a living, such as it was, producing and hustling documentaries. His big dream was to sell a pilot for a series to one of the networks. Sam always came across with the music backgrounds; sometimes original material he composed, sometimes mixed out of his tape library. If Ralph couldn't sell the film, Sam let getting paid go. Sometimes everybody got lucky and Ralph sold his idea before he went into production.

Sam didn't need the work or the money.

"Ralph, you know I don't mind helping you out, but I can't handle any extra work right now. I've got a new house going up." He looked around. "Everything here's got to be put in crates, and I'm working with Joey on my new studio." He threw his hands in the air. "I'm up against it, buddy."

"Just this once?"

Sam's low, pleasantly grainy voice became serious. "Ralph, I love you like my own brother, but I haven't got time right now for a spec job that might get flushed down the toilet. Do me a favor this time out. Go to a sound studio and have them mix some music out of the can and tell your client, if they buy, you'll put an original sound track on it. I'll help you out after August first."

Ralph reached over and took an apple from the dish. "Can I have this?"

Sam threw his head back and laughed. "Why not? You've eaten here more than I have."

Sam stood up and handed his friend the script, then put his arm around his shoulders and walked him to the door. He was confident Ralph already had someone else lined up to do the sound track, and was determined to concentrate completely on his own composing.

The doorbell rang.

Glancing at his watch, Sam said, "He's early, but I think the courier from the network is downstairs. Can you let him in on your way out?"

Sam stood at the open door waiting for his delivery of videotapes from the week's *Men in Blue* show. He was anxious to get started on the musical bed even though his deadline wasn't until Wednesday. If he finished before then, he could run up to Eastlake for a couple of days, a prospect that excited him.

The elevator door opened and Lillian stood there pressing the open button. After a few moments she slowly walked out. Nothing or nobody was going to rush her when she wanted to make an entrance, least of all the Otis Elevator Co.

Sam held the loft door open as four hours of Charles of the Ritz drifted by. Lillian walked directly into the bedroom they hadn't shared since she bought her penthouse overlooking Central Park four years back.

Sam stood leaning in the doorway, and as she slowly undressed, took a deep breath and turned his eyes away. He'd finally fallen out of love with her and couldn't understand why he was so intensely aroused. Maybe, because Lillian was so devoid of morals she could deliver pure sex.

Sam looked over and saw Lillian on her hands and knees with her silky blond hair draped from her shoulders, glaring at him like a beautiful wild thing. Pulling off his sweatshirt, he climbed up on the bed behind her and slowly slipped off his belt as he admired the shapely buttocks that sloped sensually toward the narrow waist. In seconds he was thrust inside her moving with a primeval rhythm as he gripped her smooth alabaster skin.

When he was finished, there was a split-second when he wanted to pull her down on the bed and hold her in his arms; instead, he was suddenly struck by sadness and tears welled up in his eyes.

Lillian slid down on the bed, turned around and laughed.

"You're so goddamn sentimental. It's only a fuck."

Finished in the bathroom, she seemed agitated as she quickly dressed.

"That's what I've always liked about you, Sam. *You're easy.*"

She appeared to be getting angrier as she sat on the bed to put on her nylons.

"The trouble was, you were too headstrong. Daddy could have gotten you anything. Would you take that offer he got you at *CBS*? No! You want to compose music!" Her voice was becoming shrill.

She stood up and started to pull on her jacket. "Do you have any idea...any idea *whatsoever* how embarrassed I was when people asked me what you did!"

She went right up to him, an ugly expression on her face.

"He produces all the sound tracks for *Men in Blue!*" she screamed, as she tried to shove him backward.

Unmoved, he stood there with his hands on his hips slowly shaking his head. "Lillian, we've played this scene a couple times before. That's why we're getting a divorce. There's nothing wrong with what I do. In fact, I'm damn proud of it."

He gently pulled her toward him and put his arms around her. "Lil, you can't torture yourself like this. We're from two different worlds. You tried. I tried. Hell, even your dad tried. *Finito la musical.*"

She pulled away, grabbed her purse and slammed the door behind her.

CHAPTER 5

Lynn kept looking up expecting to see Cal's ancient pick-up pull in. She glanced at the clock. Eight. He should have been there by now. He was going to help her pot seedlings and bring in some mulch and dirt with the small payloader Ken had used to help clean out the barn.

She wondered just how much activity there was going to be across the road today. Kincaid evidently hit water since they pulled his rig out the day before. The hill across from the farm looked strange, no longer a rolling meadow just turning green. The pile of cinderblocks had disappeared, no doubt into the basement, and a stack of lumber had taken its place.

Since the construction had started, Lynn felt like something had died. She had to shake off this senseless brooding. After all, she had no claim to the other side of the hollow. Even so, she had always thought of that hillside as part of the landscape of the farm, like the sky or clouds or sunrise. This ubiquitous natural element now had a black scar marring it like a gash torn in a delicate lace shawl.

Lucky's welcoming bark told her Cal was approaching.

Cal had sold his farm down the road to his son years ago, and was living in a trailer set up next to the old farmstead now inhabited by his boy, his wife and their four kids. Cal liked his son's wife. However, her domineering spirit always made him feel like he was in the way.

Cal helped Lynn more to get away than to earn money he didn't really need. Lynn knew he'd hold onto the checks she gave him until her season got rolling, just like he had in the past. The first year she hired him she was almost hysterical thinking about how she was going to juggle finances to get him paid, but by now they had settled into an easy relationship like two old friends.

The monotony of long days potting seedlings in the greenhouse was usually broken by the rhythm of Cal's craggy voice telling all the old stories of country life. With almost total recall, this man, now in his early seventies, could remember as far back as the nineteen-thirties and forties as if they were yesterday. Familiarity with the way things used to be years ago on the farms of Central New York made Lynn feel more connected to the place, and many times she'd coax Cal to retell his stories to Jess when he came in after school.

"I didn't hear you drive in," Lynn said as she poured a cup of coffee from her thermos and handed it to him.

"I couldn't make it to the house driveway so I parked in the nursery lot and walked over."

"How come?"

He bent down and scratched behind Lucky's ears. "What's the matter with you, boy? Are you getting so used to that darn commotion across the road that you don't even bark at them any more?"

At that, Lucky turned and anxiously scratched at the door until the old man let him out.

Lynn poured herself some coffee, sat down on a stool and nudged a small plastic baggie with a couple of cookies toward Cal.

"Don't you worry about Lucky. He sits at the end of the driveway like a sphinx all day watching the trucks go in and out. I think he likes the excitement." Lynn shook her head and gazed off into space. "Things have changed for Lucky. He was always Ken's dog. He used to go everywhere with him, follow the tractor into the fields, stand guard in the barn during milking. Ken had him as a pup. But ever since ...you know

... ever since then, Lucky thinks his job is to watch over me. He even lets me know who's pulling in the driveway by the sound of his bark."

She put her coffee down and went back to work, carefully tipping a seed pot upside down and letting the plant fall out. The motions were almost automatic. "He knows he's all I've got to protect me."

As she carried a loaded tray to a sunny spot, she said, "What's going on? Why couldn't you get through?"

"There's a big eighteen-wheeler flat-bed trying to make the turn into that darn driveway. Why in the heck they put that road next to a creek, I'll never know," said the old man as he finished tying on his apron.

The creek ran down the hill, through culverts under Richardson Road, emerging past the far end of the nursery parking lot.

"Yep. They're bringin' in them eighty-thousand-dollar redwoods, I reckon," said Cal as he scratched behind his ear.

"What are you talking about?"

"He's paid eighty-thousand dollars for the redwood beams goin' in that place."

Lynn stopped cold and with eyebrows furrowed studied Cal.

"Where do you *get* all this stuff?" There was more than a hint of incredulity in her tone.

"My daughter-in-law says so. Her sister works for that architect he's gone and hired. She read as plain as day they quoted him eighty thousand and he told them to go right ahead and get 'em. Just like that."

Lynn pressed the dirt firmly around a potted seedling and felt a hard rock in her stomach. She didn't even have *eighty* dollars to spend on *her* house.

Cal was like a dog with a bone. "Nope. They're not going to make that turn unless they back up in your driveway and then ease the truck around until they can go straight in. They can't take a chance on cutting that curve wrong and ending up in the creek. They'll probably figure that out before long and be in here askin' for permission to pull in your driveway."

Sam looked at the clock on the dash. Darn. The headwinds, in addition to making the trip bumpy, had made his flight twenty minutes late. The truck was going to deliver his redwood beams straight off this morning. The trucker who brought them all the way from California probably stayed at a motel nearby, got up and had breakfast at the diner just outside town, and by now was wheeling his way toward Richardson Hill.

Sam was hoping he'd be there in time to make sure the beams got up his road safely. He'd never lived in anything new in his life, but this site, thirteen-hundred feet above sea level, deserved the kind of structure he was building. Out of the two hundred acres, his architect had found the perfect location. "On a clear day, you can see the Adirondacks from here," he had told Sam. Then with a slow grin, added, "I just can't tell you how many clear days there are in Upstate New York."

But when the architect added they were anchoring each of the twenty-two steel beams holding up the A-frame structure with a ton of cement, Sam figured they were anticipating there'd be more than a few days that wouldn't be too clear.

As Sam went over the crest of Richardson Hill he saw the eighteen-wheeler stretched across the road below. A pick-up was finishing a U-turn and heading back toward him. Two other pick-ups had been stopped on this side of the loaded flatbed. On the other side, there was a row of vehicles lined up and twisting back up the hill.

Sam's heart rate quickened. There was something about this scene that was foreboding. Noticing a worker coming up along the road edge, he pressed the button to lower the passenger window and strained toward him.

"Sorry, Sir. We're going to need a few minutes to get this truck onto the driveway," the man said as he approached the rented Bronco.

"I'm Sam Reynolds. That delivery's for me."

"Good. We were lookin' for you." He motioned toward the side. "Why don't you pull in here. I've got to get up to the top of the hill and slow the oncoming traffic down or we're going to have an accident."

As Sam got out of the car and started down the hill, the balmy weather made him acutely aware of his surroundings. He felt his body jar as gravity yanked his feet downward and pulled him toward the hollow. The sudden, sharp trilling of a red-winged blackbird pierced the air and startled him. He shook off a feeling of anxiety that he blamed on the flight from New York. He was always keyed up after a bad one.

He started for the other lane, and as he came from behind one of the waiting pick-ups, he saw the rear corner of the eighteen-wheeler heading straight for the huge old maple at the edge of the widow's driveway.

The prospect of being asked for permission to use her driveway delighted Lynn. Finally, she was going to have to be considered. In anticipation, she fluffed up her ragged bangs and smoothed her hair back behind her ears.

Lucky's barking suddenly got frenetic. Then came the horrible sound, almost like a thunderclap. Lynn gave Cal a sharp glance and sent her stool flying as she raced to the door. The big maple at the end of the farmhouse driveway was lying across the lawn, branches reaching toward the house like someone lying on their side needing help.

Stunned, Lynn stood motionless in the driveway taking in the scene. When the noisy diesel engine was finally turned off, the still quietness struck her as odd. Something was wrong, she thought. Suddenly the dead silence exploded in her brain and a scream jumped out.

"Lucky!"

Feverishly, she made her way into the debris, climbing and crawling as the gnarled limbs scratched and tore into her flesh. She stopped cold at the sickening sight of Lucky's head pinned underneath a huge limb, mouth open, blood trickling out.

Crying openly, she crawled into the cavity and gently stroked his still head, then ran her hand firmly down the sleek fur to close his eyes. Strong heaves gushed forward as she dropped her head into her hands and cried for everything. For the loss of a loyal friend, for Ken, for her boy who lost one of his last links with his father, for the end of Ken's protection of her.

She hadn't been able to cry when Ken died no matter how hard she had tried. Her emotions had been frozen in time. But the ripping away of this bond to Ken brought back all the hopelessness she felt at the sight of his still body lying on the flattened grass, and a suppressed watershed of despair poured out.

She cried into the darkness of the shelter her hands made as if her lungs would burst, as strong arms lifted her up and carried her in jarring motion up and down through the maze of limbs. Before long she was on the settee in the darkened parlor.

Quiet now, her arm lay across her face, and soft, repetitive heaves punctuated each breath. She opened her eyes as someone lifted her arm and gently laid it at her side. She was incredulous as she recognized the man who opened the door for her in the post office. He had pulled up a footstool and was blotting her face with a wet cloth. Cal was standing behind him scratching behind his ear and looking concerned.

Lynn stiffly sat up.

"Cal, can you please get me some paper towels?"

When the old man left the room, neither Lynn nor the man sitting in front of her seemed to know what to say. Lynn leaned back against the settee and ran a hand through her messed hair. She felt awkward suddenly seeing this stranger in her home and avoided making steady eye contact with him.

Instead, her eyes fell upon her rumpled clothes and traced the bleeding lines criss-crossing her arms. The towels arrived and she went about the business of blowing her nose several times, then thoroughly wiping her face with the wet cloth.

"Where's your first-aid kit?" the man asked.

Lynn looked up at Cal and in a hoarse voice said, "In the cupboard over the stove."

The sight of Lucky suddenly flashed in her mind and she buried her head in the wet towel and started to sob again.

"Here, here. Please don't start that. You were doing fine," Sam said.

For the next ten minutes Lynn sat numbly as Sam carefully cleaned and bandaged the scratches. Slowly, the burning stopped as the ointment started to do its work.

"There. That ought to do it," Sam said as he started to collect everything.

There was a softness in Lynn's voice as she said, "You're a very kind stranger to stop and help out this way. I really appreciate it." Bitterness crept into her tone. "I only wish my inconsiderate new neighbor were here so I could tell him how I feel."

A trace of reluctance was now noticeable in Sam's movements as he got up and placed everything on the cluttered dining room table and then came back and sat on the stool. He clutched his hands tightly and leaned forward resting his elbows on his knees. After taking a deep breath, in a slow, mellow voice, he said, "I'm not exactly a stranger, Mrs. Richardson. I'm Sam Reynolds, your new neighbor."

Lynn couldn't get what he was saying to register and just kept staring at him.

The quizzical expression on her face made Sam feel like this encounter with the woman he'd felt somehow attracted to in the post office wasn't going to end well. He self-consciously rubbed his hands together. "I'm awfully sorry about the dog."

Lynn suddenly raised her hand to her mouth as tears exploded from her eyes.

He looked around, frustrated. "Please, don't start that again."

She took a deep breath and stared wide-eyed at him. He was obviously uneasy as he looked aimlessly around the large, high-ceilinged room searching for something to say.

Finally, "This is a nice place you've got here. No wonder you didn't want to sell."

Lynn closed her eyes tightly and took a deep breath as everything suddenly fell into place, then abruptly stood up.

Offering him her hand, in a tone laden with resentment, she said, "Thank you for your obvious concern, Mr. Reynolds."

He clasped her hand with both of his and said anxiously, "I'm so sorry I upset you this way."

She drew away. "*Upset me*? How could you *possibly* upset me?" She made a huge sweeping gesture with her arm. "You came up here from New York and tried to buy me out. When that didn't work, you put that blasted road in to mar my view.... and when *that* didn't work, down came a hundred-year-old tree. The only thing, by the way, that did anything to screen that ugly road of yours. And then you got Lucky. My boy *loved* that dog. I don't know if you're aware of it, Sir, but my husband was killed just over a year ago, and that was *his* dog..." Her voice cracked and she stopped and made an effort to regain her composure.

But she couldn't stop. She put her hands on her hips and in an accusing voice added, "You thought you could just come up here and buy and sell anything or anybody you wanted. Well, you've got another think coming."

Sam's face reflected amazement. She'd gone from utterly fragile one moment, to a fiery vixen the next.

"About that road..." he started to say.

She cut him off. "I'm sorry, Mr. Reynolds. I don't want to hear one more word about that road." Arms firmly crossed, she tossed her head toward the door and said, "*Get out.*"

The builder's foreman was waiting for Sam as he left the farmhouse. A State Trooper car was in the driveway and the truck laden with the redwood beams could be seen winding its way up the hill to the building site. Sam could hear the droning of a dispatcher as the trooper sat with the door open finishing his report.

As Sam approached, the foreman asked, "Is she going to be all right?"

"*Oh yeah!*"

The foreman had a sheepish expression on his face. "What'd she do? Throw you out?"

Sam brushed the comment aside and walked briskly toward the tree.

"Get everything out of here. Clean up the whole mess and get her another tree." He turned and looked at the foreman. "And get Conway to move the road as soon as possible."

CHAPTER 6

Dick Mitchum finished the accident report, got out of the squad car and asked the foreman to give the sheet to the truck driver. With that done, he radioed that he was on his way to Cortland.

Speed traps, petty thefts, drunken fist fights and fender-benders were the mainstay of Mitchum's daily investigations, but today he was going to represent Troop D at a briefing on the search for the Cramer girl at the Troop C barracks in Cortland.

The little girl had disappeared on her way to her grandmother's house a quarter of a mile from where her parents had been conducting a class for deacons in their small church outside the village of Marathon.

Within hours of her abduction Cortland's Bureau of Criminal Investigation had brought in every available asset in the region to search for the ten-year-old. New York State Troopers from Troop D and C converged on the site as well as thirty to forty of their investigators. The kidnapping was deemed a multi-jurisdictional incident involving the Cortland City Police Department and the County Sheriff's office. No stone was left unturned in an effort to make a quick determination as to what might have happened to the child.

That was four weeks ago. Now the investigation was focused on the follow-up of leads. The Cortland barracks was operating as the command post for one of the most intensive investigations ever to be launched in Upstate New York.

This was the kind of crime that took on a different meaning for Mitchum. A dedicated State Trooper, he'd always been able to boost himself to a certain level of commitment, but when the crime involved a child, he was able to turn the intensity up a notch or two.

Every time he'd been given a lead assignment in a case of this type, he found himself so focused time had no meaning. Even though he was stationed two counties over, he was suspecting everyone, and found his part in the investigation taking on a whole new dimension.

No one was saying anything officially, but as far as he was concerned, this was an obvious sex crime. Maybe even that of a serial killer. After four weeks, even though the child was probably dead, a major full-scale search operation was still in progress.

The troopers were operating on the theory there was always a chance the little girl was still alive. Every morning there was a briefing of the thirty or so investigators on the case in the command post and lead assignments given out. There'd be another briefing at night when the investigators trailed in to report what they had found, and then plans were carved out for the following day.

Today, Mitchum was going to a special monthly summary briefing where the entire case would be rehashed and everyone brought up to date on developments over the past four weeks. He'd been assigned to trace the movements of the known sex offenders in Oneida County and had his report ready. Oneida County was only an hour's drive from where the girl had disappeared, so everyone in the county with a criminal background, every transient, anyone on parole or probation, was a suspect.

The National Missing and Exploited Children's Clearinghouse had the case in its network, and similar cases from all over the country were being compared.

The missing girl was still dominating the front page of the papers for counties around. The first item on the nightly TV newscasts was a picture of a happy youngster holding her cat followed in pathetic contrast by desperate parents pleading for help from the public.

A control center manned by volunteers operated night and day from the church. Hundreds of people and groups were searching the woods and farmlands around the sparsely populated town. Flyers and handbills printed by the thousands were plastered all over eight counties.

Hell, thought Mitchum, what else were the parents to do. No body. No clues. Hope was all they had.

CHAPTER 7

Excited, Lynn wiggled into a shift and pulled on a cardigan. Still pitch black outside, the early morning mist carried the sound of Cal's truck pulling into the nursery driveway through her open window. She heard his door slam and the truck's back door open. Cal was loading up for her trip to the Syracuse Regional Market.

Jess appeared at the bedroom door with a wide-awake look of anticipation.

"You ready for a big day, pumpkin?"

The boy nodded enthusiastically. He had been his mother's cohort in this business since he was in diapers, listening to her plans and dreams even before he could talk as they rode the country roads in the early morning hours to farmers' markets all over three counties.

The two raced across the dewy lawn past the greenhouse to the nursery lot. Cal had left his headlights on as well as the light in the nursery shelter so they could see. They made quick business of getting the perennials into the truck before carefully loading the seed stand.

Lynn gave Cal a quick hug before she climbed into the cab of his ancient one-ton International. Cal went to the other side and helped Jess scoot in and handed him a carton. "Hold on to this, boy. It's got the cash box."

Lynn leaned toward Cal. "You should have a big day today. Robin Smith will be here by eight and I should be back by three. Why don't you go in the house and lie down on the couch until it gets light."

"I think I'll do that."

The old man closed Jess's door and stood back as Lynn took a deep breath, pressed the clutch and put the gears in first. The headlights beamed on Reynolds' new road straight ahead. Lynn eased out of the lot, shifted into second and climbed out of the hollow. As she reached the crest and saw the faint glow from Eastlake's streetlights in the distance below, she reached over and patted Jess's leg. "We'll get breakfast in Syracuse, honey. You up for pancakes?"

The boy laughed more to see his mother happy than anything.

Robin lay in bed staring at the dormer window where a soft gray light was starting to illuminate the room. She looked around the small cramped bedroom and remembered how it used to be when she was a small girl, before her brother Ben arrived and the room had to be divided.

An accident, Aunt Mary declared about the baby's coming. Robin wasn't much kinder as she recalled her embarrassment when her mother appeared at her high school graduation large with child.

Now, she wouldn't trade the energetic, devilish bundle for all the bedrooms in the world. Besides, she was away at college most of the year.

The girl tossed in bed, flipping a small stuffed animal onto the floor. She languidly reached for the teddy bear her brother had left behind and in one continuous motion got up.

After yawning and stretching in front of the mirror, she looked thoughtfully at her reflection. Only four-foot-seven. The doctor wanted to give her steroids when she was twelve, and even though her mother encouraged it, the stubborn girl had refused. "If God wants me to be small, I'll just be small," she remembered telling them.

A pair of white cut-offs was pulled from the drawer along with a navy sweatshirt. With all the bending she had to do, she liked the freedom of shorts for working at the nursery, but preferred a long-sleeved sweatshirt on top during the cooler days of early summer. She grabbed a T-shirt in case it got too warm.

The narrow back staircase opened to the kitchen. Robin was surprised to find her mother standing at the counter.

"I made you lunch," she said, handing Robin a glass of orange juice.

Robin quickly gulped the juice down and reached for the bag.

"I'll drive you over," said her mother. "Now that you're home for the summer, your dad wants to service your car."

The Richardson place was only a couple of miles down the road and Betsy Smith felt perfectly at ease making the drive in her robe and pajamas.

"I wish you hadn't taken this job again, Robin. You'd do so much better at the grocery store in town."

"She needs me, Ma."

The only sound came from the humming of the tires on the asphalt. Robin rolled the window down, put her arm on the sill and gazed out at the green hills whooshing by. "What she's doing is good, Ma. I think she's on to something. Sometimes I get so excited when someone brings in new seeds they've gotten from some old flower on their farm, that I'm... I'm electrified or something. Mom, they're even starting to bring in old rose bushes."

Robin hadn't had a chance to sit down with her parents since she came back from college, but she was planning to transfer from the Business School to Cornell's Ag School. She'd spent hours studying the history of seed hybridization on her own, and was determined to have a career searching for and preserving the old strains of grains and flowers. She believed this effort was as important as what the environmentalists were doing.

Betty Smith smiled and reached over and patted her daughter's leg. "You're a good girl, Robin. I don't think I've got anything to worry about."

Betty dropped Robin off with, "I'll pick you up at five."

By the time Lynn backed the truck into their stall at the regional market it was almost six. They let the doors in the back of the truck swing open and set up the seed stand first, then took out the sawhorses and plywood. The cacophony of honking horns, shouts of "hello," and parents hollering to their children rose by the minute as farmers started to arrive and unload. The lady who sold the jams and jellies across from Lynn's stand motioned for Jess to come over, and in minutes he returned with two strawberry tarts and a big grin.

As Lynn set about busily arranging her tables, Liz Palmer came up to her. Liz and Henry Palmer had a small truck farm in Oswego and had vied for Lynn's spot five years earlier when the banana wholesaler moved to his own building on the other side of the lot. There'd been a row in the office when the prized location went to Lynn, but the manager held his ground. He wanted to put a vendor on the highly visible corner that would appeal to the yuppie segment of his market and Lynn fit the bill.

"I'm glad to see you back at the markets again this season," Liz said. "Gotta hand it to you. Thought you'd give up after your husband's..." She glanced over at Jess and stopped. After a moment she added wistfully, "I thought I was finally going to get this spot. But I'm glad I didn't get it that way, honey. You need anything...just come over and ask me and Henry." She leaned over and tousled Jess's hair. "That goes for you too, kiddo."

This was the first time Liz had spoken to Lynn. After the accident last spring, Liz had stopped mumbling under her breath every time she looked at Lynn, but that was about as far as the relationship advanced.

The vendors rolled in like a fast-moving stream. Since it was the first week in June, orchardmen were bringing in the cherry crop from Newark and Geneva, and all the Oswego muck farmers were loaded with vegetables. A couple of them had some early corn and expected to get two and a half dollars a dozen.

The sun started to burn off the morning chill and, as the colorful flowers and produce started dressing up the tables, shoppers appeared out of nowhere. Expectations for a glorious day charged the air.

Lynn stood erect in front of her stall and made her final inspection, then carefully smoothed her hair back behind her ears and put on her big straw hat, the signal to Jess that they were open for business.

She happened to glance over at her son and when their eyes met, they both burst out laughing. The optimism in the air was infectious. Lynn went over and put her arm around her son's shoulder and drew him close to her.

These farmers' markets were their special time together. Ken had never been able to get away from the barn long enough to go with them and must have decided to let that be. Instead, he had always enjoyed sitting at the dinner table listening to the animated vignettes of their day at market.

By ten, the place was hopping. Lynn was almost halfway through the perennials and the seeds were going well. A lot of repeat business, she speculated. She was surprised so many were taking her flyer and signing up to be on her mailing list. This was a good sign. Plus, Jess had grown a lot in the past year and was a bigger help than ever.

Just as she was finishing showing a woman how to start seeds in her house, someone tapped her on the shoulder. He was holding a mike and the man standing behind him had a video camera with the local public television channel call letters on it.

"Hello. I'm Steve Cummins from *WKNY-TV*. We're doing a show on the popularity of gardening in Central New York and we understand from the market manager you raise your own perennials and also sell seeds."

Lynn automatically adjusted her hat and smiled into the camera. She felt as if she were somewhere outside her body as she threw herself into an energetic presentation of Richardson's Herbs and Seeds. Careful not to take her eyes off the camera, she even managed to reach over and pull Jess in front of her and introduce him.

After the camera crew left, she was elated when Jess told her she did well. However, after glancing beyond the crowd and catching the cold glare coming from Liz, her mood flattened.

For the first half-hour of the ride home Jess straightened out all the bills, then put them in packs of one-hundred dollars each with a rubber band around them. This was his job.

"I'll count everything again when we get home, Mom, but I think we've got over seven-hundred dollars."

When they stopped at a light, Lynn looked over and recognized the same confidence in the boy she had noticed the first time Ken walked up to her in that college bar and asked if she wanted to dance.

The mother and son didn't talk much on the ride home. Jess took a couple of sandwiches from the cooler and handed one to Lynn. They shared a soda; then Jess put the moneybox on the floor and lay down on the seat. Lynn reached for her cardigan and tucked it under his head.

As Lynn drove home, she wondered if Cal and Robin were having a busy day. Cal had promised if the traffic slowed, he'd work in the barn and clean up the winter's mess. Then her thoughts tumbled onto how she'd fallen into her fascination with old seeds and perennials.

What started as afternoon drives to explore the back roads of Oneida County with Jess in his car seat and a bag of chocolate chip cookies on the dash, eventually developed into a life-long passion. She couldn't help being curious about the tumbled-down old farmhouses that were almost hidden from view with vines and brush growing all around them. Then in the spring before these invaders took over, she'd notice drifts of daffodils and grape hyacinths and wondered what had happened to the people who planted them.

She got into the habit of pulling into the barely distinguishable driveways and taking a look around while straddling Jess on her hip. Sometimes there was just the limestone foundation or something like a pump with a broken handle to testify that the place once held a family's hopes. Nothing of value. These places had been picked clean years ago.

When she had stopped to admire the forgotten flowers, she'd been struck with the thought that at one time someone had been taken with a universal urge to make something beautiful come from the earth, and felt somehow connected to them. Who were these people? Was it the farm wife who, when the door-to-door merchant came by with his wagon full of wares, noticed a bag of bulbs among the pots and pans and suddenly felt a desire for the elegance flowers offer? Or was it the farmer himself who, while visiting one of the neighbors, noticed a striking drift of daffodils and asked to trade for any extra bulbs his neighbor might have.

Whichever way these delicate miracles had made their journey to these backwaters, they all represented one intrinsic human desire: hope.

As summer came, Lynn was drawn to these places again and noticed an abundance of tiger lilies along with other plants she couldn't identify. This led her to stop by farms and ask about them. Before long, she had a network of farmwomen, mostly older, who shared their heirloom seeds, cuttings and stories.

One of the reasons she liked going to the farmers' markets so much was because she made contact with people who were intrigued the same way she was. How could these minute little seeds turn into huge drifts of flowers? This spectacular miracle of nature alone captures the hearts of most gardeners.

Lynn recalled one family who had stopped at the nursery. The mother walked up and down the aisles of plants thoughtfully picking and choosing, while the father didn't bother to get out. Two obviously bored older children leaned against the car as a little girl of around five stepped out, her eyes like saucers. She walked in amazement, staring hard at the rows of blooms until she spotted a coreopsis. All atremble, the child tugged her mother toward the delicate yellow flowers dancing in the breeze, then pleaded to get it as if her heart would break if she didn't.

What was that ingredient that made a gardener, Lynn wondered? They were a breed unto themselves. Was it hereditary? What motivated someone to willingly take on the painstaking drudgery of fall and spring cleanup and mulching, never-ending digging and weeding, and overall backbreaking labor? There seemed no other explanation other than an overwhelming desire to create beauty.

As the truck moved along the country road, Lynn felt a deep satisfaction that she was somehow a conduit for these beautiful things of nature, linking the past with the future. She reached down and gently stroked her sleeping son's hair. She was glad for her decision to stay on the farm. This was a good life, healthy and safe.

She thought about the TV filming and reached in her pocket to make sure she had the card that told when the show would be aired. Cal and Robin will be excited about this development, she thought, and knew that without them, her dreams could never be realized. A smile spread across her face as she looked forward to getting back to the peace and solitude of the farm.

As the van drove past the nursery, a sprite of a girl in white shorts attracted the man inside's attention as she edged into his line of vision. Gary Snyder kept one eye on the road and one on Robin Smith as she set some pots on a table at the front of the nursery.

He strained to look back and scrutinize the parking lot. Only one vehicle. Could she be alone, he wondered. Then the other part of him, the part that was afraid, told him to keep moving.

A quarter of a mile past the crest of the hill, almost like a reflex, he made a sharp turn into an abandoned driveway. He sat there for a moment listening to his heart drum in his ears. Then a strange subdued grin spread across his face as he put the gears in reverse and headed back toward the nursery.

From the top of the hill, he could see the white shorts bounce around. He only wanted to get one look at her up close. Maybe she would be nice instead of a nasty bitch like all the rest!

He pulled the van onto the shoulder of the road next to the nursery and sat there for a moment staring at the cluttered dash. A bead of sweat splattered on the steering wheel. After swiping his arm across his greasy forehead, he haltingly opened the door. His movements were stiff as he got out and mechanically walked toward the lot, not daring to raise his eyes off the ground.

"Looking for some perennials?"

God! The voice was so sweet! Suddenly his eyes consumed the delicate doll-like figure.

"Is there something special you're looking for?"

That's it! Buy enough so she'll offer to help load the van!

"These will be good," he mumbled, pointing to a cluster of yarrow plants.

The man stood in the hot afternoon sun in a sweat-soaked shirt, every muscle tense, barely breathing, while Robin went over to the booth to make change.

His jaw tightened and fists clenched as the smiling figure strolled toward him. When the small porcelain hand put the change in his, ugly waves of desire consumed him and he wanted to grab her right there and then. But he was controlled by animal cunning. First, he'd lure her to the van.

Picking up one of the gallon pots, Robin said, "I hope you enjoy these. They look wonderful either in large drifts or spotted around the garden." Then handing him the pot, she said, "I'll get a cart and bring the rest over to you."

Violently aroused, Gary Snyder rushed to the back of the van, unfastened the padlock, yanked off the chain and swung the doors open. Tossing in the pot, he swung around to get ready to grab Robin when he saw an old man with a cart coming toward him.

Gary Snyder's formula for survival was suddenly triggered by dark memories of years in prison. He would do nothing to stand out. Without a word, he loaded the plants and drove away.

CHAPTER 8

WKNY-TV's production assistant tapped on the side of the opened door of her boss's office. "You got a minute to look at some of the video Steve took at the farmers' market on Saturday?"

The production manager, looking as if she welcomed the break, threw her pen on the desk and said, "Sure."

The assistant snapped the tape into the player and turned on the monitor across the room. "I want you to take a look at this woman." She fast-forwarded until the wavy image of Lynn in her straw hat flickered across the screen.

The production manager leaned back in her chair and watched the fresh-faced woman in a light blue denim shift and a wide-brimmed straw hat knowledgeably tell about how simple and rewarding it was to grow perennials. The manager liked the way Lynn projected the kind of enthusiasm that only comes from someone who truly believes in what they're doing. In fact, she was surprised to feel an urge to go out and plant something herself.

The tape was viewed several times.

"You've definitely got something there," said the manager.

"I know. We could really use her to punch up our Sunday afternoon nature show. Maybe ten minutes. She's got the look...confidence.... I think we've got a winner here."

"All right. Get her name from Steve and try and cut a deal." She started to rifle through her desk for her budget when the assistant said, "I already checked. We can go as high as two-hundred a program."

"Okay. Give her a contract that locks in that figure for a year with an option for us to renew for two more years. And make sure there's a bail-out clause with thirty day notice in case we want to dump her." The production manager, aware of the disapproving expression on her assistant's face, added, "You never know. She may turn out to be some kind of *prima donna*."

Lynn came in from the greenhouse to make some coffee, when the phone rang. She pulled up a chair and sat down as Mindy Templeton, the assistant production director of *WKNY-TV*, told her how pleased they were with the video.

"We'd like to know if you would be interested in a ten-minute segment on our nature show every Sunday afternoon."

Lynn was speechless.

"We'd give you two-hundred dollars."

"How many shows would I have to do for that?"

There was a short chuckle. "That's per show."

"How many shows?"

"Hopefully it'll turn out to be every week."

"How would we go about this?"

"Lynn, why don't you start by making a list of ... let's see.... Ten programs. Describe what you'd talk about.... show.... That kind of thing, and bring it down with you so we can talk about a contract."

"Sure. I could do that."

"How about two days from now? Let's see..." The assistant flipped through her calendar. "Ten o'clock?"

"I'll be there. Ten o'clock on Thursday."

Lynn put the phone down and paced nervously. Her mind was spinning. She stopped abruptly, then ran over to the desk and pulled out her budget and quickly multiplied two hundred times fifty-two weeks. Just as she thought! Ten thousand four hundred dollars in one year! The ramifications of this windfall were too much to absorb, so she shoved the budget back under the blotter and dialed Shelly.

"Can you believe it? Me? On TV?"

"Thank God for that! I haven't been able to sleep nights worrying about you."

"Oh, Shelly. If only Ken were here. He would have been so proud. His mom and dad too."

"Don't think about that, honey. Right now, you've got to do something about your nails. They do close-ups of hands on these shows."

Lynn gave out a hearty laugh. "I love you, Shelly. You never lose sight of the real priorities."

Lynn's mind raced through a series of program ideas and she barely listened to Shelly as she ran on about the town gossip, that is, until Lynn picked up on the name Sam Reynolds. "What was that you said, Shelly?"

"Barb McMasters. Remember? Our old school chum. She's got her trap set for him."

"Who?"

"Sam Reynolds! Aren't you listening? He's big in the music business in New York and is building somewhere in the country. Anyway, all the music people in Syracuse are ga ga over his coming here. Barb's on the symphony board so she's throwing one of her big parties in July with him as the guest of honor. I understand his place isn't quite finished yet, but he's moving in any day now to supervise the installation of his sound equipment."

"How do you know all these things?"

"It's Pete, honey. He does everyone in town's teeth and hears almost everything. I told him if he doesn't land us an invitation to this party, I'll never forgive him."

"I happen to know Mr. Reynolds."

"*Really.*"

"He's building right across the road from me."

"My God, Lynn! He's not the guy you threw out, is he?"

"The very one."

"Lynn, you're your own worst enemy. You've got to do something about that temper of yours. This guy would be a perfect catch for you. Honey, you've got to get back in good graces with this Reynolds fella right away."

"Forget that! He's an arrogant.... I won't say it."

"What am I going to do about you!"

"Watch me every Sunday afternoon on TV. That's what. Gotta run."

Returning to the greenhouse with Cal's coffee, Lynn decided not to say anything about the TV show until Jess got home from school. It didn't seem right to talk about this without him, so she got back to work, barely listening to Cal as her mind reeled in excitement.

They'd been planting new seedlings to winter over in the greenhouse before she went into the house and were still at it when Jess came in after he got off the bus. Without being asked, the boy jumped right into the assembly line after snatching a cookie off the table.

Finally Lynn asked Cal and Jess to stop for a minute so she could talk to them. Then she washed her hands in the sink as they pulled up stools. She tried hard not to get carried away as she told them about the call, just in case something went wrong. But there was no holding Jess back.

"Two hundred dollars a show! Gezz, we're gonna be rich! I can't wait to tell everyone at school my mom's going to be a TV star!"

Lynn reached over and put her hand on the boy's shoulder. "Wait a minute, buddy. The lady said something about a contract. Let's not tell anyone anything until we get it."

"You sure she didn't mean two-hundred for all them shows?" Cal asked cautiously.

"She told me specifically it was per show."

Everyone was quiet until Jess finally said what they all were thinking. "I wish dad was here to see this."

Cal leaned over and put his arm around the boy and they all sat there, each trying to cope with their feelings in a way, which they had somehow discovered, worked for them over the past year.

Finally Lynn slapped her legs and said, "Let's get back to work, everyone. *We're not rich yet.*"

Lost in thought about the unusual turn of events, they all worked in silence. After a while Cal started in with the day's gossip, his habit during late afternoons when everyone was too tired to think about anything else. As usual, he began by bringing everyone up to date on the affairs of Cricket Johnson and her husband Squeak who lived with their four kids in a trailer on Woodcock Road.

"Nope. He isn't going to give her another chance. He swore if she ever ran off with Jeb Dunes again, he wouldn't take her back."

"Who's he ever going to get to take care of those kids? After she's tired of running, he'll take her back just like he did the last time," Lynn said as she swept the droppings from the day's work into a pile. She leaned on the broom and worried about the two girls now going into their teens. Robin's mother had told her one of them was wild, just like their mother. "Cal, I've got some clothes that might fit those girls. You know. Things I wore in college. If I put them together, would you take them over?"

He nodded, then said, "Everybody's talking about that little girl that's missing in Cortland. The troopers aren't saying anything official, but..." He scratched behind his ear. "Nobody's holding out much hope for her being alive." He turned to Jess. "You be careful now. I know Cortland's two counties over, but it'll still pay to watch, now." Everyone sat there, again mulling over the news of the day, until Lynn broke the silence with, "Cal, how much do you know about the man across the road?"

"How much do you want to know?"

"First off, why don't you ever talk about him?"

Cal and Jess looked at each other and each knew what the other was thinking.

"Didn't see any point in gettin' you riled."

"They say he's getting ready to move in."

"Yep. He's letting Sauterfield rent the fields like he did from Mrs. Reichert. Then, once all his things arrive, Sauterfield and his wife are going to help him uncrate them. Meanwhile, Reynolds is gonna sleep on a cot while they work on his studio."

"What kind of a studio does he have?"

"Mom, Nora Sauterfield told Billy's mom he makes all the music for *Men in Blue*...and movies too."

Lynn looked inquiringly at Jess.

"He's real nice, Mom."

Lynn sprayed a tray down as she asked, "How would you know that, Jess?"

The boy's eyes darted over to Cal who was slowly shaking his head and rolling his eyes.

"Well, Jess? I'm waiting."

Cal spoke up instead. "I took him up there when I delivered some straw my son sold Reynolds for his lawn. You know, the day you asked me to watch the boy. We met him then."

"Mom, you should have seen the place! It's humungus! And the view was super. I could see all our fields, the house, the woods in back. Gosh, it was great!"

The boy suddenly froze as he noticed his mother throw a squinty glare at Cal. Then he went over and nudged Cal with his elbow. With a disappointed look on his face, he said, "We'd better get back to work."

Cal, never able to leave well enough alone, said, "You know now, Lynn, he did move the road just to make you happy. And that tree and Lucky.... You know.... None of that was necessarily his fault."

Lynn walked up and down the aisles gently spraying the newly seeded pots and was embarrassed all over again for loosing control that morning in front of so many people. Even Shelly had heard the gossip in Eastlake. If only she could get over the senseless anger she felt every time she thought of Lucky. She knew Sam Reynolds wasn't directly responsible. But if he only hadn't come to the hollow with all his money to begin with, this never would have happened. But evidently he was here to stay, and more importantly, Jess and Cal liked him. She promised herself she would put her resentment aside and let them both enjoy a normal relationship with the man even though she didn't think she'd ever find it in her heart to forgive him.

Once Lynn's silence told Cal the coast was finally clear as far as the subject of the man across the road was concerned, there was no stopping him.

"Yep. Sauterfield told my boy that Reynolds asked him how much he thought it would cost to put a chicken-wire fence around his property." Cal waited a moment for that to sink in and then winked at Jess. "Sauterfield told him he didn't know how much it would cost, but if he did put it up, all he'd keep out was the chickens."

That was too much even for Lynn. She joined in the hearty laughter.

CHAPTER 9

Mindy Templeton took a moment to rearrange the piles on her desk, then glanced at her watch and saw she had fifteen minutes until Lynn Richardson's appointment. She hit the rewind button and watched the tape one more time and wished like hell she looked as good as Lynn. After thinking for a moment about the twenty pounds she needed to shed, she chalked it up to genes.

For the past three years, in addition to her job, Mindy had been slugging away at her doctoral thesis in Women's Studies at Syracuse University. By the end of the year, she expected to be finished and finally teaching full time. Right now, all she could manage was teaching one night-course each semester at the local community college. With two kids at home, the effort was a struggle, but she needed to beef-up her resume.

Mindy was struck by the fact that Lynn Richardson was exactly the kind of woman she was chronicling for her thesis. As she listened to Lynn explain how she started her business after marrying a farmer, she saw a classic thumbnail sketch of the struggle most women go through trying to make a place for themselves. They look for their own meaningful work, their own money and want to be in control of where their life is going. Mindy felt empowering as she realized that she was probably playing a pivotal part in this woman's life, then shut her eyes tightly and prayed to God the lady wouldn't blow it.

Lynn pulled into the television station's parking lot. The place had been easy to find, just like the receptionist had told her. She reached over and her trembling hand picked up the file folder with her program outlines. She wasn't taking any chances; there were twelve.

Getting everything into Robin Smith's computer the night before had been a struggle with her little brother's sticky fingers constantly reaching for her pages. Robin, who had been helping her mother with a sewing project, finally put him to bed so Lynn could type unfettered.

When the unmistakable voices of the Eleven O'clock News anchors drifted from the living room, she'd worried so much about the Smiths asking her to leave she got a splitting headache. But a half-hour later, when the crisp pages were finally spit out of the printer and Robin handed her the sheets, the whole episode became worthwhile.

Sitting in the car, Lynn wished she had a briefcase instead of a manila folder, but quickly dismissed the thought. She was determined not to clutter her head with anything that wasn't one-hundred-percent posi-tive. What they're looking for, she recalled the lady telling her on the phone, is "someone who projects well on video." She nervously took a look at herself in the mirror and wished she'd gotten more sleep.

Once inside, Mindy Templeton appeared in the "no frills" reception area and led Lynn through a labyrinth of narrow hallways to an office that barely had room for a desk and chair.

After they were seated, Lynn pulled the outline from the folder and handed it to Mindy who put on her glasses and began to read. Within minutes her expression reflected obvious approval.

While continuing to read, Mindy said, "I see here you're using your nursery as a backdrop."

"Yes. Possibly your crew can do several shows in one trip."

Just then, a man poked his head into the office. Mindy looked up and introduced Bob Caldwell, the station's video director. When he reached over and gave Lynn a vigorous handshake, she was struck by his blond, thirty-something good looks.

"We're all looking forward to working with you," he said with the kind of lingering smile that could make one think he had something else on his mind. His demeanor turned professional. "Our Sunday show needs a shot in the arm. We've been floundering ever since we lost our host."

Lynn didn't know how to take him, but his obvious response to her made her feel important.

He glanced over at Mindy and asked, "Do you have those storyboards for me?"

Mindy tossed Lynn's outline on top of a pile of illustrations, and as she handed them over to Bob, said, "Can you do me a favor and get copies of Lynn's program plans to everyone who's going to sit in on our meeting?"

"Sure thing," he said, giving Lynn a wink.

After he left, Mindy said, "I don't know how closely you've been following our show, but our anchor had a stroke and, frankly, we don't expect him to come back. We've kept the show limping along with guest hosts, but we really need to get someone permanently on board by September."

Mindy stood up and glanced at her watch. "Our production team is going to meet in the conference room in about twenty minutes and go over your outline. But first, I want to show you around. We're not taping this morning so you can get a look at the *Nature Show* set."

The studio, basically an expansive open space with several small sets and a bunch of cameras and banks of lights, was surprisingly sterile. Mindy walked over to a table sitting on a green platform with a scenic backdrop. "As you can see, our set's not too appealing. That's why I think the staff might be enthusiastic about shooting some of the show at your place."

Lynn nodded thoughtfully, but inside brimmed with excitement.

After the tour, they grabbed some coffee and went into the conference room. Like the rest of the building, it was strictly functional: TV monitors, stacks of tapes on a well-worn table, mismatched furniture. The video director, who was leaning against a wall holding a cup of coffee, gave Lynn another reassuring wink as she took a seat. Mindy got things rolling by introducing her boss, Kim Wood, who was obviously in charge.

"Why don't you tell us something about yourself," Kim said as she sat there like an unbiased judge obliged to size Lynn up, something she was extraordinarily good at and what probably got her where she was today.

"I started Richardson's Herbs and Seeds nine years ago on our farm in Oneida County." Lynn looked directly at Kim and stated very matter-of-factly, "I've got a nine-year-old boy and my husband was killed in a farm accident just over a year ago."

Kim's eyes instantly flashed upward at Bob and then back at Lynn.

What could that mean, Lynn wondered? She decided she had said enough about herself. She folded her hands in front of her and asked, "Have you had a chance to look over my program ideas?"

"Yes. We were talking about them before you came in. You evidently have a pretty good fix on what the public is looking for. I'm sure it's based on your experience with your customer base." She tapped her pen impatiently on the table and asked, "Do you think you can keep your spots close to ten minutes?"

"Oh, yes!" Lynn said as she pushed forward in her chair barely stopping short of adding that she'd practiced in front of Cal the day before.

"Are we going to have scripts for each segment in advance?" one of the staff asked.

The video director cleared his throat, drawing everyone's attention. He rubbed the back of his neck, obviously keyed up, and paced slowly as he said, "I don't think that's a very good idea. She's got a naturalness in front of the camera that makes her believable. I don't want to change that. She's not a pro and a script would only make her delivery stilted."

He went over to the table and picked up a copy of Lynn's outline. "By the looks of this, I'm convinced she's got a pretty good handle on what we're looking for. I say we take a camera out to her nursery and tape a couple of segments. Then after we edit them, see what we've got."

Like spectators at a tennis match, everyone's eyes automatically switched to Kim Wood.

"I agree," spoke Kim as she studied Lynn. "Has Mindy discussed the terms of our contract with you?"

"I thought we'd do that after we're done here," interrupted Mindy who'd been on tenterhooks during the entire meeting.

Kim stood up and with a warm smile extended her hand to Lynn. "I hope the two segments Bob is talking about work out. You'll certainly add a breath of fresh air to this program. I wish you well." As she snapped her daytimer closed, she said, "Please excuse me. I've got to get to another meeting." With that she left the room and in an instant the atmosphere became more relaxed as everyone interpreted Kim Wood's words as a blessing of the newcomer.

"Can you be ready for us to shoot two segments early next week?" Bob asked.

"Oh, yes!"

"Would you mind my coming out to look the place over first? So I've got an idea of what the location actually looks like."

"Sure."

"How about tomorrow around one?"

Lynn thought for a moment, but her mind had gone blank the instant Kim Wood disappeared. She wasn't used to being stared at so intensely and was stunned at how fast they had moved.

"One o'clock should be good," she said blindly.

Mindy tapped Lynn on the shoulder. "Come back to my office so we can talk about the contract."

On the trip to Mindy's office, Lynn felt as if she were floating in space. The whole wondrous proposition of being on TV had suddenly become a reality. Dumbfounded, the only concrete thought she could pull together was how she was going to celebrate with Jess and Cal that afternoon over milk and cookies and a fresh pot of coffee.

Lynn scanned the two-page contract with her name and the date hand-written in the blanks along with two years and two hundred dollars per segment. When Lynn asked Mindy about the thirty-day notice, she brushed the article aside as something that was rarely used, mostly in the event of illness. Lynn knew better and forgave Mindy for soft-pedaling the delicate issue.

No. Lynn didn't want to take the contract to her lawyer. Was this woman kidding? This piece of paper was going to make the difference between her and Jess eking out an existence and living like normal human beings!

Lynn barely listened to Mindy explain the major points. Instead, she stared blankly ahead. When Mindy tried to get her attention, Lynn shook herself out of her trance, reached for the pen and said, "Where do I sign?"

CHAPTER 10

With the dinner dishes done and the kitchen picked up, Lynn put on the water for a cup of tea. Outside, Jess and his friend, Billy Barnhill, hollered to each other as they raced their bikes up and down the driveway. Lynn stood by the window and knew the sun was starting to set behind the house when she saw the dark shadows in the grass and the orange glow on the rolling green fields. Even the sweat on the boys' faces glimmered like rose gold.

For the first time in a long time Lynn felt at peace. She couldn't wipe the grin off her face as she thought about the little party she'd had that afternoon with Jess and Cal to celebrate the contract. In an instant she had gone from not knowing how she was going to get through the year, to being absolutely positive she was going to make it. That is, if her show was a success. Cal had been quick to point out the contract allowed the station to cancel her with thirty-day notice.

That just wasn't going to happen. By some act of God she'd gotten her foot in the door and she wasn't going to let it slam shut even though preparing for the show segments and handling the business at the nursery would definitely be a challenge.

The whistling kettle got quickly turned off. Instead of tea, she was going to treat herself to a quiet moment with her thoughts before the race to get through the summer swung into full-gear. She was going to take a walk down the lane between the meadows and watch the sun set like she and Ken used to do when they wanted to be alone.

She yelled to the boys not to go into the road and noticed the swallows darting at Queenie who cautiously made her way to the barn. Cal had run the bush-hog along the lane to keep the grass down so she and Jess could get to the back woods to pick apples and berries later in the summer, but she could still feel the coolness of the evening dew as the grass brushed against her ankles. The frogs, detecting the sun starting to set, sent up early fragments of the night's music.

While she strolled along the lane, the air cooled by degrees as the red orb lowered. She noticed that the blue larkspur growing wild in the hedgerows on either side of the lane had taken on a vivid fuchsia glow as it reflected the crimson sky. The majesty of this spectacle made Lynn feel small, almost minute, and she understood why farmers felt a part of the land. They knew they were temporary caretakers, existing just a millisecond between the generations that were on the land before them and those who would follow.

She thought about the Indians who must have roamed this land, and could see why they had such a deep reverence for nature. The realization that she was a link in a long chain made her feel like she belonged to something bigger than herself. This thought both humbled and comforted her. Her mind lingered on the emptiness she had always felt as she and her mother shuffled from run-down apartment to run-down apartment. She shuttered at the thought of her boy feeling that way and became more determined than ever to see that he would get this land.

The stark white interior of the fridge was empty except for a carton of orange juice. That would do. Sam poured some into a glass along with a few chugs of vodka and went over to the bank of windows that ran to the peak of the A-frame. His footsteps echoed in the massive space, empty except for a cot with a few blankets and his tarp-draped grand piano, one of two which had to be brought in before the house was fully enclosed.

By the first of June, nothing was holding Sam in New York, and even though everything wasn't finished in the new house, he had packed enough clothes for a couple of weeks and gone to Eastlake. Most of the paintings and sculpture in his New York loft were already crated with movers scheduled to do the rest. Sam was counting on Ralph to show up and make sure everything got on the truck. Joey Schwartz had already disassembled his studio equipment.

The red-orange sun was spectacular as it sank behind the green hills, washing the room with a golden-pink glow. After a lifetime of watching the sun disappear behind skyscrapers while reflecting onto thousands of panes of glass, Sam was feeling eerily out of place when the boys on the bikes caught his eye. They looked like miniature dolls from that distance, but their joy was apparent by the way the bikes sped down the drive and then made slow graceful turns circling the barn and nursery lot.

He liked her boy. Yes, that's it. Jess. His blond hair was unlike his mother's. Sam tried to imagine what the father must have looked like.

He took another gulp of his drink and just as he was turning from the window spotted someone in a white sweatshirt bobbing down the lane toward the barns. Something gripped his insides as he instinctively recognized Lynn Richardson.

She disappeared for a few moments but then reemerged from between the barns. As Jess whizzed by, she playfully grabbed the boy's hat and continued to run after him. Sam watched intently as the friend was waved off, the bike put away and mother and son disappeared into the house.

Sam stood at the window rubbing his beard; eyes fixed on the white farmhouse, wondering about the woman inside. Over the past few months, whenever he was able to get up to his new house, he'd been drawn to this window and by now knew her routine. No boyfriends.

Just long hours of what seemed like hard work. Even from that distance he could tell she was driven.

Once, he'd caught sight of her stocking the hardware store in town with her seeds. She'd been so intense that she didn't noticed him staring at her from the middle of the aisle. Other than when he had carried her into the house, this was the first time he'd had a good look at her. In spite of the loose-fitting shift, he couldn't help noticing the curves as she moved. After she left, he went over to her rack and picked up two of each.

God, he wished their dog hadn't been killed. Then he had an idea. Tomorrow he'd drop into the nursery and ask the old man to help him find them a new one. Something irresistible. He felt a pang of shame at the blatant ploy, then laughed out loud as he slapped his thigh in glee.

He went over to the piano and flipped the tarp aside. Sitting with his back to the window, his fingers danced across the keys now reflecting the pink cast of the sunset, and even after the room became dark the sound of the notes continued to echo in the empty room.

The sun was yet to rise from behind the horizon. Lynn, in a pair of shorts and a T-shirt, was outside turning on the sprinklers for the forty or so rows of flowers and herbs in her permanent garden, her pride and joy. For the past nine years she'd scoured the countryside looking for these heirloom plants, carefully qualifying each one, making sure they weren't from hybrids someone ordered out of a seed catalog.

Most of them came with a story. The first year of her search she'd found Ella Rockwell, a seventy-year-old farmwoman who'd been widowed for years and lived on the same farm her great, great, grandparents had bought. Seeds from the flowers and herbs her distant relatives had brought over from England had been carefully reaped every season and passed on from generation to generation. Ella was the one who taught Lynn the almost forgotten secrets of how to choose the best seeds and store them over the winter.

Many of the plants in Lynn's permanent garden were in full bloom and she and Robin were already taking seeds for the dryers. This was one of the most backbreaking chores of the summer but the heart of Lynn's business. Robin, with her small, fine-boned fingers, was excellent at picking out seeds, and the only one Lynn could trust to get it right. Scrupulous attention had to be paid to handling the seeds so there'd be one-hundred-percent certainty every one was identified correctly. But first, they'd select and mark the plants with the most beautiful flowers, so they'd know which to pick from once the blooms went to seed.

Lynn waited until the garden was watered, then went over to the potted perennials in the nursery lot. Some were on wagons or makeshift tables, others in neat clusters on the ground. She turned on the hose and systematically started watering them, marveling at how clean and fresh everything looked in the clear early morning light.

After waving to neighbor driving by on his way into work, Lynn's eyes drifted up to the top of the hill. The house stood out on the horizon like a pyramid. She hated the self-conscious feeling she got as she wondered if Sam Reynolds ever looked down at them.

Cal pulled in around seven and Robin arrived at eight, and the three of them scurried to beef up the inventory for the weekend crowds and the farmers' market.

Lynn let Robin and Cal handle the trickle of buyers who were strolling through the lot, while she went into the barn to see to the seeds and straighten up since the guy from the TV station would be there at one.

When Lynn went back to the lot, she eyed Sam Reynold's green Blazer pulling out and felt strangely disappointed that she missed him. As she straightened out the seed stand, she casually asked Robin if he'd bought anything.

"No. He just wanted to talk to Cal."

Lynn looked over at the old man who was unloading a wagon full of plants. Probably wants some more straw from his son, she thought.

Then remembering something that had bothered her, she pulled a cigarette butt out of her pocket, walked over to Cal and showed it to him.

"You know where I found this?"

He looked at her blankly.

"Last night I took a walk down the lane and found it just before the woods." She let it roll around in her palm "Who could have been smoking back there?"

Cal picked up the crumpled Marlboro. "That's nothing. Just blown there by the wind."

Two cars pulled in and Lynn tossed the butt into the garbage.

That morning Sam had awakened with a longing he hadn't felt since the days before he and Lil had gotten together. While looking down at the activity in the nursery lot, he couldn't get Lynn Richardson out of his mind as he sipped the coffee he'd gotten from the diner in town.

Joey Schwartz would be there by one with all his equipment. What a dependable guy. He had scheduled a crew, mostly his brothers, to start loading everything in Manhattan at six that morning. He'd be on the road by now since he was personally accompanying the equipment to Eastlake. No wonder he was so much in demand by the studios. Nothing was left to chance.

Hopefully, the electrician would finish a couple of the extra things Joey had asked for before the truck got there. Knowing Joey, Sam expected him to jump right into the job and work non-stop all weekend. Sam checked his watch when the electrician pulled in, hoping once the man got started, he could cut out and take a look at the dog Cal had told him about.

That spring, Glenn Bacon, a farmer down the road, had kept one of the pups from a litter his Rottweiler had had with his German Shepherd. Even though his farm was practically overrun with dogs, there was something about this one the farmer hadn't been able to resist. Cal had suggested Sam stop by during milking so Glenn would be sure to be there. Maybe he would be willing to part with the dog if he knew it was for Ken's widow.

When Sam pulled up to the barn and got out, three dogs ran up and sniffed him but he didn't spot the puppy until he walked into the dark, dank barn. The pungent odor of manure and the blaring radio disoriented him at first, but then he eyed a pup lying on the floor next to the farmer who was disconnecting a milking machine from a cow's teats.

As Sam approached, the dog slowly rose emitting a threatening growl from his sneering mouth. The farmer turned, and noticing Sam said, "That's okay, boy." The menacing expression quickly faded and the dog sank down on the straw.

The farmer stood up, wiped his hands with a rag, then reached over and shook Sam's hand as he said, "You're the fella who bought the Reichert property, aren't you?"

"That's right. Sam Reynolds."

"I hear tell you don't like chickens."

Sam was embarrassed. He stood with his hands on his hips and looked away and wondered if he'd ever live down his gaffe about putting chicken wire around his property.

The farmer folded his arms and grinned; obviously pleased he'd been able to land that remark.

"That's quite a place you've built up there."

"Yes. Everything's turned out real well."

Sam crouched down and petted the dog that questioningly looked up at his master.

"I was talking to Cal Wilkinson and he told me about this little guy."

The farmer shook his head. "*Oh, no.* There's no way I'm going to part with *him*. There's something special about that dog."

"I don't want him for myself."

Sam thought carefully about what he was going to say next. He had to have this dog.

"I feel partly to blame Lynn Richardson's dog was killed a couple of months back, so I'm kind of obliged to get her a new one."

The farmer was listening intently, a good sign.

"Yeah. I know. Lucky belonged to Ken."

"I don't think just *any dog* will replace him."

The farmer looked around like he was mulling something over. "I thought his wife would light out of here the minute she had the chance, but she's working harder than hell to keep that place."

Sam knew from experience the local farmers weren't big talkers, so he just waited for him to say what was on his mind.

Finally, the farmer pointed to a tractor and said, "That's the one that crushed Ken. I didn't want any part of something with that kind of history, but when no one was bidding at their farm auction, I looked over at Lynn and the boy... and hell, I needed a tractor and they needed to sell it."

He picked some baling string off a nail, bent down next to the dog, and tied it around the pup's collar. "Here. Keep him on a rope for a few days or he'll high tail it right back here. I don't think I'll be letting him go a second time."

"How much do I owe you?" Sam said as he reached for his wallet.

"That's okay. If Sauterfield ever decides he doesn't want to rent your fields, I'd appreciate you giving me a call."

"Sure thing."

"His name's Commander, by the way."

Sam led the pup to the Blazer, then rode with the windows down to get rid of the barn smell. The boy would be getting off the school bus around two-thirty, he thought. By then he could give the dog a bath. Sam recalled what the farmer had said about Lynn trying to hold on to the farm and bit his lower lip in angst. No wonder she resented his offer to buy her out.

Sam kept glancing over at Commander. The dog had the coloring and face of a Rottweiler but wasn't as chunky. He had a certain dignity as he sat at attention looking straight ahead. Definitely an Alpha male.

Sam scanned the nursery lot before he swung into his driveway and was surprised at how disappointed he felt when there was no sign of Lynn. Before Sam reached the top of the hill, he faced the fact that he wanted this woman more than any he'd ever known.

The kitchen sink was too small for Commander and there was no hose to wash him with outside, so Sam led him to the enclosed shower in the bathroom, stripped and then pulled the reluctant pup in. Forty-five minutes later, with that sloppy ordeal over, Sam was at his piano experimenting with a melody that had been running through his head all week while the dog sat in the corner contentedly gnawed on a stale bagel.

Even though there was no time for anything but a peanut butter and jelly sandwich and a cup of coffee before Bob Caldwell showed up, Lynn managed to have a little talk with Cal.

"Now, whatever you do, don't interrupt me when I'm talking with the TV guy. Especially not about some customer complaint. And above all, don't jump in and contradict me."

As Cal sat mumbling to himself, Lynn got up and went over and gave him a big hug. "I love you Cal. I just don't want anything to go wrong. I really need this money." Then she turned and ran up the back staircase to change yelling, "And don't offer any information, either!"

The BMW pulled into the nursery lot fifteen minutes early but Lynn was ready in a pair of jeans she'd pressed the night before and a new T-shirt she'd splurged on in a shop in Eastlake. Bob, with a digital camera slung around his neck, got out holding a clipboard and light meter and gave Lynn a warm handshake.

"This is beautiful country up here."

She stood smiling pleasantly.

"Can I look around?"

"Be my guest."

The shoppers couldn't help but notice the tall, handsome man. He appeared to be genuinely interested in the plants, picking one up every once in a while and examining it closely. Lynn stood back and watched him take some Polaroid shots of Robin standing behind a huge skid of blooming lavender plants. They were joined in conversation by a couple of ladies, with Bob's mirthful laugh rising above the rest.

After a while he came over and told Lynn he'd love a guided tour. He busily jotted down readings from his light meter as she showed him the heirloom garden and rows of potted perennials that were just over a year old and wouldn't be sold until the following year. The tour finished in the greenhouse where hundreds of new seedlings were growing.

In each location Bob took several shots of Lynn from different angles, more interested in the locations than his model. The power source also got checked out and amps noted. Surprisingly, in less than an hour they had covered the whole gamut.

The last stop was the nursery lot. Bob put everything in his car, closed the door and strolled toward Lynn.

"Is there anyway I can get something cool to drink?"

Lynn was embarrassed by her lack of hospitality.

"Of course. Why don't you come into the house."

Entering the kitchen, Bob let out a long, slow whistle. "This certainly is a big, old place." He turned and smiled at Lynn. "Mind if I look around?"

"No, go right ahead."

She followed him into the dining room where the cluttered table glared at her.

"This is where I prepare my mailings," she said apologetically.

Bob wasn't paying attention as he meandered into the front parlor. "Wow, this is the real McCoy. The furniture's got to be rosewood." He glanced over at the staircase. "Is that *beautiful*. What is it? Cherry?"

Lynn went over to the staircase and lovingly ran her hand down the banister she'd polished a thousand times. "Yes. And so is all the woodwork and fireplace mantel."

Bob crossed his arms and kept nodding as he became lost in thought. "Come in the kitchen and I'll give you some lemonade."

Lynn got out two of her nicest placemats and arranged them on the table with a napkin, then poured two glasses of lemonade, after which she put out a dish of her homemade cookies and sat down.

Bob kept fidgeting with the glass as he watched her eat, carefully studying her face. This didn't bother Lynn since, after Kim Wood, she'd come to the conclusion that TV people were in the habit of studying peoples' faces almost as if they were inanimate objects. Two could play this game, she decided, and as she sipped her lemonade didn't take her eyes off him. She hadn't thought she'd ever meet anyone as handsome as Ken, but this man was an Adonis. In fact, he was almost too perfect and definitely prettier than she was.

Joey arrived in the truck around one, followed by his two brothers in a van. Just like Sam figured, after announcing they had already stopped for lunch, Joey started unloading. He took out his measuring tape and compared the actual dimensions in the studio room with his marked-up blueprint and was pleased at what he found. While his brothers did the grunt work, Joey met with the electrician and went over every breaker and outlet to make sure the power was right. Sam was surprised when Commander growled at Joey. The pup sure delivered a lot of loyalty in return for a stale bagel.

While Joey was busy with the electrician, Sam decided to trim his beard before going down the hill with the dog. He studied himself in the mirror. Everything was turning out the way he had planned. The house would be finished in plenty of time and he knew Joey would have his studio up and running by the end of the next week. Thank God he wouldn't have to do another *Men In Blue* segment until August. The foreign film script had arrived and a melody was already whirling around in his head.

Sam rubbed his jaw and stretched his neck as he stood erect and examined himself in the mirror. None of what was happening to him was really luck. The success he was experiencing seemed like a natural conclusion to a lifetime of labor. However, Lynn Richardson was another matter. Just the thought of her made his heart beat in his throat. Suddenly, the image of Lil repulsed him and he quickly pushed her out of his mind.

Until now, he figured his empty emotional life gave him the freedom he needed to be creative. He'd always had his work to feed off. However, a need he'd pushed beyond his consciousness for years was now surging to the surface. By some strange twist of fate he'd been brought to this beautiful hollow with the charming farmhouse and the strong woman struggling to keep it. He was moved when he thought she was having a hard time. He'd fix that. The dog was just for openers.

He could laugh now when he remembered how feisty she was when she threw him out. That's what he liked about her. The thing he saw in the post office. There was a self-possession about her, like someone with a dream bigger than themselves. Yet she was tender with the boy and the flowers. He fleetingly wondered how tender she'd be with someone she loved, then he fixed on the image of her watering the plants that morning as he slapped on some after-shave lotion.

When Sam pulled into the nursery lot, the boy, who had just gotten off the school bus, was talking with Cal. The two watched Sam come toward them carrying the dog.

"Hi, Mr. Reynolds," Jess said enthusiastically.

"Hello there, son."

Cal gave Sam a big wink, then quickly jerked his head toward the boy to nudge Sam along. Sam looked around for Lynn but she was nowhere in sight as he placed Commander at the boy's feet.

Sam knew he had to get this right. He was counting on the dog to break the ice with Lynn. Mercifully, the dog didn't growl like Sam worried he would, and instead licked the boy's face.

"This fella's name is Commander and he's yours. That is, if your mother says it's okay."

"He's beautiful," said Jess. Then he looked up at Cal with a questioning expression.

"Do you think Mom will let me keep him?"

"You won't know unless you ask."

The boy swooped up the dog and raced toward the house, then stopped and shouted for Sam.

"Hurry up! Let's go ask her!"

They both excitedly ran up the porch steps when Jess stopped cold and said in an almost panic, "No! Let's not take him inside!" He put the dog down and told him not to move with the sort of kindly authority that only someone raised with a family dog could impart.

Jess swung open the door to the kitchen and Sam followed behind. Startled, Lynn quickly turned toward them. Everyone froze at the unexpected scene except Bob, who casually lifted his drink and eyed Sam.

Things weren't going as well as Sam had planned.

Jess ignored the uncomfortable feeling that permeated the air and went over to his mother and whispered urgently, "Mom, can you come out on the porch for a minute? I've got something important to ask you."

Lynn was so disconcerted to see Sam in her doorway she brushed aside the idea of making introductions and, instead, turned to Bob and told him she'd be right back. As she stepped out onto the porch, Jess was lovingly caressing the dog.

"Isn't he beautiful, Mom?"

Lynn was speechless as she turned and stared incredulously at Sam who was still holding the screen door open.

An image of total destruction flashed across Sam's mind.

"I'm sorry, Mrs. Richardson. I'm afraid I've come at the wrong time."

"No! Everything's fine!" the boy shouted anxiously.

Sam couldn't believe it was happening all over again. Why couldn't he get this right? He should have asked her before he brought the dog over. "I just felt you might take him as a gift," he said. "My feeling responsible and all." He felt himself redden.

"Please, Mom! *Please* let me have him."

Sam couldn't believe how awkward Lynn's stiffness made him feel. She was like a cat with an arched back. "I don't mean to come between you and your boy," he said apologetically, disappointment on his features.

Lynn started to respond, but stopped after catching sight of Cal who had come up to the house and stood with a trace of concern on his brow. She stepped back and her eyes fell upon the boy. After taking a deep breath filled with resignation, she looked at Sam and said coolly, "Thank you, Mr. Reynolds. It was very thoughtful of you to bring us the dog. We're delighted to accept."

Cal's face melted into a smile and the boy quickly snatched up the pup and ran down the stairs yelling, "I love you, Mom! Thanks, Sam!" as he ran to show Robin his new pet.

Lynn passed Sam close enough to get a whiff of the after-shave lotion and looked him square in the eyes before going inside.

As Sam started down the stairs he blew out a long-held breath.

"Yep," said Cal with a huge grin on his face. "She's warming up to you. She didn't throw you out this time."

CHAPTER 11

Mindy Templeton enjoyed the ride to Eastlake as she gazed out the window from the passenger's side of Bob's BMW. The cameraman was in the back, every once in a while checking out his equipment and supplies. He hadn't said anything, but Mindy was sure he wasn't looking forward to working with an amateur. This shoot could take all day, and if they weren't lucky, followed by another day of agonizing editing.

No wonder they called this the Uplands of Central New York, Mindy thought as she estimated they'd been climbing uphill for at least half an hour. Eastlake's quaint little shops looked interesting, but as the car sailed toward the farm on Richardson Road, the countryside seemed incredibly beautiful, the way it can look only after a night of gentle rain with the earth dark and the still-moist green hills glistening under the morning sun.

Mindy glanced over at Bob who was lost in thought and couldn't help noticing how spiffed up he looked. Not the usual well-broken-in Dockers and khakis. A small worry elbowed its way into her consciousness as her mind rested on the coed that interned with him last summer. The door to the building had to be locked until they got the hysterical kid under control while she kept screaming, "He told me to get rid of it!" at the top of her lungs.

Everyone expected Kim Wood to fire him, but instead she fell back on the "use better judgment" directive after calling around and learning they weren't going to replace him with another warm body for the kind of money he was making.

The BMW glided into the lot and was greeted by Lynn who, spotting them coming over the hill, had told Cal and Robin to look busy. But Cal was transfixed as he clutched a pot and watched them get out. Robin's mother, who was coming to help at the sales lot, pulled in behind them. After all the introductions, Lynn led the crew into the house.

There were the usual oohs and aahs about the furniture before they finally settled down at the table. Lynn passed around the papers she'd copied at the record shop in town for twenty-five cents a page and Robin poured everyone coffee as they looked them over.

Mindy suppressed a smile as she studied the stick figures Lynn had drawn in all the scenes. Naturally the ones wearing straw hats were Lynn. Mindy was impressed with how Lynn explained every scene like a seasoned pro. Lynn hadn't grasped the buzzwords yet, but Mindy was sure she'd have them down pat by the end of the shoot. What had she been so worried about? This lady was going to do *just* fine.

After a scene-by-scene discussion of the two segments, the cameraman took off his glasses and rubbed his face in relief. Then he put them back on, slapped his hand on the table and confidently announced, "Let's roll!"

Everyone trooped out to Lynn's heirloom garden that looked spectacular. The day before, Lynn and Robin had removed all the seeds they wanted and then deadheaded all the spent flowers, after which Cal had finely cultivated between each row.

Lynn brushed off her denim shift and checked out her T-shirt before carefully adjusting her straw hat. She was counting on this first scene to turn out to be her signature beginning for every segment.

With the camera rolling, Lynn started down the wide center row that had a mowed path of grass. Mindy put her hand to her mouth and felt her throat tighten as she listened to Lynn say, "Welcome to Richardson's

Herbs and Seeds just outside Eastlake, New York. I'm Lynn Richardson and this is my heirloom garden."

Bob, who was standing with arms folded clutching Lynn's script, smiled and kept nodding his head in approval, then turned and gave Mindy a big thumbs-up.

They went from scene to scene, shooting each two or three times, some just once. Robin assisted on-camera in some of the scenes, while Cal, who was supposed to stay at the nursery lot and help Robin's mother, kept showing up until he was gradually absorbed into the crew.

The second segment, with Lynn in a pair of jeans, kicked off with "Today, I want to introduce you to a couple of my favorite herbs."

By one-thirty they were finished. Right after the Beamer disappeared over the hill whooping broke out. Lynn gave Cal a big hug and playfully admonished him for not staying in the garden center. She took a deep breath, obviously pleased with the way things had gone. Robin's mom was anxious to get back to the house and start calling everyone about Lynn's spot at the farmers' market airing on Thursday. Since she wanted to make sure everyone watched the first *Nature Scene* segment on Sunday in which Robin would be seen; she feverishly started collecting her things from behind the counter.

As Lynn stood rehashing the day's events with Robin, Jess caught sight of a white van slowly passing by. For an instant he made eye contact with the man inside and something about the sullen look on his face made Jess shiver.

"Is something wrong, dearie?" asked Robin's mother.

"No. I'm fine." His eyes remained glued to the van until it disappeared over the hill.

By two, things had slowed down at the nursery. Lynn, tired from the stress of the shoot, decided that Cal should go home early and she would rest. The garden center was left in the care of Robin and Jess.

After Cal and Lynn left, business picked up for a while and Robin had to send Jess in for more change. Two old ladies wanted some advice from Lynn, but were content once Robin found them some plants for their patio. Someone in town had told them a TV crew had been out that morning, so Robin brought out the Polaroid shots that Bob Caldwell had taken of her on his first visit.

When Jess returned with the change, he noticed the white van he'd seen drive by earlier sitting in the lot. The man with the sullen face seemed to be milling around next to the women as they prattled on about the photos. Jess went up behind him and asked, "Can I help you?"

Startled, the man turned around and glared at Jess, then mumbled something and took off in the van.

During the TV shoot, Sam had followed the activity through his new binoculars. Sam knew Lynn couldn't afford to produce a TV commercial, no less have it aired, and figured they must be doing a show. He kept focusing the binoculars on the director. The handsome figure in the round circle of the lens had made Sam's jaws tighten. He studied the fuzzy image and guessed his age somewhere in the mid-thirties. That's why he was here last week, Sam said to himself. The feeling was groundless, but he disliked the guy, especially since the stranger had witnessed the way he'd bumbled the whole dog thing.

At noon, Joey insisted they drive the five miles into town for lunch. The scrambled eggs and sausage from breakfast hadn't moved much past Sam's throat but Joey was used to conducting business during meals, so he reluctantly went along.

That's the way dinner had gone every night since Joey arrived. He ate, drank, and breathed the music business, epitomizing the brilliant but frenetic New York pace that Sam was trying to escape. As they drove back to the house, Sam rubbed his hand on his stomach and recalled the image of the lean, wide-shouldered man he'd seen that morning through the binoculars.

They worked straight through until eight. After begging off dinner, Sam waved to Joey and his brothers as they headed into town to their motel for a quick shower and then a restaurant. Sam laughed to himself as it occurred to him that Joey had already conquered the whole restaurant scene in town, everything from Pete's diner to the five-star Eastlake Inn. The minute he walked through the door flashing his broad grin and making eye contact with everyone in the place, they knew he loved to eat out. He was on a first-name basis with every waitress, owner and regular patron. After a few more days they'd probably be inviting him to join the Rotary Club.

The phone rang.

Sam crunched up his brow as if he were in pain as he recognized Barb McMaster's baby-doll voice. The last thing he needed was a relationship with another rich, spoiled socialite. He regretted he'd agreed to be the guest of honor at her annual symphony shindig. Everything had happened so fast. The conductor of the Syracuse Symphony had introduced her to him when Sam dropped in to say hello, and in minutes Barb was all excited. Of course his old buddy from Julliard couldn't offend one of the symphony's wealthiest patrons, and therefore encouraged her. Sam had been there before and just smiled and thanked her.

Her offer for a game of tennis at the Eastlake Country Club had some merit, though. He patted his stomach and got the directions.

Lynn hadn't remembered being so happy in a long time as she sat at the foot of Jess's bed listening to him tell about the party celebrating the last day of school. She was glad they'd now have more time together. He was growing up to look and act so much like his dad she felt more and more like Ken had never left her. She was thankful their only child had turned out this way.

While Jess went through a play-by-play description of the fight Billy Barnhill had with Stevie over the last chocolate cupcake, her thoughts drifted to what other children would have been like had she and Ken had any. They'd wanted another but had been disappointed month after month. The doctors couldn't come up with an explanation no matter how many tests they took. Doc Green told her these things happen sometimes. Could even be a psychological block on her part. After two years, Ken convinced her he was happy with the one boy God had blessed them with. How much of a disappointment for him was it really, she wondered.

Outside, they heard Commander bark. Lynn went to the window and looked out at the dog straining on his leash toward the back of the property.

"It's just the deer he smells," said Lynn. "He'll stop after we turn the lights off."

They were quiet for a while as Lynn gently rubbed the blanket where the boy's legs lay.

"You're a good boy, Jess. Did I ever tell you how proud I am of you?"

"Gezz, Mom. A hundred times!"

They both laughed and were quiet again.

"Mom?"

"Yes, honey."

"I really like Commander. Sam was nice to get him for us."

Lynn felt a pang of guilt. She was grateful Jess would be home everyday now. She'd kept the pup tied to Lucky's old doghouse next to the kitchen door all week while he was at school. But even in this less than authoritative position the pup growled at all the strangers that came to the house.

Lynn gazed off in space as she said, "He's a good dog. He knows his job... and is proud of it." She reached over and squeezed the boy's hand. "Do you believe that in less than a week he knows who belongs and who doesn't?"

The room had a comfortable look with the soft light from the yellowed lampshade atop the rope-swinging cowboy that had been Ken's as a boy. In fact, the room and all its furniture had been Ken's. Lynn lovingly rubbed the worn quilt as she listened to the sound of the crickets and frogs and the soft whimpering of the pup. Suddenly, maybe because of the quiet from the room above, Commander let out a blood-curdling whine, his final effort at being let in before he settled down for the night. The dog's boldness made them both laugh.

Lynn stood up and said, "We'd better be getting to sleep, honey."

She looked down on the face that reminded her so much of Ken's she didn't want to turn off the light.

The boy fidgeted with the edge of the quilt as he said, "Sam likes you, Mom."

"Of course, darling. We're neighbors."

"You know what I mean, Mom."

Lynn was suddenly embarrassed and felt herself blush.

She quickly bent down and kissed Jess on the forehead and turned off the light.

"Mom?"

"Yes, sweetheart?"

"Can I please bring Commander up. He'll be good. I know it."

Lynn remembered how much the boy liked having Lucky sleep next to him after his father died, and couldn't say no.

Later, undressing in her room, Lynn caught sight of herself in the full-length oval mirror on the Victorian vanity. She slowly took off her bra and looked at the full breasts as the nipples started to contract. As she lifted the nightgown over her head, she looked in the mirror at the reflection of her flat stomach stretched between her hip bones and remembered how Ken would put his arms around her and pull her onto the bed before she could slip it on.

She snuggled between the sheets and was pleased. The day had been good. Maybe Sunday afternoon she and Jess could take something up to Sam Reynolds to thank him properly for the dog. She thought for a moment. Maybe some rosemary plants and a few different kinds of thymes. She'd look his place over and send Cal up later to dig him a small herb garden and afterward arrange everything herself. She wondered what she would wear and then remembered when Ken was alive taking a long bath every Sunday in the late afternoon and putting on a pretty dress for dinner.

After a few minutes, she wiped the tears from her eyes, turned over and fell asleep.

Even though Gary Snyder had been careful coming from the back, the pup's barking had surprised him. They must have just gotten it, he had thought. Hidden downwind for a while, he was about to turn and go back when the farmhouse door opened and the snoopy little kid took the dog in.

The lights in the house had been off for quite a while, so Gary Snyder moved stealthily toward the garden center on the path between the two barns and the heritage garden. He knew the way well.

Commander, lying on the floor next to Jess in the room at the back of the house, shot to attention and started to growl. The boy reached over, put his arm under the pup's big round belly and pulled him up onto the bed. After some comforting, Commander cuddled up against his new master and fell back to sleep.

Gary, now in the garden center, had to hide in the shadows of the booth while a car passed. The headlights gave him a clear shot of the sales counter and the lock on the cabinet door. Damn it! He had to have one. Just one! After the car passed, he fumbled with the lock, then rocked the doors as much as he dared, but no luck.

Another car came over the hill, so he crouched down behind the counter. Waiting for it to pass, he noticed something on the lawn next to the waste bin. He reached over, then got out his lighter. Suddenly the stinging scratches from bramble bushes all along his arms and legs were worth it as he slowly broke into a queer grin at the small child-like figure in the Polaroid.

Lynn held the sales lot phone between her shoulder and jaw while she patiently listened to Ella Rockwell and at the same time fiddled with the security-light timer. The phone had been ringing all day, mostly sweet old ladies who'd given her seeds, cuttings and advice, and who'd seen her on the farmers' market special.

Shelly's car came cruising over the hill. Since there was no way Lynn could rush Ella, she threw Shelly a wave and watched Jess run up and help her with two pizzas. Finally, Lynn's old friend closed with, "I'll be watching you on Sunday."

Lynn decided to take advantage of the lull in the traffic at the garden center and have everyone eat at the picnic table next to the heirloom garden. Once settled in, Shelly ran her hand across Jess's hair. "You don't mind if your mother and I eat inside, do you, baby? Just a little girl-talk between old friends?"

"No, it's okay, Aunt Shelly." Jess scooted toward Robin and gave Shelly a big grin.

"No, just one piece!" squealed Lynn playfully as Shelly piled two on a plate for her. "Now that I'm a television star I've got to watch my figure!"

Robin and Jess snickered as the two women ran into the house in a fit of giggles.

"Well, what'd you think of the show?" burst out Lynn as she settled into a chair.

"Not bad. Not bad at all." Then Shelly propped her chin in her hands. "But, honey, you've got to do something about your hair. You can't just pull it back behind your ears. You need some style."

Lynn took a bite from the slice of pizza and then picked up the long string of cheese that spun from it, and with her pinkie in the air popped it in her mouth.

"Oh, Shelly, I can't wait to see my first segment of *Nature Scene* running on Sunday. Mindy Templeton from the station phoned yesterday and said the show looks great."

After rehashing Lynn's three minutes of fame until it got stale even to them, the two women finished their pizza and Lynn got up to make some fresh coffee. She stood at the sink rinsing out the pot while Shelly started in on the town gossip.

"Guess who I met a couple of days ago?"

"Lay it on me, Shelly."

"None other than Mr. Sam Reynolds."

Lynn went to cupboard and got out a can of coffee and carefully placed it on the counter so she wouldn't miss a word.

"That guy *moves* me," Shelly cooed.

"Where'd you see him?" said Lynn, trying hard to sound casual.

"At the club. He was playing tennis with Barb McMasters. You should have seen her. She was wearing a short... and I mean *short* tennis skirt and a little sleeveless thing. Her blond ponytail was swinging from the back of her visor as she bounced around the court. Let's forget any designs we had on that guy for you, baby. I'm afraid you're no match for that!"

That night, after laying out her clothes for the farmers' market, Lynn picked up Ken's old baseball cap from on top of the dresser, put it on, and used a hand mirror to get a look at her profile in the vanity mirror. She definitely looked like a Tomboy. Shelly was right, she had to do something about her hair. Then she hated herself for the big dose of jealousy the vision of Barb McMasters' ponytail flitting around the tennis court gave her. Suddenly her idea of putting in an herb garden for Sam Reynolds appeared incredibly presumptuous and she felt ashamed. What am I thinking? Why in the world would he want her barging in on his life and putting in a garden. Sure, he brought over the dog. Why wouldn't he under the circumstances?

She pulled the cap off and hugged it as she gave herself a long critical look. Her freckles were out in mass and her complexion as ruddy as ever. She dropped the cap on the dresser and for the hundredth time that day focused on her dream. She was going to make a go of

Richardson's Herbs and Seeds, or die trying. I've got to keep my head screwed on, she commanded herself. She nodded as if she'd made up her mind about something. Yep. If Mr. Sam Reynolds is going to get an herb garden, he's going to have to plant one himself. A nice card. That's it. We'll send him a nice card.

Sunday, they started to close the garden center at four-thirty so Robin could be home in plenty of time to see the show and Lynn and Jess could get cleaned up before it started. Cal, who was invited for the evening, stayed behind.

The first one out of the shower, Lynn snapped on the TV in the parlor on her way into the kitchen, then got out a bottle of wine she remembered was in the back of the fridge. The screen door opened and Cal walked in and sat down, exhausted.

"Here, this should mellow you out," said Lynn as she poured him a glass of wine.

Just then she heard a faint whimper at the door and saw Commander with his nose pressed against the screen.

"*Okay*, you can come in *too*."

Cal laughed out loud as the dog proudly ran to him. "I see you finally found a spot in your heart for this little cuss," he said as he rubbed behind the dog's ears.

Jess appeared at the doorway. "Come on, Mom! The show's gonna start!"

The beginning of the show was as dull as Lynn remembered. After listening to an elderly professor spend fifteen minutes discussing summer plant diseases while sitting behind a desk, she was thrilled to hear him announce anything, no less, "Lynn Richardson will now talk to you about her wonderful heirloom garden in Oneida County."

Lynn was delighted at how colorful the garden looked. Probably because of the rain the night before. She looked a lot older than she was, and there were dark circles under her eyes. She'd have to get some make-up. Strangely, she didn't hear a word, instead saw herself as an inanimate object, just like the TV people had.

The small TV Sam had bought the day before was sitting on his kitchen counter. He watched Lynn walk down her garden path and a melody instantly streamed into his head. He closed his eyes tight and memorized the melodic tone of her voice.

In the rundown farmhouse on the Milestrip, Gary Snyder, who had heard all the talk about the show in the hardware store in town, sat shirtless with his fist around a can of beer watching a set on the table in front of him. But it wasn't Lynn who got his attention. He never took his eyes off little Robin Smith.

CHAPTER 12

Even before he started up Richardson Hill, Gary Snyder knew he could get lost in the Saturday crowd at the nursery and the snoopy Richardson kid and his mother wouldn't be there. Two weeks ago, he'd heard Robin tell a customer they went to the farmers' market every Saturday.

From the crest he saw the lot was full, so he pulled to the side of the road and parked behind a truck.

A guy on the radio belting out a song about a lady in a blue dress made him angry, and he quickly switched it off. There'd been one like that back in Montana. At least at the beginning there was. There had always been three parts to every one of them, a beginning, a middle, and an end. He erased all the endings from his mind. They were still there though, just pushed way back to the same place where all the things that had happened to him as a kid got stored.

He got out of the van and looked around. The hot sun was a change from the musty house. He quickly tucked in his wrinkled flannel shirt, then pulled his jeans up underneath his bloated belly. His face was still burning from the shave with the dull razor.

A few people carting their plants to their cars passed him, and he could feel the nervous sweat oozing out of his pores as he hurried to disappear into the crowd in the nursery lot. Every once in a while the sound of a ringing cash register rose above the low hum of conversations between friends who'd just bumped into each other during a day's outing.

Gary lowered his head as he slowly made his way through the nursery trying to look as if all the clutter interested him. He was startled when the man next to him suddenly shouted, "Honey, come and take a look at this," and he had to take a moment to get his bearings.

He didn't dare look up, but he recognized the voice, soft and precise, not lyrical like Lynn Richardson's.

He moved toward the voice, but not too close. Once they get skittish you've lost them. He picked up a plant and steadily kept moving until he heard, "Is there any way I can help you?" Afraid she might remember him, without looking up, he nervously reached for his wallet and mumbled, "I'll take this one."

"That'll be three-ninety-seven with tax."

Someone bumped against Robin and as she turned away and laughingly said, "That's it, Brenda. Just push me around," Gary stole a glance at her. Robin chatted with her friend as she waited for Gary to get out his money. He couldn't believe his luck. His eyes devoured her. She was small like a child, and her skin white and flawless. Keep talking, he screamed to himself. But when she turned and looked directly at him he dropped the five-dollar bill in her hand and turned his back to the crowd as he waited for her to bring back his change.

By the time he got to the van he could hardly breathe. He had to stop doing this or she was just going to end up like all the rest! He hated himself as he remembered the pathetic little sobs that came from Marylou Cramer. After he was finished he had no choice, the little snot would tell everything. The car shook as he pounded the steering wheel with his fist. No matter how nice he had been to them, the little bitches all looked down their noses at him like he was dirt. He had to keep away from them or he'd end up in jail again and those same terrible things would happen.

Customers started swarming all over their stall at the farmers' market before Lynn and Jess could get properly set up. "Aren't you the one on TV?" a woman asked Lynn, as she tried to concentrate on making change from a fifty-dollar bill. Why would someone hand her a fifty when they were purchasing a one-dollar package of seeds? Now she'd have to have Jess run to the office to get more singles before the end of the morning.

Lynn sensed a change in the way people were talking to her. Suddenly they seemed aware of her as a person. Jess even noticed this as he nudged his mother during a brief lull and said, "I think the TV show was a good idea."

Jess had no sooner gotten this out when another surge of customers came at them. Lynn pawed through her cash box and handed Jess the fifty. "Here, honey, go to the office and get some change."

A hand grasped the bill and Lynn looked up and saw Bob Caldwell in a pair of jeans and a V-necked sweater. She couldn't help but notice the dark, curly hair on his chest.

"I'll get it for you. You guys are swamped."

Lynn quickly introduced Bob to Jess, and said, "Get singles."

After he left, Lynn wiped the sweat off her forehead with her sleeve and tried to get the dirt off her hands with a rag she kept under the table.

When Bob came back, he said, "You take care of the customers. I'll help the boy with this," then grabbed two pots from Jess who was emptying out the last of the perennials from the back of the truck.

The extra hand eased the stress in the booth and by noon they were sold out and leisurely packing up. Lynn caught sight of Liz Palmer for the first time that day as she strolled over to the booth.

"Saw your show last Sunday," she said as she pulled a small manila envelope out of her apron and shyly handed it to Lynn. "Them hollyhocks seeds are from plants that have reseeded at our place in Oswego County for generations. I can vouch for them. My mother told me they were originally brought over from England by her great, great grand-mother. They're not fancy, puffy ones, but they're real homey like."

Lynn thanked her and carefully wrote on the outside of the envelope before putting it in her cash box.

"Can I buy you two lunch?" Bob threw over his shoulder as he wres-tled the last tabletop into the truck.

Just as Lynn was about to accept, Jess said, "Mom, we gotta be getting back. They're going to need us at the nursery."

"That's okay. Some other time," said Bob as he latched the door closed. When he turned and looked at Lynn, she didn't know what to say. She felt Jess's resistance as he stood next to her looking up at Bob with his arms folded across his chest.

"Thanks for all the help," she said, embarrassed, and started for the front of the truck. Bob opened the cab door and put his hands around her waist and helped her up, then waved goodbye as the truck headed out of the lot. Lynn didn't know exactly what happened back there, and decided to think about it later.

Jess sat quietly until they were cruising on I-81, then he carefully opened the cash box on his lap and conscientiously started counting the money.

After he finished putting the bills in neat little rubber-banded bun-dles, he closed the box and kept patting it with his hands. Finally, he said, "We did it, Mom. This is the first time we made over a thousand." Lynn glanced over at him. He looked so much older than last year. His blond hair, moist with sweat, had curled behind his ears just like his dad's. Lynn reached over and gently squeezed his shoulder.

She shook her head ever so slightly as she thought about how wrong it would have been to accept the lunch offer. They had just had the biggest market day of their lives and it was now their time to savor this triumph. Jess had bought into her herb and seed business just like she had her husband's farm. And as she glanced at him one more time, she saw the confidence and pride they'd been searching for.

They didn't speak. Except for the whooshing sound of the air rushing past the partially opened windows, the truck was quiet. For the first time since they started the little business, mother and son both felt a taste of professional respect, recognition and success. For years they'd been fueled by a dream, experiencing just enough progress to keep their hopes alive. But with the TV show, they were suddenly at the threshold of a whole new plateau. Today had proven that. They both knew there'd be new dreams now, but before the new dreams, they both wanted to savor the satisfaction of a job well done.

Then, as was their custom, the boy reached into the cooler and handed his mother a sandwich and took one for himself.

CHAPTER 13

The computer was making Lynn so nervous her fingers trembled as she gingerly hit the keys. Why on earth had she let Robin talk her into putting all their bookkeeping on the computer at the peak of the season!

Now if I just hit Okay, we should have it. Darn! Nothing! She hit Okay again and when nothing happened she wanted to scream.

The kitchen clock was visible from where she sat at the dining room table. Eleven. Did she dare call Robin?

"Hello, Betsy? I know it's late. I'm really sorry to be bothering you but I'm in the middle of payroll on our new computer and I'm stuck."

Lynn's frustration must have been obvious, because before she could ask if Robin was up, she heard, "I'll get her."

A moment later, a faint, groggy voice said, "Where are you now?"

"I did everything like you showed me, but when I hit the Okay button nothing happened."

There was a pause during which Lynn felt guilty about waking Robin up, but there was so much demand on her time. Tomorrow they'd be taping two more segments at the farm, and with a farmers' market on Wednesday and restocking the stores on Thursday, the payroll just had to be done tonight.

"Is there an Apply box anywhere?"

Lynn studied the screen. "Yes!"

"Hit it."

"I did."

"Now hit Okay."

"Bingo," Lynn purred as Cal's payroll ledger instantly appeared with every deduction neatly in columns and the weekly total at the end.

"Thank you, darling. See you tomorrow."

After Lynn finished writing the checks for Cal and Robin, she booted up her outline and slowly blew out the breath she'd been holding when the draft popped up.

She looked it over again and listened to the contrasting waves of song from the frogs and crickets that drifted in through the window as the lace curtains fluttered in the gentle night breeze. The air, laden with the sweet aroma of newly cut hay, made her yearn to be curled up between the sheets in her bed upstairs. However, by the time she finally set her alarm for five and wearily dropped into bed, the clock read one.

Lynn crept out of bed and snapped off the alarm so Jess could sleep late. As she swiftly pulled on a pair of shorts she sensed someone was looking at her. Her eyes flashed toward the door and then darted down to Commander whose thick legs set under broad shoulders were firmly planted on the braided rug.

"Okay, boy. Let's get started. Another day, another dollar."

Once outside, Lynn dragged the hose to the heirloom garden. She wasn't going to turn on the sprinkler since these plants were in the ground with roots deep enough to keep them well nourished. She'd just hit the thirstier ones.

The potted plants in the garden center were another thing. They needed to be watered at least twice a day. Cal pulled in as she was dragging the hose over.

"You want me to get this, Lynn?"

"No, that's okay, Cal." She looked around. "Why don't you beef-up the inventory here. We could use more of everything."

"Have you looked back there recently? We're starting to run low."

Lynn thought for a moment. "Maybe we should bring out some of the one-year-old plants. We won't be able to sell them for three-seventy-five like we would next year, but we should be able to get a buck-ninety-five. I stopped by Robert's Nursery last week and that was what they were doing."

"You'll be cutting into next year's inventory."

She thought again, but they had no choice. "Tonight, let's pull out... let's see ... a quarter of next year's plants and start mixing them in with the matured ones we've got left. If that doesn't tide us over for the season, maybe I can get some from the nursery in Richfield Springs. By the time we haul them over here we won't make any money on them, but at least we won't lose our customers."

"Girl, this business of yours is really taking off. You've got to start thinkin' ahead."

Lynn knew Cal well enough to know he already had a plan.

"What'd you have in mind?"

"You're going to need a lot more plants than you've got growing in that old greenhouse of yours."

Lynn turned off the water and listened intently.

Cal scratched behind his ear as he said, "If we buy one of them big greenhouses out of the magazines you get, my boy says you could probably find someone to put it up right quick."

"I don't know, Cal. I've got so many things on my mind right now I can't think. But you're right. I'm just going to have to put aside the time to figure this out."

By breakfast she told Cal to look over the catalogs and pick out a couple of greenhouses and she'd call around for prices.

The crew arrived for the third shoot of the summer at ten o'clock sharp and everything went so smoothly they were packing up to go by noon. Bob, who'd come in his car by himself, was the last to get ready to leave.

Up on the hill, Sam, who knew their routine by now, had been spo-
radically watching the shoot on the new telescope he'd picked up on his
last trip to New York. He watched Mindy and the cameraman load up
their car and pull out, then locked onto Bob. Sam squinted into the
lenses trying to glean everything he could from the expression on Bob's
face as the man loosened his tie and walked over to Lynn.

"Can you get away for lunch?" Bob asked.

He stood with his hands on hips giving Lynn the same suggestive
look she'd remembered from the first time she met him.

She blushed, then looked around at the nursery and said apologetically, "Not really."

"How about dinner?"

Lynn folded her arms across her chest and cast her eyes downward as
she disappointedly kicked the dirt in front of her. Sam picked up on this
and grit his teeth as a sickening wave of fear went through him.

"Not tonight. I've got too much to do," Lynn said.

"I shouldn't take that as a no, should I?"

Just then, Jess tugged on his mother's arm. "Come on, Mom. I put the
stew on like you told me."

Sam slapped his side. "Atta Boy, Jess!"

As Jess pulled Lynn toward the house she glanced over her shoulder
at Bob and said, "Call me."

After the BMW pulled out of the lot, Sam watched Lynn disappear
into the house with the boy. He stared at the deserted parking lot and
slowly rubbed his beard becoming lost in thought. Suddenly, as if he
had made up his mind about something, he swung around and went to
his desk and punched in the number for Wally Silverman, the *Men in
Blue's* production director.

"Wally, it's Sam."

"You all set up for us?"

"Yeah," he said sarcastically. "I can hardly wait to get the first show."

"Hey. You're making good money, Bud."

"I'm not knocking it, Wally." He hesitated for a moment. "I need a favor from you."

"Sure. Shoot."

"I want you to check someone out for me. I don't know the guy's name, but he works for a small ETV station up here in Syracuse. *WKNY*. I think he's their video director. Mid-thirties, tall, blond."

"You're not swinging in the other direction are you?"

"Don't worry. If I were, I'd save myself for you."

Sam shook his head as he heard the wicked snicker on the other end.

"Okay. Give me your new number again. I'll get back to you."

Now that three of her shows had aired, Lynn noticed people she passed on the street in Eastlake were beginning to stare at her as she went about her business. First, she went into the post office with a big batch of seeds. By now, orders should have been slacking off, but instead were rolling in at a record pace. Even the postal clerk mentioned he'd seen her show the previous week.

Lynn was ashamed that some of the orders had sat for over a week. In fact, if it hadn't rained so badly the day before, they'd probably still be lying on the dining room table. Suddenly she felt ungrateful. The memory of sitting at the kitchen window and praying the mailman would bring her some orders was all too recent.

She was going to have to reorganize everything once the garden center officially closed down in late September so this sort of thing wouldn't happen again.

God, she wished Ken was there. She was getting so stressed out and confused. She used to talk everything over with him, sometimes into the night, until she knew the problem inside and out and weighed every option. But now she was beginning to feel brain dead. If Cal hadn't been there, she'd really be in bad shape.

Things weren't totally out of control though. She was still holding everything together even though she was dog-tired and items like the mail order business were getting a little frayed around the edges. The shows were getting better each time and everything at the nursery was fine. All she had to do was hang in and ride this thing out. Her business was growing, and just like Cal had warned her, she had to think ahead if she was going to keep on top of things. As tired as she was, she felt exhilarated. The sudden realization that her dream was becoming a reality hit her. The big question was, did she have what it took to hold on to it.

Lynn parked the truck next to Citizens Bank. Jim Hughes said he'd see her at three. She couldn't make up her mind if she should just ask for eight thousand for a new greenhouse or get six thousand more and add an office-warehouse space. How much longer could the dining room handle the mail order business? Cal told her adding one later on would cost twice as much.

A poster of the missing girl from Cortland was taped on the bank's door. These grim reminders were all over town, and lined the roads on telephone poles all the way into Syracuse. From that distance, they were more of a warning to parents than anything else.

When Betsy's sister waved at her from behind the teller window, Lynn was jolted with the gnawing thought that if she got the loan everyone would know about it in a couple of days. Lynn started to take a seat in the lobby when Jim Hughes who was sitting behind his desk motioned for her to come into his office.

"So you want a loan to build a greenhouse?" he said cheerfully as he stood and shook her hand.

Lynn nodded and sat down. At the same time she decided she might as well get the office and warehouse also.

"Fourteen thousand would do it," she said.

He opened a drawer and pulled out some papers. "Here's a financial statement you'll have to fill out to get a mortgage on the farm."

She reached over and picked up the papers. The banker leaned back in his chair and said, "My wife tells me you're quite a celebrity. I'm sorry I haven't seen your show. I watch golf on Sundays if I watch TV at all." He tapped his pen on the desk for a moment and finally said, "Do you have a written contract with the station?"

"Yes." Lynn stopped herself as she was just about to add she could be dropped with thirty-day notice. Sensing which way the conversation was headed, she added, "I've been talking with Farmway about shelf space for my seeds. Just recently their marketing director called me and is trying to set up an appointment with their merchandising manager."

She nervously cast her eyes downward and noticed the dirt under her nails, which no matter how hard she scrubbed, wouldn't come out. Then, deciding to make this development with Farmway sound as positive as possible, said, "He was quite friendly. Asked me about the farm. How I got started with heirloom seeds." She looked up at the banker and with a confident attitude tossed her head and said, "I've got a hunch I'm going to be doing business with them."

While the banker appeared to be mulling a possible deal with Farmway over, Lynn felt relieved to have been able to throw that tidbit into the conversation.

"We're going to need your tax returns for the past two years. Is that going to be a problem?"

"Well, Jim. Last year, with Ken ... you know...I had to sell the equipment and livestock to pay off everything we owed you. In the end I showed a loss. The year before, even with Ken being there, with all the depreciation and the way milk prices were, we had another loss."

"Don't worry. Fill out the statement as best you can and we'll take a look. Just be sure to include a copy of the contract from the television station."

Lynn started to get angry. As good a farmer as Ken was, he had never been able to make good money. They'd kept having to buy bigger equipment and more stock to make ends meet. The survival formula had always been, get big or get out, and it seemed like the only one ever getting ahead on the deal was the bank. In the end, all the auction money went to Citizens' Savings to pay everything off.

Lynn's temper started to get the best of her. "If they can give twenty-thousand-dollar car loans to all these college kids right out of the chute, I feel there should be no problem with my getting this fourteen thousand."

The banker slowly sat upright. "Lynn, the bank can always repossess a car, but what are we going to do with a greenhouse."

Lynn started to blink back tears, then somehow managed to get a grip on herself. She stood up and said, "I'll fill these out and get back to you."

As Lynn left the bank she felt her heartbeat throb in her head and heat radiate from her ears. When she got back into the truck she looked at her flushed face in the rearview mirror. No wonder Ken was always so quiet after a visit with Jim Hughes.

That night, Lynn labored to make her financial statement look as good as possible, even throwing in ten thousand in antiques in the asset column. The next morning she went to the Radio Shack in town and had her contract and tax returns copied and dropped them off.

The phone call that afternoon from Jim Hughes sounded promising at first. Then, came the mention of the contract's thirty-day cancellation clause. With no firm means of support, Jim Hughes explained, she would need a co-signer to get the fourteen thousand.

Lynn put down the receiver and yelled to Cal to watch Jess as she ran to her truck. She'd be back in an hour.

No one answered the door at Shelly's house, so she went around the back to the pool where she found Shelly lying on a lounge chair and her two girls splashing in the water.

Lynn smiled and waved to the girls.

Shelly took off her glasses and sat up.

"To what do we owe this honor? You haven't dropped by the house since Jennifer was born!"

Lynn ignored the comment, pulled up a chair and sat down next to Shelly.

"I need a favor."

Shelly jumped up waving her hands in the air. "Wait a minute. Wait a minute. I know this is going to be good." She put her hand on Lynn's shoulder. "You just sit there while I get us drinks."

Lynn looked around in exasperation as Shelly disappeared into the house. The two girls smiled knowingly at Lynn who went over to the edge of the pool, knelt down and kissed them both.

"I love you two."

"We love you too, Aunt Lynn."

Shelly came back clicking the heels of her clogs and balancing a tray of drinks.

"Come on out girls and have some juice. Then I want you to go upstairs and get changed."

After handing Lynn a whisky sour complete with a maraschino cherry, Shelly sat down, put on her sunglasses and made herself comfortable.

"Okay, darling. Shoot."

Lynn took a long swallow, then embarrassed, looked at the two girls and then down at the ground.

"Okay, girls. Take your drinks upstairs and get dressed. Mommy and Aunt Lynn want to talk."

"Thanks, Shelly," Lynn said as the two girls departed.

"Well...don't keep me waiting."

Lynn stuttered her way through the whole story of the greenhouse and the visit to the bank, then stopped.

"They're not going to give you the money, are they?"

Lynn rubbed her hands nervously. "If I get a co-signer."

Shelly tossed her head to the side and rolled her eyes. "I don't believe you're here doing this. You can't expect me to throw in with this nutty scheme. I'd have to have my head examined if I helped you do this crazy thing!"

Lynn rocked forward running her hands through her hair. "It's *not* crazy. Believe me, Shelly, it's the only way I'm going to find dignity for Jess and me. I know I can make it if I can only grow enough plants over the winter. You've got to believe in me."

"Oh, baby," Shelly said, her voice becoming sympathetic. "You're such a mess. Your life would be so simple if you'd just quit that god-awful business, sell the farm and move into Eastlake. If you can't make it with what you already have, why go deeper into debt? Why in hell you have to do everything the hard way, I'll never know." She threw her glasses on the table, took a sip of her drink and thought for a minute. "You know how cheap Pete is. He'll never go for this."

"Tell him, if my business doesn't make it, I'll work for him for the rest of my life to pay him back."

Lynn tried desperately to bat back the tears as she got up and paced. "Shelly, you're my only hope."

Lynn walked over and plopped down on her chair and let the tears fall down her burning cheeks. After a few moments, she turned to her friend. "Shelly, I'm begging you. I know I can do this. All I need is a chance."

When Lynn spotted the two girls standing in the doorway, eyes wide open and crestfallen, she wiped the tears from her face, smiled and went over to them. "Aunt Lynn is all right. Don't worry."

Lynn turned to Shelly. "I've got to go. Let me know tomorrow if you can."

CHAPTER 14

The soft crunching of the tires on the dirt roadway drifted into the van's open windows. The noise of crickets and peepers filled the air, but were so much a part of the night that Gary Snyder took no notice of them. He was too intent on reaching his destination.

With the headlights off, there was only the light of a half moon. The van floated to a stop at the turn-around area on the logging road Ted Brown used to get to his woods.

Gary Snyder studied the thicket in front of him. He planned to use a different path tonight. He didn't want the farmer to suspect someone was using the road to park while they made their way to the clearing. He slid off his sneakers and pulled on a pair of rubber boots identical to the ones he'd seen Ted Brown wearing in town. Unusual footprints could arouse suspicions.

The air was cool but he was on fire. He tugged at the T-shirt stuck to his sweaty back, then tightened his belt. A long-sleeved flannel shirt was put on, then a liberal spraying of Deet.

His eyes, which had finally adjusted to the darkness, zeroed in on a possible route. The thick thorny brambles between two maples were carefully spread apart and he pressed toward the clearing fifty yards away. His huge paw swiped across his perspiration-drenched face to chase the mosquitoes from his eyes. A grove of hemlocks suddenly stood in his way. Undaunted, he turned and backed his way through.

A noise startled him. Not moving or breathing, he strained to listen. Way off in the distance, a deer snorted. Satisfied that was what he had heard; he kept going toward the clearing ahead. Just a few more yards and he'd reach the lawn.

The stirrings were already beginning in the pit of his stomach as he moved cautiously toward the Smith's house. He crouched down low and crept toward the second-floor back window with its golden light reaching into the darkness. From past nights he knew the best view would be next to the lilac bush where he'd catch sight of Robin whenever she walked across her room.

He couldn't take his eyes off the window for a second. Her appearances were like unexpected explosions.

A gnawing fear that tonight something was going to go terribly wrong kept surfacing. A flood of resentment rolled across him as he remembered how the new pup at the Richardson's had surprised him, and he smacked his fist into his hand.

Suddenly, Robin was standing with her back to the window motioning with her hands. Someone must be in the room with her. She was still for a moment, then started moving around with the casual motions of someone getting ready for bed. Gary's gaze was unbroken.

Slowly, he unzipped his pants, but in seconds, the deep exhilarating desire was replaced with a sickening feeling of emptiness, then violent anger. Just like all the other nights, once the light was out, saturated with disappointment, he turned and started toward the woods.

Halfway through the thicket, the shrill laugh of a girl made him stop. He crouched down and crept cautiously through the pitch black. Now two voices! They sounded young, like teenagers.

Emerging from the thick brush, he almost bumped into their car. Remaining crouched, he listened.

"Whose van is this? Why is it parked here?" the girl asked.

"There's no mistakin' this hunk of junk. It belongs to that big retard that gets gas at my dad's station. You know. One of them hill people."

They both laughed.

"You should see him. The dirtbag's never had a bath, and I'd be surprised if he can even talk."

"Let's set it on fire before we go," the girl giggled.

"Naw. We're already in enough trouble. My father's going to kill me when he finds out about the baby."

"That old man of yours thinks I'm nothin' but white trash, doesn't he?"

"Lucy, you have no idea what a mean son of a bitch he is. I'm tellin' you, he'll kill me."

"Well, since he's goin' to kill you, why don't we have a little fun first. That's why you brought me here, isn't it?"

The boy's eyes nervously searched the woods. "Sure. That guy can't be around. Probably, ditched the van after running out of gas or somethin'."

They knew who he was, Gary screamed to himself. What if they tell someone about seeing his van on the logging road? Would they start asking questions and link him with Robin? Maybe even bring him in for questioning about the missing girl in Cortland?

The sounds of panting and moaning told the man he could get to his van without being noticed. He went around to the passenger side, reached in, and careful not to make any noise, opened the glove compartment and took out the Smith and Wesson.

Crouching low, he moved cautiously toward the obvious sounds of lovemaking. A muffled crack sounded as he put his weight on a fallen limb. The reek of perspiration odor enveloped him as his heart pounded in his throat. But the sound went unnoticed.

A few more guarded steps and Gary stood next to the writhing figures. The hand gripping the gun had gone numb.

The girl was startled when the boy on top of her stiffened. He slowly stood up with the cold metal against his temple.

"Wait a minute, buddy," the trembling voice uttered.

"Shut up."

Gary nudged the girl with his foot. "Get up."

The girl started to put on her blouse, when Gary grabbed her by the arm and shoved her toward the car.

Poking the gun into the boy's back, he told him to keep going. Gary opened the car door, reached for the keys, and then told the boy to get in.

"You fuckin' breathe wrong and the bitch is dead."

Moments later, the sounds of pathetic begging, then crying echoed in the clearing. The boy pounded the steering wheel and cried, "Awh, mister. Please, don't do this. Oh, God! Please don't let him do this."

There was a sickening silence. Then a harsh whisper. "Get dressed, you little whore!"

Gary suddenly appeared at the passenger door and threw it open. The hysterical girl buttoned her blouse with erratic jerking motions then managed to stuff her blouse into her jeans.

After throwing her into the car, Gary jumped into the back seat. All was silent except for the girl's short, mindless outbursts. The smell of gunpowder filled the air as the boy's head was flung to the side. Gary ignored the girl's shrill screaming as he painstakingly wiped the gun, wrapped the boy's hand around it and carefully aimed. Silence fell like a thud.

Using a towel he found in the back seat, Gary Snyder wiped off all traces of his fingerprints and put the keys back in the ignition. He turned the van around, snapped a branch off a nearby maple and carefully brushed its path. In the two or three days it could take before Ted Brown would have time to cut more wood, it could rain and disturb the site even more. No matter, after the farmer drove his tractor and wagon into the clearing, all traces of the van's tire marks would be destroyed.

CHAPTER 15

"Just what is that thing anyway?" asked Rusty Sauterfield after he climbed down from the ladder.

Sam, who was getting down from another ladder on the other side of the huge Jackson Pollock painting they'd just hung, stepped back and nodded in approval. "Why, this is modern art."

"Does it have a name?"

"Yes, as a matter of fact. *Rhythm in the Fields No. 27.*"

Rusty shook his head and mumbled something about that morning the cows must have gotten out and messed it all up. Sam laughed. He was happy and at the same time anxious to get Rusty and his wife out of there.

For the past three days they'd been uncrating and arranging furniture and wall hangings and now he was finally starting to feel at home. Every waking moment up until then had been spent either getting the studio ready or working on the score for the new foreign film.

Rusty's wife marched down the stairs and sternly announced, "I changed the sheets on that trampoline of yours."

"Come on, Nora. You know you're dying to have a waterbed," her husband joked.

"Heck! If I bounced around in that thing all night I'd get sea sick."

Rusty's mood changed as he started to collect his tools. "I'm awfully sorry we can't make it again tomorrow, but like I told you, we've got to go somewhere."

"Yeah," piped in Nora. "His cousin's son went and shot himself."

Rusty nodded thoughtfully. "Yep. We weren't that close, but still, we're obliged to show up at the funeral parlor tomorrow."

"That's a shame," Sam said.

"That's only the half of it," Nora scoffed. "He went and shot his girl friend too. A kind of Romeo and Juliet thing, they're sayin'. The autopsy showed the no-account girl was pregnant."

Rusty snapped his tool chest closed and slowly rose, saying, "My cousin was always too tough on his boy. The police figure the kid was too afraid to tell his father about the girl's condition, and in a panic, went the murder-suicide route."

No one spoke as the last of the crates were put in a pile. Sam pulled out his wallet and handed them each a crisp hundred-dollar bill and then helped Rusty carry the debris to his truck.

Even though she was bigger than he was, Sam gave Nora Sauterfield a boost up and thought the two hard-working country folk were a good match. Nora matter-of-factly said, "Be up to clean your place next Thursday," and tucked the bill in her bra.

"If I've left for Spain, the key'll be under the mat and you know the security codes," Sam yelled as they started down the hill.

The phone was ringing as he walked into the house.

"Hello! Sam! I'm about five miles from the thruway exit in Canastota."

Sam grimaced as he instantly recognized Ralph's voice.

"I'm on my way to Rochester and thought I'd stop by and see your new digs."

Sam was tempted to tell Ralph to catch him on his way back until he heard, "I told Wally I was coming up here and he gave me a message for you." Sam quickly gave him the directions.

"You got to be kidding. I knew you were in the boonies, but Christ, I'll never find it."

"Yes you will. Just remember when you see a little nursery on the right in the hollow at the top of the hill, make a left onto a gravel roadway and start climbing. I'm at the top overlooking the nursery. If you get lost, give me another call and I'll walk you through."

The MG convertible looked small next to Ralph as he got out and reached in the back for his briefcase. Sam winced as he realized there had to be a script in it. His mind was filled with the theme for the new film and he was anxious to get most of the melody down before the *Men in Blue* tapes started arriving.

Ralph appeared to be in a rush as he walked in the house and quickly glanced around. "You got class, Sam. This place is sharp." With those niceties over, he said, "Where's the studio?"

Sam casually walked over and handed him a glass of ice water. "Sit down. Let's have the message."

"Oh yeah!" Ralph made himself comfortable in a cushy chair and said, "There's not much to tell." He picked some lint off his slacks. "The guy's name is Bob Caldwell. He's basically your friendly neighborhood heel. Knocked some college kid up last summer and told her to go whistle. He started out as a hot-shot video director, but from what I understand, he'd be a lot further ahead right now if he'd only been able to keep his pants on when he worked for a station in St. Louis. Do you believe he was dumb enough to screw around with the station owner's married daughter?"

Wrapped in thought, Sam sat down and scratched the beard under his chin for a while. Finally, he leaned forward with his elbows on his knees. Cracking his knuckles, he said, "I need a favor."

Ralph's eyes narrowed.

Sam looked down at his hands and said, "I want you to get this guy a job offer somewhere like LA or New York and get him out of here."

"You gotta be fuckin' kidding!"

"No. I need you to do this."

Ralph kept shaking his head while looking off into space. Finally, as if he was thinking out loud, he bit his lip and said, "Remember that guy we did the documentary on Cape Cod for... Tucker ... Jack Tucker." Ralph gave Sam a moment to think. "He's a big producer with *WGBH* now. I had lunch with him last week and he was telling me he'd landed a big grant and was going to be looking for some talent. It's a hell of a long-shot, but I could give him a call."

"That'd be good."

"Yeah. He mentioned you. Everyone knows the Cape Cod score you did for him boosted him into the big leagues. By the way, he heard you were working on the new Sandini film."

Ralph put his briefcase on his lap and snapped it open. He took out a videotape and before Sam could open his mouth, said, "I know! I know you told me not to bother you until August. But I sold that documentary, and like I figured, they want an original sound track. All I'm asking is for you to take a look at this and give me a call." He tossed the tape onto a stack of magazines on the table in front of him.

Sam stood up. "Let's go see the studio."

He led Ralph down the hall, then stopped abruptly. Without turning around he said, "Are you going to get this guy out of here for me?"

Ralph, who'd been thinking about it non-stop since Sam asked, said, "Don't worry, I'll get him out of here even if I have to hire him myself." He placed his hand on Sam's shoulder and said, "You're really stuck on some chick, aren't you?"

Before Sam could answer, Ralph burst into the studio. "Wow! Baby!"

Sam motioned him to a chair and sat down behind the controls. The lights lowered and the music came up. A woman in a straw hat started down an emerald green grass pathway in slow motion on the six-foot screen. Drifts of vividly colored flowers waved eerily in the breeze. From the Dolby Surround-Sound in the studio, an almost Victorian-sounding theme mirrored the rhythm of her ethereal slow-motion walk. The music went under as the speed normalized and the lyrical voice said, "Hello, I'm Lynn Richardson of Richardson's Herbs and Seeds outside of Eastlake, New York and this is my heirloom garden."

Sam watched Ralph lean back in his chair and cross his legs at the ankles. When the spot finished and the lights went up, Sam knew Ralph had been enthralled because Ralph wouldn't have sat still for ten minutes unless he was.

"You got an extra copy?"

Sam tossed over the video he was planning to send him in hopes Ralph could find a station that might want to syndicate a show starring Lynn.

Ralph started to rise when Sam said, "Sit down. I want you to hear this." Sam went over to the studio Baldwin and played the score he was working on for Sandini.

When the music stopped, Ralph shook his head. "This is the best thing you've ever written."

In spite of all Ralph's wheeling and dealing, at heart he was a musician, and Sam knew by the sound of his voice the theme had grabbed him.

"How are you going to produce the score?"

"I'm going to Spain next week to visit the set and play what I have so far for Sandini. If he likes what he hears, I'll start composing the entire opening score and have a draft produced right here using musicians from the Syracuse Symphony. Once I get the edited version of the movie, I can work up the final score in a couple of months. We'll probably record it in New York or Toronto."

Ralph thought about that for a moment and then grabbed the tape and got up. "I've got to get moving."

When Ralph reached the main hall he hesitated and said, "Can I just take a look at the view since I schlepped all the way up here?" and walked over to the window.

"Holy shit! You can see forever!" Then he bent down and peered into the telescope aimed at the nursery and saw a woman in shorts coming toward him. "Hey, the scenery across the road ain't bad either." He looked hard and then said, "Is that the nature girl in the video? Damn! It is!"

Ralph looked over at Sam and said, "You dirty dog, you." They both let out a hearty laugh and walked to the door with their arms around each other's shoulders.

Oh, God, please don't let them say no, thought Lynn who was sitting at her desk in the kitchen as Shelly pulled in the driveway. She quickly shoved a stack of bills into the desk drawer.

"Where'd you get the computer?" Shelly sang out as she dropped the bag of groceries on the table.

"Mindy Templeton from the station found it for me," Lynn said, trying to sound as casual as possible. "Whatcha got there?"

"I was cleaning out my kitchen cupboards. These are canned goods we're never going to use. Pete can't pass up a bargain."

When Shelly started taking the cans out of the bag and putting them in the cupboard, Lynn's heart sank as she figured the gift of the food was intended to soften the blow of their not agreeing to co-sign for the note.

"Before I tell you what we decided about the loan, you're going to have some tea with me." Shelly put the kettle on and continued with the cans. When she finished, she turned abruptly and leaned against the counter.

"You *owe me*, baby. I got Pete to agree to this harebrain scheme of yours... but I'm telling you... only after giving him one night he's not going to forget *anytime soon*. Believe me, Lynn, if his patients knew what went on in our bedroom last night, they'd *never* let him put *his hands in their mouths again*."

With her elbows on the table, Lynn covered her face with her hands and slid forward. "Oh, Shelly. Thank you. Thank you. Thank you. You'll never know how much this means to me."

Shelly put the cups on the table, then poured the hot water while Lynn reached for the box of tea bags.

"Pete's going over to the bank this afternoon to take care of everything."

Shelly's tone became serious as she sat down and played with the tag hanging over the side of her cup. "Do you know why I'm doing this, Lynn?" She wasn't looking for an answer and continued. "It won't be the end of the world if we lose fourteen thousand. That boat sitting in Alex Bay that Pete just bought cost over a hundred grand. But it will be a tragedy if you spend the rest of your life futilely struggling to make ends meet on this godforsaken piece of dirt. We're not doing this to encourage you. It's worth fourteen thousand to put a final end to this hard life you have."

Shelly grasped Lynn's hand. "I want you to promise me if you fail you'll get the hell out of here and come work for Pete. You don't have to sell the place. Rent it out or something. We'll help you get a small place of your own ... or an apartment ... whatever."

Lynn dismissed the thought of failure. She would never let that happen no matter how hard she had to work. "Don't worry, Shelly. I'm not going to fail. I know I can do it."

"*Promise me?*"

"I promise."

Lynn was surprised when Shelly's interest quickly switched to the town gossip.

Deliriously happy, Lynn was unable to concentrate on what Shelly was saying until she felt her friend tugging on her arm.

"You look like hell, baby. When was the last time you got some sleep?"

"The price of fame, Shelly."

Shelly got up and poured more hot water over the tea bag. "Pete says everyone in town's talking about you and your show."

"Everybody's always talking about somebody around here."

"Lynn, I don't mean to go on and on, but I'm so excited! You should see my absolutely gorgeous new dress! I had to have something smashing for Barb McMaster's big luau this Saturday. I've never spent four hundred dollars on a dress before and Pete's going to kill me when he sees the credit-card bill, but I don't care."

"Four hundred dollars for a dress? I hope he does."

Shelly was sorry she had mentioned the price of the dress the minute she saw the expression on Lynn's face. "Awh, honey, you'll never know how competitive it is out there since you'll probably never be invited to a party like this. Trust me, I had to have this dress or I'd look like the poor relative."

After Shelly finally left, Lynn felt a little like the poor relative herself but shook it off. Just wait. In a couple of years things will be different, she thought. Then remembering the promise she'd made to Shelly, a sickening fear gripped her. There was absolutely no way she could fail.

Then as she went to join Cal and Jess who were potting seedlings in the greenhouse, her mind drifted to what Mindy had said about Barb's party. She wanted to kick herself as the jealousy rose when she thought of Sam Reynolds dancing with Barb wearing some drop-dead dress.

"Anybody check on Robin?" she asked as she entered the greenhouse.

"Things are slow today. She'll be okay," Cal told her. Then he reluctantly asked the question. "Well? Are they going to sign?"

Lynn clasped her hands and jumped into the air. "Yes! Yes! Yes!"

There were smiles and hugs all around until the threesome were startled by a truck that pulled into the driveway next to the house. They listened for Commander's bark but, instead, the greenhouse door opened and Sam Reynolds walked in with the dog following behind, his tail thumping against the door.

Jess called Commander over and when he told the dog to sit, he immediately obeyed.

"You're doing a good job training Commander," Sam said to Jess.

The boy looked proud as he bent down and hugged the animal. Cal smiled and stopped his work. Lynn, who at first ignored the visitor, couldn't resist seeing her boy happy, so she stopped potting, wiped her hands on her apron and pulled Jess close to her. With her arms folded across the boy's chest the two of them listened to Cal and Sam make small talk.

There seemed to be a lull as Sam stood there staring at Lynn not quite listening to Cal. The old man finally noticed this and stopped talking.

The room became silent and all eyes fell on Sam. He shifted his weight from one foot to another and said, "I'm invited to a party in town this coming Saturday and I just came down to see if you'd go with me."

"What party is that?" asked Lynn. She stopped breathing. This couldn't possibly be the symphony splash! Suddenly she cursed herself for not doing something about her hair, and then cursed herself again for thinking it.

"Barbara McMaster is having some symphony patrons over."

"We know about that party!" shouted Jess as he pulled away from Lynn. "It's all my Aunt Shelly ever talks about!"

Lynn wanted to die. She felt her cheeks get warm.

"I'd love to go, but I have nothing to wear on such short notice."

"Sure you do, Mom! You've got that fancy blue dress you bought for Shelly's sister's wedding! You look good in it, Mom!"

"What do you mean, on such short notice, girl," admonished Cal. "You can drive into town and get somethin' in less than an hour. He's being a gentleman and giving you a whole week."

Sam threw his head back and laughed. The greenhouse became quiet as Lynn's eyes jumped from Cal to Sam and then the boy. Jess excitedly grasped his mother's shoulders. "Please go, Mom! You're just as good as all those fancy people Shelly's always talking about."

Lynn nervously ran her fingers through her hair. "Okay, Jess. That's enough." She looked up at Sam and said, "I'll go."

Cal swung around on his stool and told Sam, "That wasn't so hard, was it, son?" and everyone laughed.

"Aren't you going to offer him something to drink?" Cal prodded. But just as Lynn started to speak, Sam told them he was having trouble with his new truck and had to take it to the dealer and that he'd pick her up at six on Saturday. The door started to close behind him when he peeked back in and said, "I'll put my money on the fancy blue dress."

CHAPTER 16

Lynn agonized about the party she was getting ready for while her hands soaked in the bowl of warm, soapy water. She hadn't been able to bring herself to tell Shelly she'd been invited. She'd read too much into Sam's neighborly gesture, and insist on a new dress, hairdo, the works. No, she wasn't going to pretend to be anything she wasn't. She was just a farmer's widow trying to make a go of a small nursery with no business spending money she didn't have. She was still sick over getting Shelly and Pete to co-sign for her loan.

Lynn took a final stab at getting the dirt from under her fingernails, then emptied the bowl she'd been soaking them in into the sink. Robin was right in insisting she take a nap after she and Jess got back from the farmers' market. She felt renewed.

Jess sailed past the kitchen window on his bike as she looked up at the clock. Five. Cal should have the garden center shut down any minute now. I'll serve the two of them dinner, she thought, and then go up and get dressed.

The spaghetti was enthusiastically received by Cal and Jess, so she poured them each some lemonade and went upstairs. When she spotted the dress lying on the bed, she remembered dancing with Ken at the wedding. She picked it up and buried her face in the soft cotton hoping to get a trace of him, but there was only the faint scent of mothballs.

She slipped off the robe and put on a pair of plain cotton panties and a bra, then some nylons. In the bathroom, she blow-dried her hair, which had grown to shoulder length during the summer, and curled it under with an iron. When she slipped on the light blue dress she saw how tanned she'd gotten and how lean her arms were.

Back in the bathroom, after lightly powdering her face and putting on some rouge and lipstick, in a moment of defiance she picked up the brush, fluffed up her bangs and swept her hair back behind her ears. That's better!

When she walked into the kitchen, Jess froze. Cal, who almost dropped his fork, said, "Is that you?"

Lynn sensed someone else's eyes were on her and turned and saw Sam across the room. The light-blue seersucker jacket and white shirt made his luminescent blue eyes stand out from his handsome face. She suddenly felt relaxed as she fixed on his shirt, open at the neck.

"You ready?"

She nodded.

Cal winked at Jess when Sam put his arm around Lynn's waist before they walked out the door.

Sam could hardly believe he actually had Lynn sitting next to him. He looked over, smiled and was pleased with the gentle, friendly smile he got in return. He didn't know what to say. Things were going so well, he didn't want to put his foot in his mouth, and yearned for the day they would be at ease with each other.

Lynn crossed her legs and pulled her dress over the knees that no matter how hard she scrubbed wouldn't come clean. For a fleeting moment she wished she were strolling through the back lane in a pair of comfortable shorts instead of sitting on pins and needles waiting for utter doom.

As the scenery whizzed by, Lynn remembered inviting Barb McMasters to her wedding and hearing, "You're not marrying that country bumpkin, are you?" Barb never showed up, and when Lynn ran into her in town she was hurt even more when her old schoolmate pretended not to know her. Lynn held her breath for a moment as she thought of how awkward introductions were going to be.

"You doin' okay?" Sam asked.

"Well, actually I'm a little nervous. I'm not exactly a socialite. Ken and I used to go to the Slabside Inn on Friday nights in the winter ... and an occasional wedding ... that's about all."

Sam looked over at Lynn who appeared so vulnerable he wanted to pull to the side of the road and hold her. He reached over and squeezed her hand. "You want to skip this shindig? We can go out to dinner somewhere."

"Good Lord, no! If you don't show up tonight, Barb McMasters will just about die. She's not my best friend, far from it, but I wouldn't do that to my worst enemy. We're going!"

Sam burst into a grin. "That's the spirit! You and me, the Richardson Hollow Gang, against the world!"

Two miles on the other side of town, they spotted the McMasters' spread on top of the hill overlooking the lake. Fluttering pennants lined the driveway and the crowd on the sprawling lawn looked like a mixed cluster of flowers. A parking attendant shepherded Sam's truck into a space on the mowed field next to the estate. When Sam opened Lynn's door and the sound of the symphony's string quartet wafted in, Lynn's heart sank.

Reading the anxiety on her face, Sam said, "Don't worry about a thing. I'll take good care of you."

Lynn's walk was stiff until Sam offered her an arm that she gratefully took. She eyed the crowd looking for four-hundred-dollar dresses but never recognized any. Instead, she saw everything from simple summer suits to flowery long dresses, and from sportscoats to colorful slacks and golf shirts, all of which made her feel better.

At the top of the hill, the house loomed like a castle flanked by gorgeous perennial borders. Pennants were snapping in the breeze and the tables, draped in white with swags of garlands, groaned with food.

All the anxiety was worth seeing this, thought Lynn. Just then, one of her loyal patrons at the nursery sang out in a high-pitched voice, "There she is! Lynn Richardson!" In a flash, Lynn was surrounded by a bevy of elderly women cooing about how absolutely wonderfully fantastic her show was. Lynn's apologetic glance at Sam was met by a big wink.

After chatting for a while, Lynn was able to break away. While searching for Sam in the crowd, she caught a glimpse of Barb McMasters introducing him to an enthralled cluster. He kept looking over his shoulder and when he eyed Lynn, motioned for everyone to wait a moment and ran back and got her.

"I'd like to introduce my date, Lynn Richardson."

Barb stood there with her mouth frozen slightly open, emitting an attitude from her toes up. "Well, how nice to see you're out of the barn, darling. You clean up well."

Lynn was stunned, but Sam threw back his head and laughed. Then he put his arm around Lynn and pulled her close to him. Looking over at Barb, he said, "Excuse us while we get something to drink." As he led Lynn away he leaned toward her and laughingly whispered, "I see you two girls know each other."

After the stress of the ride up, Lynn felt oddly giddy and the whole thing struck her as funny too. "She should have seen me after I got back from the farmers' market!"

The minute the waiter handed them their drinks, a crowd sucked in Sam and drew him away. Simultaneously, another troop of gardening buffs swarmed over Lynn. In between all the adulation, she kept scanning the crowd for Shelly and Pete.

Eventually the quartet started to pack up their instruments and an orchestra that specialized in the music of the forties and fifties took over. Lynn made her way to the edge of the crowd that by now had either settled on lawn chairs or blankets in front of the chanteuse crooning out *"Blue Moon, you left me standing alone, without a care in my heart ... without a love of my own..."* Lynn was charmed by the older couples dancing cheek to cheek to the music of their younger days as if time had stood still, when Sam slipped his arm around her waist and swept her to the lawn in front of the band.

The music and the genuine joy of the moment made her feel truly happy and she was oblivious to the approving faces in the crowd as she rested her cheek against Sam's. When the music stopped and he started to lead her away, they bumped into Shelly and Pete. Lynn had just finished the introductions when the orchestra director pulled Sam away, and Sam, refusing to leave Lynn behind, dragged her along with him. Lynn gave Shelly a feeble wave and felt badly about the disappointed look on her face.

By the time Sam and Lynn ran into Barb McMasters again she had accepted the fact Lynn was the sweetheart of the gardening set and introduced her to a circle of friends as an old college chum. Sam gave Lynn a soft nudge with his elbow and she had to bite her lip to keep from laughing.

After the orchestra stopped playing, the crowd thinned and the two said their good-byes and started down the hill.

"I never thought someone who just came out of the barn could steal the show," chided Sam.

"I clean up well."

"If that lady's like that with an old school chum, hell, I don't want to be around when she goes after an enemy!"

They both laughed. Sam wanted to hold Lynn close to him and kiss her, but she ran ahead laughing. All the nervous energy Lynn had felt about the party was released. She jumped into the front seat just as Sam was about to open the door, then pressed down the lock and made a funny face. He quickly unlocked the door and reached in and grabbed her. He froze with her in his arms as she pushed against his chest. They stared into each other eyes and listened to each other breathe. Lynn looked away, almost as if she was ashamed of her joy, and Sam slowly loosened his grip and let her slide back onto the seat.

They didn't speak on the way back to the farm. The tires made a soft crunch on the gravel driveway as the truck gently rolled to a stop next to the house. All the night sounds were magnified and Lynn felt her nose flaring as she struggled to draw her breath.

Sam wanted to reach over and put his arm around her but he knew he'd never be able to stop. Suddenly the light from the kitchen startled them and they looked over and saw Cal standing behind Jess who was in his pajamas with his face pressed against the window.

"Why don't you come in for a few minutes, Sam. Jess would love to see you."

"You got any food in there?"

"Uh-huh."

"You've got yourself a deal. I'm starved."

"So am I!"

Lynn jumped down from the truck and raced Sam into the house laughing. When the porch door swung open Jess rushed into his mother's arms and Commander excitedly pranced around her.

"Did you have fun!"

"We sure did!"

"Aunt Shelly just hung up. You're to call her the minute you get in, no matter how late."

Jess nudged Sam and said in his most manly tone, "Aunt Shelly's like that. Everything's kind of an emergency."

Lynn kicked off her heels and went over and gave Cal a hug.

"You sure do look pretty," he said as he gently hugged her.

"Thanks, Cal."

"Okay, everybody. Let me take your orders."

Lynn spun around and laughed at Sam who'd taken off his jacket and rolled up his sleeves. Lynn took one of her aprons from a hook and tied it around his waist.

Looking over the contents of the refrigerator, Sam spied a dish of eggs and said, "Is everybody ready for my specialty of the house..." and in an outrageous rendition of a French accent added, "*herb soufflé?*"

With much fanfare he continued with "Will *moi assistant* please present the *fromage.*"

Lynn whipped out a stick of cheddar and a few leftover pieces of Swiss with an exaggerated flourish.

"*Ooh la la! Fantastique!*"

As Sam separated the eggs, he leaned over and whispered loudly to Lynn, "*Vous* got any herbs?"

"*Moi? Beaucoup!*"

He gave Cal and Jess an obvious aside. "I can see she passed French 101 with flying colors."

Lynn put her hand up to her mouth to shield Sam's view and whispered, "I can see he flunked."

Lynn swung around and got some tarragon, burnet and chives out of the crisper and started chopping them on a wood block with as much flare as she dared without risking cutting off a finger.

Jess giggled as he leaned against Cal and watched his mother and Sam put on a show.

"First, *le sauce!*"

Sam deftly melted the butter in a pan and added the flour and milk.

"Zen...*le eggs!*"

Lynn squealed with delight as he adroitly whisked the whites with one hand and the sauce with the other.

"Zen... we mix zeet all together and *voila!*" He gently poured the mixture into a soufflé dish Lynn had whipped out, and put it into the oven.

"*Trentes minute...and finis!*"

Everyone applauded. Jess ran over to Sam, grabbed his hand and pulled him to the table while Lynn put on coffee. Cal and Jess were delighted to hear Sam tell what a hit Lynn was at the party. "Boys, you've got to be careful when you go out with this lady. She's a big celebrity now."

Lynn couldn't help smiling at this remark. She kept looking over at Sam as she carefully went about setting the table, and caught him glancing up at her several times. They all laughed and chatted until Sam proudly brought the soufflé to the table and dished it out.

Everyone enjoyed the treat, mopping up every last bit with bread. Finally, Cal got up and said he had to be getting home to feed his two cats and it was high time Jess got to sleep too.

"That's right, honey. You be a good sport and go on up."

Jess looked down at Commander and then put his hands together as if he were praying.

"*Okay*. He can go *too*."

Jess hugged his mother, then ran toward the back staircase with Commander bounding behind as he shouted "Good night, Sam. Good night, Cal," and disappeared around the corner.

"Well, that's all for me, folks," Cal said.

"Thanks for baby-sitting, Cal. You want us to walk you to your car?"

"Nope. I'm not *that old* yet."

After Cal left, Lynn went back and sat down. With her elbows on the table, she nestled her chin between the palms of her hands and looked at Sam as if to say, I'm all ears, tell me about yourself.

Sam picked up on the cue, but first poured himself another cup of coffee.

"Well, go on... tell me about yourself," she coaxed. "Are you really famous?"

He brushed the comment aside with, "I've been nominated for a few Emmys, but I'm working on a project now that's got me real excited."

He slowly stirred his coffee. "I'm doing a score for a foreign film about a woman who loses her husband and can't let go."

Lynn felt the blood rush to her head and gasped for air. Sam quickly reached across the table and squeezed her hand. "I'm so sorry. I didn't mean to hurt you."

When Lynn saw how watery his eyes had become, she knew he was sincere and abruptly changed the subject. "Have you lived in New York City all your life?"

"Yes. I'm from a family of cops. My grandfather was a cop, my dad was a cop, and my four brothers are all cops. The oldest is the chief of detectives for the seventeenth precinct."

Lynn chuckled as she gently said, "Your becoming a musician must have gone over big."

"Awh, they didn't take my not going into the force that hard. All my brothers resemble my dad to a tee, sandy-colored hair with hazel eyes. But from the get go I was just like..." His voice slid into an Irish brogue. "... Me Irish mum."

Lynn was moved by the obvious special bond Sam seemed to have had with his mother.

"That's where I get the black hair and blue eyes. She gave piano lessons and taught me from the time I was four. I guess everyone just knew I'd be a musician and that was that."

He leaned back on the arm of the Windsor chair and took a sip of his coffee. "But I'll tell you, my dad never let up on me. I got boxing lessons in the backyard just like the rest and had to train all winter in the basement with my brothers. I'm grateful for that. Working out still helps me relax. I like to compose on the piano in sweats and when I'm stuck or want to think something through.... Lifting weights clears my head."

Lynn held her cup and swirled around her coffee as she said, "I hear you're separated from your wife."

Sam leaned forward as if he was in pain. "News really travels around here."

Lynn laughed, "I'm convinced they have a satellite watching our every move and some kind of sound truck going up and down the road picking up conversations."

"Tell me. Am I ever going to live down the chicken-wire incident?"

"*Never*. That's etched in stone."

She started to giggle. "They'll probably put it on your gravestone..." She punctuated her words with her hand in the air, "Here lies Sam Reynolds of Richardson Hollow ... he asked the man if he was for hire ... cause he wanted some chicken wire..."

Lynn loved the fake embarrassed look Sam was putting on.

"I can hear school kids chanting the rhyme as they play hop-scotch on the sidewalks in town," she laughed.

Sam folded his muscular arms across his chest and a satisfied look spread across his face. He sat there for a moment, then rested his crossed arms on the table and slid forward. "I like to hear you laugh. The lyrical tone of your voice is very pleasing."

Lynn blushed.

"After I saw you in the post office I couldn't remember exactly what you looked like, but the sound of your voice was imprinted on my mind."

This was only half true. He remembered precisely how she looked, down to the tint of her green eyes.

Lynn felt herself blush again and couldn't look at him. She kept running her fork around on her plate. Finally, she said, "You didn't tell me about your wife."

Lynn watched him carefully and noticed an almost crestfallen look on his face that quickly faded as he said, "I guess you could say we were incompatible. I just never fit in with her crowd ... not successful enough."

He resettled himself in the chair as if he were uncomfortable. "I was willing to stick it out ... raised Catholic and all ... but she wanted out.

Next month we'll be separated a year, and our divorce final a few weeks after that."

"Are there any children?"

Sam answered simply, "We never got around to that."

Lynn thought that fact pained him more than the divorce.

"Do you still love her?" Lynn asked with a hint of nervousness in her voice.

Sam stretched his neck and scratched under his chin as he said, "No, I'm over that part." He stopped and looked Lynn in the eyes as if he really wanted her to understand. "But I guess I'll always worry about her. I need to know she's all right."

The room fell silent except for the hum of the refrigerator that had just kicked on. The chair made a sliding sound on the wood floor as Sam stood up and carefully put it back under the table.

"I guess I better be going."

Lynn walked with him onto the porch, careful not to let the screen door slam and wake Jess. The sweet aroma of the wild sage that grew in the fallow spots at the farm permeated the air. Sam paused just as he was about to go down the first step. Lynn came up next to him and could feel his firm muscles on her bare arm. They stood there looking out on the barnyard lit by a lone sodium vapor light. The edges of the cloud hiding the moon glowed white against the black sky.

Sam felt paralyzed, not even breathing. His body refused to leave. Hell, Sam said to himself, then slipped his arm around her waist and pulled her to him. When he felt her go limp, he slowly brushed his lips across her forehead then down her cheek. He held her so close his insides felt liquid except for the hardened area under his groin which he pressed against her, the only way he was going to be able to keep himself at a tolerable level. He ran his hand down to the small of her back and drew her in tight to his body. He gently pressed his mouth against her ears and breathed in the perfume of her hair.

She clung to him. The firm warmth pressing up against her made the muscles deep inside ache and brought her to a place of intense desire.

His face could be made out now that the moon had come from behind the cloud. His eyes were glistening and the gentle smile gone, replaced with an intensity that made her turn her eyes away as if she were ashamed of how she felt. He studied her face for a brief moment and knew she wasn't ready and slowly loosened his grip.

"I better be going."

She said nothing as he released her, just leaned back against the railing post with her arms behind her back.

As Sam pulled out of the driveway he saw the pattern of light dance as the screen door opened and then closed. Lynn, please let go, he begged, then slapped the steering wheel in joy as he remembered the taste of her.

CHAPTER 17

Three hours later, Sam Reynolds got up from the piano to watch the breaking of a new dawn and was alarmed to see the silhouette of wildly bending trees on the dark horizon.

At the farmhouse, a sound like the roar of a train made Lynn fly out of bed. In seconds she was nervously gripping Jess and running down the front staircase. Amid the howling sound, a tree crashed against the house. A bizarre shadow of a huge maple tree lying on its side feverishly danced around the parlor walls, but the old house stood firm. In minutes an eerie silence fell.

Lynn and Jess ran out the front door and were thunderstruck by the devastation. With the dawn just breaking, they could see that the old greenhouse was gone and the big barn leaning over. Only the horse barn was standing. Lynn ran down the porch steps, and dazed, stepped backward as her eyes traced the outline of the house, untouched except for the storm gutter yanked off by the falling tree.

Sam's truck skidded to a stop as he slammed on the brakes and jumped out. Just then, they heard a crack like a gunshot coming from the leaning barn.

"That baby's about to blow," Sam shouted.

"Sam, my seeds are in there! I've got to get them out!"

"Not unless I brace it up, you're not! Do you have any planks?"

"Yes, in the horse barn!"

Lynn, barefoot and wearing a nightgown, ran into the barn. She flipped on the light switch but the power was out so she grabbed a flashlight hanging on a nail. The beam of light jogged along tools and equipment, finally landing on a stack of thick old floor planks. Sam rushed over and picked one up, obviously heavy as evidenced by his straining neck muscles.

"Do you have any stakes!"

"I don't know!"

"Two by fours?"

"Yes!"

"Go get them!"

Sam started dragging planks to the leaning barn while Lynn and Jess fetched some two-by-fours.

"Where's your saw?"

"I'll get it!" Jess cried out.

Moments after Jess came running with the saw, Sam feverishly cut up the studs as he yelled, "Get me a sledge hammer!"

Lynn hugged Jess and watching in terror as Sam dragged the first plank to the corner of the leaning barn and jammed it tightly under the roof eave at an angle to the ground. Then he pounded in a piece of studding at the foot. Sam systematically repeated this maneuver in eight to ten foot increments until the barn's sixty-foot length was secured, then started over, putting another brace in between.

While Sam completed the backbreaking task, Lynn and Jess ran into the house and put on jeans. When they returned, they all walked around the barn and could see there was no way to slide the crushed doors open.

"Do you have a chainsaw?" Sam asked.

Lynn swallowed hard. Her throat had gone dry. "Yes! In the basement of the house."

"Where's your main power box?"

"In the basement!"

"Turn everything off and bring the saw. I'll try to do something about the water."

"I can turn that off from the basement too!"

Minutes later, Lynn held her breath as Sam, walking to the front of the barn brandishing the whirring chainsaw, quickly carved out a doorway. Lynn flashed a light into the dark cavern and saw everything leaning sideways.

"Oh my God! I've got to get my seeds!"

"Oh no you're not. I'll get them!"

Lynn clutched desperately at Sam's shirt. "No! The containers need to be handled carefully. I don't want anything mixed up. I've got to go. Please!"

Sam checked out the braces one more time and said, "Okay, but for God's sake be quick!"

Lynn crawled through the small doorway with the flashlight and made her way into the barn by climbing under and over fallen tables until she reached the shelf area where the dried seeds were stored. She was stunned to find the whole shelf structure lying face down.

"I can't get at them!" she screamed. "They're buried."

"Get out of there!"

"No! Not without my seeds!"

"Don't move! I'm coming."

Lynn could hear Sam's heavy breathing as he inched his way toward her. The smell of the sweat pouring off his body permeated the air as he carefully started up the chainsaw. The shelf was sliced in half, exposing the sealed cartons. The two kept sliding them ahead little by little as they made their way out of the barn, retrieving fourteen of the seventeen cartons.

Lynn's legs were wobbly but she managed to get to the grassy knoll next to the porch steps before collapsing. Sam dropped down next to her.

Wearily, Lynn asked Jess to take the seeds into the house in case it started to rain. The boy jumped to the task.

As she wiped her face, first on one sleeve and then on the other, Lynn said, "We've got to get the tractor out before the barn collapses."

Sam went over and flashed the light to the left of where they had gotten the seeds. A huge timber that had been holding up part of the second floor was lying at an angle over the Ingersol. This hand-hewn beam was the only thing keeping the floor from crashing down on the tractor. If they had an opening big enough, he could drive it straight out.

He yelled over, "Do you have another tractor?"

Lynn shook her head dolefully.

"How about rope?"

"In the horse barn!"

"Get it!"

When Lynn came back dragging the thick, oily rope, Sam was backing his truck up to the unbraced side of the barn. He pried off a board and, while standing in the truck bed, tied the rope around the corner post. He jumped off and tied the other end around the truck tow bar.

"Tell me when the rope's taunt!" he hollered.

Lynn signaled for him to stop and he threw on the emergency brake and jumped down.

"That ought to help hold her while I cut another door."

The chainsaw started up again and a hole big enough to get the tractor through was carved out. Sam stepped through the debris, taking great care to snake around so he wouldn't bump against anything. Once on the seat, the tractor started on the first try. After giving Lynn a smile and a thumbs-up, he put the gears in first and slowly pulled out. After some clapping and whooping Lynn started toward the barn. Sam quickly jumped off the tractor and pulled her back.

"Let the rest go. Consider yourself lucky you got what you did."

Lynn kept straining toward the broken barn and then suddenly relaxed as if she realized he was right. She turned toward Sam. "I'm sorry. I didn't ask you about your place."

"The tornado didn't hit me. The damn thing just tore a swath across the hollow."

"I wonder if Cal's trailer got hit."

Lynn yelled over to Jess to give Cal a call and make sure he was okay, and if he was, to ask him to come right over.

While Sam unhitched his truck from the barn, Lynn walked over to the fragments of greenhouse lying all over the garden center lot, clearly visible now that the sun was up. She stoically started collecting any pots which were miraculously unharmed or could be tamped back together, putting them in a grove of trees on the edge of the cluttered nursery lot.

Jess ran shouting toward her.

"Cal's son's barn roof was torn off! They've got to move two thousand bales of hay to Jim Cary's empty barn. Cal's driving one of the tractors."

"Okay, Jess. Let's just get rolling," Lynn said wearily.

Their hearts leapt for joy when they saw Sam grabbing up pots as he walked toward them.

By two, only a quarter of the plants were resettled in a shady grove next to the lot. When they found themselves picking up the same pot over and over again, Lynn dragged herself over to the tractor, plopped down on the wagon and said, "We're done. We've got everything that's worth getting."

Sam took off his gloves and wiped his face on his sleeve. With his hands on his hips he surveyed the scene. His closely cropped beard had a red tinge in the sunlight and his sunburned face and arms glistened with sweat. Particles of dirt and hayseed from the barn had stuck to his oily flesh. Lynn's eyes rested on him and she recalled the urgency in his caress the night before.

Jess started hollering that Shelly was coming over the hill. Lynn laughed out loud when the familiar white deli bags emerged from the back seat.

"Do you want to eat out here on the picnic table or go inside and wash up a bit?" Shelly called out.

"The heck with that!" shouted Jess impatiently. "I'm starving!"

The picnic table got tipped right side up and everyone collapsed as Shelly proudly went about serving everyone.

"I knew Shelly would show," Lynn said. "She's been to every tragedy and triumph in my life since I was eighteen."

"Well, if you're properly insured, honey, this will be one of the triumphs."

The remark sounded like the beginning of one of Shelly's lectures. Resigned, Lynn propped up her head with one hand and ate with the other.

Sam came to her rescue.

"Didn't I meet you at the party last night?"

Shelly, obviously delighted, flew into a gushing wrap-up of the evening. They liked hearing her prattle on like that. No one paid any real attention, except Sam nodded politely from time to time and every once in a while threw out a friendly comment.

Lynn fell into a catatonic state after she downed a chocolate brownie.

"You poor baby," Shelly said as she gave Lynn's slumped shoulders a squeeze. "There's nothing more you can do today. You've got to get to bed."

Then Shelly went over to Jess and brushed his blond hair back from his forehead and said enthusiastically, "How would you like to go to the Adirondacks with me and the girls for a couple of days?"

"I don't think I should, Aunt Shelly. Mom's going to need me."

"Nonsense!" She looked around. "Your mother's got to get a team of professionals in here with big equipment."

"Shelly, you *know* how nervous I get when he's not here."

"*Mom.*"

"Lynn, for Pete's sake, you're a wreck. I won't take my eyes off him for one lousy minute. Besides, he'll be safer with me than here with everything that'll be going on to clean this place up. I'll bring him back Thursday."

Noticing the excitement in Jess's wide-eyed stare, Lynn couldn't deny him the holiday. "Maybe you're right. But he's got to call me every day."

Jess gave his mother a big hug. "Don't worry, I'll be careful." Then he went over, put his arms around Sam and said, "You were great. Thanks for everything."

Sam put his hand on the boy's shoulder. "You take care now, son."

"I will. Bye, Mom."

As Shelly led Jess away saying, "Let's just get you packed. You can take a shower at our place," Lynn looked at Sam who was brushing the debris from his shirt. She reached over and picked something off and placed it in the palm of her hand.

"This is a hollyhock seed. See how it has the fuzzy edge around it? Seeds are just like people ... they all have different characteristics and personalities."

He gazed at her as she spoke, his eyes now slowly skimming across her features. Nothing really special, just all put together in a pleasing way.

"There's a miracle in every seed. Give it a little water, some sun and the most marvelous thing happens ... a genuine miracle of nature."

She laughed. "You probably think I'm crazy, just like my friend Shelly does." She looked around. "But I have a dream ... and maybe I'm going to die trying to make it happen ... but I just can't let it go. I'm going to get this place up and running again and make it pay so we'll never have to worry about having to give it up again."

Sam thoughtfully rubbed his beard and spoke. "I know what it's like to run after a dream. Hell, I've been doing that for years. It's the last thing you think about when you go to sleep and the first thing that jumps into your head when you wake."

She looked at him sheepishly. "So you don't think I'm crazy?"

"No. Not really." They were silent for a moment. He wanted to tell her that he respected her for it, but his mind jumped to why he'd come to the hollow in the first place: to chase *his* dream.

Lynn interrupted his thoughts. "I must be really tired, spilling my guts like this. But, somehow I've got to make a go of this place. I want it so bad..." She laughed. "It's like a big mountain I've got to climb. Everyone's telling me to go around it. But I can't. It's always going to be there ... and I'm not going to be happy 'til I get to the top."

Sam looked past the sweaty face with its flushed cheeks, and into her green eyes. He'd always liked what he saw, but witnessing at close range the intense determination he had gleaned from his telescope, touched him. They were kindred spirits. And at that moment he knew he'd never rest until they were one.

Lynn rose stiffly from the table as if all her joints had frozen and went over to the heirloom garden. The flowers were reaching up for the sun as if nothing in the world had gone wrong.

Sam was filled with emotion as Lynn stood with her back to him while taking in the peaceful scene. As he came up and stood next to her, she said, "Isn't this red in the Maltese Cross the most truly beautiful red you've ever seen?" Lynn pinched off one of the cross-like florets and placed it in Sam's hand. "Here, Sam Reynolds, I'm awarding this to you for going above and beyond the call of duty."

Lynn drank in the image in front of her. She didn't know why, but she felt it was important to remember how he looked at that very moment. Her eyes carefully ran over the sunburned cheeks and deep creases at the corner of his eyes.

Sam self-consciously shifted his weight, as he stood with one hand in his back pocket and the other holding the floret. Finally, his eyes focused somewhere off in the distance. That pleased her, because now she was free to let her eyes roam along the soft curls across his forehead, then the aquiline nose, and finally the lips that had been so warm. At that moment she was struck by the notion she and Sam were somehow going to be a part of each other's lives forever.

She reached over and touched him. "I'll never forget you for saving my seeds, Sam."

He wanted to hold her, but knew if he did, it would kill him to stop.

The spell dissipated when Jess and Shelly came out of the house shouting their good-byes. Lynn threw them a kiss.

Suddenly there was a loud crack. In one big whoosh the huge barn collapsed, filling the air with a bevy of swallows and flying hay bales. The familiar horizon became stunningly naked with the massive land-mark now lying in a heap. Shelly and Jess froze for a moment as they took in the scene, then the boy was gently prodded into the car.

Lynn and Sam broke into a resigned chuckle and walked together toward the house as the Porche disappeared over the hill. When Lynn started to put Commander on his chain, Sam stopped her.

"You go on in. I'll take care of him."

The dog didn't put up a fuss. He was probably grateful to be getting some rest after a day of running back and forth chewing on discarded pots. As Sam latched the chain onto the dog's collar, the screen door slammed, followed by a tired good-by and thank you from Lynn.

Once in the truck, Sam leaned back and sat for a while looking at the house. The warm, comfortable feeling he'd had the night before poured over him. His eyes scanned the windows upstairs and he wondered if she were in one of the bedrooms by now.

With every muscle in his body aching, he started the truck and backed out of the debris-strewn driveway.

Jess rested his head on the pillow one of Shelly's girls gave him as the SUV cruised along the New York State Thruway towards Utica at the foothills of the Adirondacks. Now that the thrill of going had subsided, guilt was setting in. Even though he was just a boy, ever since his father's death he had fashioned himself in his mind's eye as his mother's protector and now he was leaving her during a crisis. Then he remembered the relief he felt when Sam helped gather up the seedlings. It seemed so natural, as if the man was being sucked into their life like lamp oil into a wick. The boy forced away an avalanche of hope that sprang from his gut. More than anything in the world, he wanted his mother to be happy and he was afraid if he prayed for her and Sam to get together he would jinx it.

Somewhere in the back of his mind he heard one of the girls ask him if he were awake, but he just let himself drift off into a sound sleep.

CHAPTER 18

Hal Jenkins of Jenkins and Smith Insurance walked quickly to his car after taking a photograph of the silo lying on its side at the Brown's farm. He hurriedly thumbed through a stack of claims and decided to do Lynn Richardson's place next. He tossed the clipboard on the seat and headed straight for Richardson Road.

Hal ran a nice friendly little independent agency, insuring most of the farmers around these parts and a lot of families and businesses in Eastlake just like his father before him. The Smith part of the company had been gone for years but they never got around to changing the name.

To Hal, insurance wasn't just a living. He believed he was bringing together a large collection of hard-working people willing to throw some money into a pot, so in case of a disaster no one person would get hurt too badly. He was still sorry he hadn't been able to sell Ken a life insurance policy and sorrier the struggling farmer couldn't afford one to cover his notes at the bank.

The damage to the Richardson's farm was apparent the minute he rolled over the hill. The trees looked like broken sticks thrown on a green carpet and the sun reflected feverishly off of thousands of pieces of glass. From that distance, the huge barn resembled a smashed toy.

First, Ken, now this, he thought as he pulled in the driveway. Hal, who'd been on the road the night before until sundown and back at work before sunup that morning, couldn't afford the time to knock at the door. He just reached for his Polaroid, shoved an extra pack of film into his shirt pocket and got out and started taking pictures.

Commander's barking brought Lynn out of the house.

"Did you get a hold of Aetna's emergency people yet?" Hal shouted.

"Yes. A woman at that eight-hundred number authorized getting someone in here to take care of the trees."

"Their adjusters are out and about now and somebody should be coming by here today. Do you have names of tree removal services?"

"Aetna gave me some yesterday. I'm waiting for a call."

Finished, Hal jumped into his car, shouted he was going to Cal's place next and pulled away.

"Tell him to call me!" Lynn yelled after him.

The phone in the house rang, sending Lynn running up the porch steps.

"Hello. Is this Mrs. Richardson?"

"Yes!"

"This is Mark Cherto from American Indian Tree Removal."

"Oh! Thank you so much for getting back to me."

"How many you got."

"Two big maples."

"Are any of them on the house?"

"No, but there are broken limbs hanging over the back of the house."

"You want us to clean everything up?"

"Yes! As soon as you can."

"Those big ones run four-hundred dollars apiece."

"Aetna told me to get them removed."

"Okay, we'll be out sometime between now and midnight."

"Midnight! It'll be dark!"

"We've got lights."

He got the directions and hung up.

A lot of the morning was spent on the phone. Mindy told her she put a rush on the studio set Bob had ordered for the winter tapings. The guy promised it would be ready by the following Tuesday.

So many calls were coming in from friends and patrons she was tempted to take the phone off the hook. Instead, she went outside and started picking up, but finding the task hopeless, went back in, took a couple of aspirins and lay on the settee. Thank goodness Shelly took Jess, she thought. Just as her headache started to fade, Commander started barking at a huge truck with a crane trying to back into the driveway.

"We got the call over the radio and since we were near here decided to do you next," yelled one of the two men who jumped out. Shirtless, he had on a pair of shorts and high-top boots with his long blond hair tied back in a ponytail. Another truck with a huge rack pulled up and two more men leapt out and got chainsaws out of the back. Although deeply tanned, they didn't look any more like American Indians than Lynn.

Since Lynn wanted all the wood for her stove, they agreed to trim the limbs so they could easily be cut up and split later on. The small branches and debris would be hauled away. In minutes, three chainsaws were busy at work in the front. The guy with the ponytail adroitly climbed the tree in back, roped one of the broken limbs to a pulley, then sawed it off and lowered it down.

"You sure are good at that," Lynn yelled up to him.

He grinned like someone who took pride in his work and shouted back, "I ought to be. Do all the limbs for the City of Syracuse."

With all the commotion, Lynn hadn't noticed the man coming from the nursery parking lot with a clipboard under his arm.

He offered his hand saying, "I'm George Atkinson. Aetna sent me." Not wasting time to chat, he walked over to where the trees were being carved up and efficiently jotted some notes on his board.

"Did they give you a price?" he asked Lynn.

"Yes. Four hundred dollars each." She stood next to him watching him write the figure down. "They're going to leave the wood, but take away the branches."

"Did you ask them to grind the stumps?"

"I didn't think of that."

He went over and talked with the fellow with the ponytail, then returned and told her he'd authorized the stump removal.

Lynn started to relax.

Although, Hal Jenkins, as well as the tree guy on the phone and Aetna's adjuster had all been cool under pressure, their polite air of urgency made Lynn understand without being told this disaster went a lot further than her and Cal's son's losses.

The adjuster measured the barn with a wheeled apparatus he'd taken out of his car. However, the greenhouse foundation just got a quick glance.

"Can I come in and use your kitchen table while I figure this out?"

"Please do."

While the adjuster busily punched figures into a calculator, Lynn nervously straightened up the kitchen. She had no idea what would happen next. Finally, he asked her to sit down and started going through the measurements of the barn and the replacement cost.

"You're sure lucky the barn was insured for the replacement value," he said. "If not, we wouldn't be giving you much after depreciating a hundred-year-old structure." He paused for a moment, then added, "I'm afraid there's nothing on the greenhouse or its contents."

Lynn bit her lip. "I know. We got it used and couldn't afford to increase our insurance."

He passed Lynn the clipboard and asked her to sign, then tore off the bottom third of the top sheet and handed it to her.

"What's this?"

"A check for eighteen thousand."

As he was going through the kitchen door, he mentioned clean-up was covered. All she had to do was call the amount in and they'd issue her a check. He went back to his car one more time, got out a camera and quickly photographed everything. In minutes he was cruising up the hill.

Cal phoned and let her know Hal Jenkins showed him the pictures and that they had talked briefly about the tornado and how many farmers had been hit. Lynn told Cal she'd phoned an ad in to the Eastlake *Republican* saying she'd be closed until further notice. When Cal fell silent after she told him about the check from Aetna, she pictured him scratching behind his ear and thinking.

Finally, he told her to sit tight. He'd get someone up there with a bulldozer and ask the Smithfield Volunteer Fire Department to burn what was left of the barn.

They talked over the possibility of salvaging more from the barn and decided that Cal and his son would come down with a couple of pry bars and help her pick through the debris. Friday, maybe. He mentioned Jess had told him on the phone Sunday Sam Reynolds was helping her out and thank God for that. Lynn could tell Cal was exhausted, so she said good-by and hung up.

The phone rang the minute she put it down.

"Jess! How's my boy doing?"

"Great, Mom! We went to the Water Park! Aunt Shelly and the girls are being real nice."

"You sound so good, baby."

"Aunt Shelly wants to talk to you."

"Have you heard anything from Aetna?" Shelly asked.

"Yep. I'm clutching an eighteen-thousand-dollar check as we speak."

"That's all?"

"Yep."

"Pete and I have been talking. This is a sign from above, sweetheart. Take the money and run. Get yourself a nice little house with a garden in Eastlake. You can still do your show. Lynn, just say, 'Aetna, I'm glad I met ya' and get the hell out of there."

"I can't *do* that, Shelly."

"You can still save the farm for Jess. Rent out the land and the house and pay your new mortgage with it. You'll break your back getting started again... and for what!"

There was silence as warm tears streamed down Lynn's face.

"Are you still there?"

More silence.

"Awh, Lynn. I didn't mean to upset you. Honey; just promise me you're not going to do anything foolish with that money. We'll be back Thursday night."

"Okay. I'll see you then."

Lynn chatted with Jess for a while, hanging onto every word. His voice had a soothing effect on her. Finally, she said good-by so as not to run up Pete's bill any more. The phone rang again.

"How you doin'?" Sam said.

"Okay. How about you?"

"I don't want to bend down and pick up another pot anytime soon."

Lynn laughed softly and then fell silent. Sam sounded relaxed and she pictured him sprawled out on a comfortable couch with his arms folded casually across his chest and the phone resting between his shoulder and jaw.

"I wanted to come down all day but could see you were busy and didn't want to get in the way."

"The tree removal people were a trip."

"You got to admit they were fast."

Neither of them said anything. After a while the silence seemed natural and took on a life of its own. Lynn ran her finger slowly around the buttons, not wanting the call to end.

"Can I make you dinner tonight?" he said.

"Sounds good, but I'm too tired to chew. I'm just going to go to bed."

She didn't mind the long silence that followed, just held the phone and closed her eyes and saw the sun glistening off his face and his eyes blue as the sky in the fall.

"Tomorrow?"

"I can't think that far ahead."

"Come on, you can't say no to the recipient of the Maltese Cross."

She gave out a short, tired laugh and said, "All right. You got me. What time?"

"Six?"

Her voice became soft. "Okay... and thanks again for yesterday."

"That was nothing ... that is, nothing a week of Swedish massages won't fix."

"Good night, Sam."

CHAPTER 19

There's something about the stillness in the early morning hours before the birds wake that makes one's thinking as clear as a bell, and this morning would be no exception. The sun had yet to rise but Lynn Richardson was wide-awake and all her senses keen. Like some kind of strange omen, she heard a hoot owl and shivered.

The air coming from the open window was filled with dew so she slid into a pair of jeans and a sweatshirt and ran down the back staircase in her socks.

Only in the quiet of the early morning could all the sounds of the old house be heard, the pendulum in the grandfather clock in the parlor swaying back and forth, and every once in a while the creaking of a contracting floor board.

She put on coffee, went over to the desk and took out a fresh legal pad, a new fine-point pen and her calculator, then carefully placed them on the table. Next, she brought out the folder with all the information on greenhouses. Finally, she poured some coffee into an oversized cup and sat down.

Methodically, she arranged everything from the folder on the table in neat stacks, and then picked up the pen. How much was the most she could pull together? She carefully wrote down the figures. There was the fourteen thousand line-of-credit Citizens had given her after Pete and Shelly co-signed, eighteen thousand from Aetna and two thousand she had squirreled away since April. Almost thirty-four thousand. Barely enough.

She was so tense she had to force herself to breathe. Would this spread her too thin? She leaned back in her chair and became wrapped in thought. For the next ten months she and Jess could survive on the eight hundred she was getting from the station and still make the mortgage payment if they were careful. They already had the wood supply and wouldn't have to pay that much to get it cut and split.

Next season she was really going to be hurting for plants that would bring three-seventy-five, but she and Cal could put in some annuals over the winter just so there'd be stock out there. Then there was the fifty acres of woods. Maybe they could rent a tree digger and bring out a hundred or so maple seedlings to sell. They could also dig up a couple hundred of the five hundred blue spruce Ken put in six years back. Fortunately, Ken had insisted on getting a company to trim them every year at a cost of fifty cents apiece. They looked wonderful. She could send letters around to landscapers as well as sell them to the public for around sixty dollars apiece.

If somehow she could get a big greenhouse up...bigger than the one she and Cal had settled on... the following year would be good, so good, she felt she'd finally be truly established as a major nursery.

The first step was going to be getting the greenhouse up. After several attempts on graph paper, while going back and forth to the brochures, Lynn settled on a steel building twenty-eight by forty for the seed warehouse and office, and a greenhouse running another sixty feet. She spent three hours laying everything out. Shelly kept creeping into her mind making her feel like a thief in the night.

Then, almost like the birds found her out, they started their morning cacophony. So she slipped into some shoes, poured the last of the coffee and went outside. Commander sat proudly next to his doghouse knowing he'd be next. Once off his chain he stood beside her like a sentinel.

The sun was promising to appear on the horizon but a bat still dared to fly out of the horse barn to grab more insects before dawn. Lynn walked with Commander across the dewy lawn to the pile of rubble that once was a barn and recognized Jess's mangled bike in the wreckage. Shelly was right. This storm was a sign from above. She just had to read it right!

So many things were gone or had just changed. Ken, Lucky, now the barn. But that's how things had always been. Ken's dad had told her when he was young they grew hops, but with prohibition, they had no choice but to turn to milking. In fact, the horse barn was a converted hop house and the puffy lantern-like blooms still grew in the hedges at the edge of the fields.

In order to survive, the Richardsons had always done what they had to. A never-ending chain of change and survival. Now it was her turn, and she wasn't going to cut and run. Instead, she was going to bank the whole thirty-four thousand on securing a place for her and Jess.

She ran into the house and feverishly thumbed through the material on the table looking for the name and number the greenhouse manufacturer had given her. The Bedesky brothers, he had told her, do a fine job and come well recommended. They were mountain men from the Adirondacks, and built quality. He said they specialized in steel buildings but were the best installers of greenhouses around.

Even though the clock read six-fifteen, she nervously dialed the long-distance number. At around the twelfth ring a gruff voice answered and Lynn flew into a hurried apology for calling so early. Then she explained about the tornado and how badly she needed the greenhouse.

He didn't say anything, but made a lot of noises Lynn interpreted as his thinking process. His hand must have been covering the mouthpiece but she could still make out the muffled shout. "Hey, Mark. You want to go to Oneida County and put up a greenhouse?"

"Just a moment, Lady."

The phone made a soft thud.

A few minutes later, "Yeah. We're interested. We're scheduled to start a big barn in three weeks but could put that back a few days. We're all set to go fishing, but if we can order the materials right away we'll start on your project when we come back. Otherwise, you'll have to wait until October. When can we meet with you?"

"Now."

Again, the muffled shout. "The lady says she can see us now."

"Okay. Where do you live?"

Lynn got so wound up waiting the two hours for the Bedesky brothers she paced the nursery lot like a penned up animal. Watering the plants distracted her for a while, but when she noticed she was actually talking to Ken out loud, she hugged herself and tried to calm down. At that moment she felt close to him, knowing he'd agree with her decision to build the greenhouse. He'd always supported her efforts as if he knew she needed to make her own mark on the farm.

When she asked if she could have the space behind the barn for a garden, instead of telling her it was too full of old parts and used barbed wire to be worth anything, he pitched in and helped her clear it out.

After she started hundreds of herbs in the dining room and sun parlor that first winter after his parents passed on, he went to the attic and brought out some books from his days at Cornell's Ag school for her to study. Two years later, when she put the three-hundred dollars in front of him she made on her first weekend of selling her plants, he placed her hand over the pile of greenbacks and gently squeezed as he said, "Honey, that's yours to do with."

That's what really got her started in the seed business. The money paid to print labels, buy supplies and come up with a mailer and some ads.

She stared absent-mindedly at fragments of broken glass and remembered the day Ken drove in with the old greenhouse he'd found for her. Painful images of the strong, handsome man assembling the pieces exploded in her head.

Lynn's thoughts were mercifully interrupted when she eyed a two-ton truck barreling over the hill. The minute it slowed down, she ran waving and hollering.

The two brothers, both in Carhart overalls, couldn't be told apart with the exception of the one wearing a leather hat with a long pheasant feather swooping down toward the back. Their faces were hidden behind bushy blond beards and their kinky blond hair covered their foreheads, hiding their penetrating blue eyes in a sea of fluff. Somewhere in their thirties, they were short and stocky and obviously as strong as oxen.

Lynn ran into the house for her plans and showed them where she wanted everything. She was in awe of how naturally they grasped what she wanted and how lucidly they discussed the project. No wonder they came highly recommended. When the three of them trooped into the house, it was like Julia Childs meets Paul Bunyon and his twin and falls in love with them. She listened in ecstasy as the brothers discussed the entire project, first, with her, and then over the phone with the manufacturer. Their confident, laid-back demeanor dispelled all Lynn's doubts.

All morning she made them coffee and kept loading up a plate with muffins as they put the figures together. There were a few more calls to the manufacturer and one to the company that would pour the floors. Lynn was impressed with the Bedeskys' style. They had a formula for figuring the price of everything, and she decided right then and there she'd do the same with her business.

Finally they showed her the contract with a total price of thirty-one thousand without a bathroom, and thirty-four with. This wasn't surprising. A structure a third of the size of this building, Cal had figured, would cost fourteen thousand without the frills.

"Is that with the shutters on the warehouse windows and the cupola?"

After they pointed out the items on the contract, Lynn slapped the palms of her hands on her thighs, said she wanted the bathroom and asked where to sign.

"Do you want to look this over for a day or so?"

"No."

Before handing her the pen, the brothers explained she had to give them half when the materials arrived and half the day they completed the job, and that the site had to be cleared and graded level before they started. There was another call to the manufacturer. The materials would arrive in seven days and they'd have the buildings completed in another twenty.

As she walked the brothers to their truck, Lynn said, "You guys probably won't believe this, but this is one of the most important moments of my life. I don't think I was this nervous when I got married."

The brothers looked at each other and laughed, and then told her that's what almost everyone says.

"We'll be fishin' for a week or so, then we'll bring our trailer down."

"Trailer?"

"Yeah. You don't expect us to drive four hours back and forth each day, do you?"

"No. Of course not."

"We bring our dogs too."

"Dogs?"

"Yeah."

The one brother gave Commander a look like he was sizing him up and said, "Don't worry. Thelma and Louise won't bother this little fella. They know they're guests and behave themselves accordingly."

CHAPTER 20

The Ford pickup rolled to a stop in the parking lot of Morrisville Feed. Lynn got out toting a carton of seed packets and gave a black Lab in the back of a pickup a friendly "hi, boy." Two steps inside and the lingering scent of mildew hit her nostrils, probably seeping up from the old boards under the worn linoleum.

There weren't that many customers, but being past three, that wasn't so unusual. Most farmers would be out haying on such a sunny July afternoon. The seed slots were mostly filled but she freshened everything up a bit and was relieved to see things were finally slowing down some.

Lynn swung around as Jake Walker put his long arm around her.

"You mean to tell me that even though you're a big TV star you're still putting up stock in my store?"

As Lynn bent down and picked up the carton, she said, "I'll never get too big to take care of Morrisville Feed, Jake. You were the first guy to give my seeds a chance."

The older man, still handsome for his age, pinched her chin and said, "They say you never forget your first, don't they?"

Lynn feigned indignation as a couple of men waiting at the counter grinned.

"Sorry to hear about your place getting hit, but I can see that hasn't stopped you."

"No, Jake. In fact, I'm going to expand."

"Atta, girl! I knew you were a fighter the minute I laid eyes on you."

Before Lynn left she decided to get a paper and check out her ad.

"It's a damn shame about the missing little girl in Cortland," Jake said as he handed her change.

Lynn glanced at the front page with the headline announcing a hundred-thousand-dollar reward for information leading to the whereabouts of the child.

On the way home, she decided to keep a closer eye on Jess. There were no homes for over a mile between their farm and the Barnhill place. Anything could happen to him on his way to visit Billy and no one would know.

As she went over the crest of Richardson Hill, she couldn't push the dinner with Sam out of her mind any longer. The clock on the dash said four-thirty. If she was going to cancel, she'd better do so the minute she hit the house.

There was no point pretending going up there for dinner wouldn't lead to anything. Not after the way he came on to her the other night. Suddenly, something gripped her insides as she remembered Ken holding her that same way, and for the first time since his death she wanted to force those memories from her mind.

Hell, she'd just jumped into the nursery business with both feet and there was a lot on the line. What was she thinking! She'd have to work night and day to get the nursery set up and seedlings started. A major distraction and the whole house of cards could collapse. The minute she got home she'd call Sam and somehow beg out of the dinner.

The light was blinking on the answering machine as she rushed into the kitchen with Commander heading straight for Queenie's dish. She quickly skimmed through the calls and then slowly sank into the chair as she listened to the beautiful melody played on a piano. The music stopped and the mellow voice disguised as an announcer said, "Don't miss the dramatic ending to this masterpiece tonight at six... played by one of the unforgettable and talented members of the infamous Richardson Hollow Gang."

The logic from five minutes earlier dissipated into thin air. Lynn took a deep breath and decided to make a masterpiece of her own to take over. She opened the refrigerator and spied a jar of her homemade pesto. That's what I'll do! A basil pesto salad!

While the rigatoni boiled, the dog got fed and put out on his chain. Lynn tossed the cooked pasta with the pesto, put the container in the fridge, then went up and took a shower. Jess called and she sat down on the bed and dried her hair with a towel while devouring every word the boy rattled off about the events of his day.

Suddenly Shelly was on the phone.

"You're not doing anything crazy are you?"

"No, Shelly. I've never been saner in my whole life."

"Good. We'll see you tomorrow night."

Lynn glanced out the window and the deep shadows in the grass told her the day was slipping away. Everything seemed to fade out of focus as she stared at the fields now starting to turn gold. She looked around the large bedroom in which she and Ken had made love for the first time right after their wedding. She smiled, remembering the ceremony had to be scheduled between chores. Afterwards was the first time she had helped Ken with the milking. When they finished he took her up to the loft, fluffed up a soft bed from hay and made love to her again.

Lynn went over to the dresser and picked up the picture of herself holding baby Jess while standing next to Ken and his prize-winning Holstein. This was the first time Ken had taken her to the county fair in Brookfield, and she remembered feeling like she was back at the beginning of the century. All the buildings were at least that old and the slow, friendly pace with everyone calling out to each other by their first names harkened back to an earlier era. Ken had proudly introduced her and their baby to friends and neighbors from all over the county, making her feel like she was wearing a First Prize ribbon herself.

Lynn slid down on the bed and tenderly picked up the picture of Ken she kept on the table. Overwhelmed with guilt, she couldn't help wondering what she'd do with this precious image if she ever remarried. When she thought of his beautiful face buried in some dark drawer she felt her heart would break. She lovingly ran her hand across the picture, wiping away the tear splattered on the glass.

After he showered, Sam checked out the house one more time. His disc library was carefully considered, but there was no contest. This was definitely going to be a Frank Sinatra kind of night.

He glanced at his watch. Ten to six. He happily hummed the melody he wrote for Lynn while he uncorked the wine and set it on the counter to rest. The kabob skewers loaded with lamb and vegetables passed his inspection, then he flicked off the stove burner with a grand gesture, knowing the rice would steam to a fluffy finish.

The table on the patio in front of the house received a final once over, the glasses buffed on his shirt, and the daisies pushed around in the vase just enough to look unplanned. The herb garden he had planted was inspected and an errant weed pulled.

A stray cat that'd been hanging around appeared. Sam coaxed his visitor over to the kitchen door and put down a plate of meat scraps in hopes this possible distraction would disappear before Lynn arrived.

Sam walked through the house excitedly rubbing his hands and rearranging things. He checked out his hair in the hall mirror, after which he sat down at the piano in an effort to relax while he waited for Lynn.

He couldn't concentrate on the melody he was going to play for Sandini in Spain because of the uneasy sensation creeping up on him. Finally, he gave in and glanced at his watch. Damn it! Six-thirty.

He went over and agitatedly poured himself a finger of scotch and swirled it around in the glass as he looked pensively out the window at Lynn's truck in the driveway below. As he noticed the sun was setting, a sickening fear that she was never going to be able to let go of her husband shot through him.

He put the drink down, and the screen door slammed behind him as he jumped in the truck and started down the hill. He pulled to a stop and saw the curtains gently blowing against the screen in the front upstairs bedroom window. Commander sat up, but didn't bark. His tail just thumped against the doghouse.

The screen door squeaked softly as Sam went inside. His eyes darted around the room. No one, just the cat eating at its dish. The house was quiet except for the pendulum swinging in the grandfather clock. As Sam climbed the staircase, the cat scampered past him and disappeared into the front bedroom.

When Sam peered in, the cat was already nestled on the bed next to the still figure in a bathrobe hugging a framed picture. Lynn's swollen, tear-stained eyes were fixed on Sam but she didn't move.

He rested his hands on either side of the doorframe and leaned in. Neither of them knew what to say. Finally, Sam looked around in frustration and then said impatiently, "I've got the wine breathing, the table set, the kabobs marinating, and the rice is done..." He walked over with a determined expression on his face, firmly took the picture and placed it on the table, then bent down and put his arms under her and picked her up saying, "... I just don't have you."

He lumbered his way down the staircase and through the house into the kitchen and shoved open the screen with his knee. Suddenly Lynn grabbed the doorframe and screamed, "Stop!"

Sam looked down at her with a furrowed brow. She calmly said, "My basil pesto salad's in the fridge."

He threw back his head and laughed, then carted her over to the refrigerator and waited as she reached in and protectively nestled the salad in her arms.

On the drive up the hill, Sam kept one eye on Lynn and one on the road, and almost veered off a couple of times, laughing joyfully all the while. When he pulled up to the house, he was pleased to see she was finally beginning to cooperate as she opened the door and started to get down. Sam ran around to her side and couldn't help noticing the lithe thigh peeking from the robe as he picked her up and carried her over the crushed stone.

When he put her down in the front hall he saw she was self-consciously clutching her robe closed. "Just a minute. I'll be right back," he said, and raced upstairs.

Lynn's eyes took in the expansive living room filled with art and exquisite furniture while she waited.

"Here. Put these on."

Lynn shyly backed up toward the staircase then quickly turned and ran up. Moments later, she descended wearing an oversized T-shirt and a pair of jersey shorts. When she saw Sam's eyes riveted on the outline of her ample breasts under the draped T-shirt, she blushed and nervously tried to cover herself.

"I'll be right back," Sam said, and took the steps two at a time.

He came back holding a brocade vest and helped her as she placed her arms inside.

"I saw your trampoline," she said teasingly as he poured two glasses of wine and then turned up the Sinatra.

"You already heard about that?"

"*Uh-huh.*" She motioned toward the Pollock with her glass and said, "The picture that the cows messed up too."

They both laughed.

"Sam, I don't know how to tell you this, but you've got the chief artery in the Lenox Township Information Super Highway cleaning your house."

"You mean, my Nora?"

"*Your Nora.*"

Lynn took a deep breath and looked around.

"Why don't you go in and look the house over," said Sam.

Lynn went to the Baldwin and struck a key then looked up and gave him an approving smile.

She strolled casually through the room and picked up a photograph that caught her attention and studied it. "So these are the Reynolds boys?"

Sam looked pleased to have her touch his things. "Yes. *The Men in Blue*."

She carefully put the picture down and walked over to the window and looked out. "No wonder Jess was so excited. This view of our farm is wonderful." Out of the corner of her eye she glanced down on the rubble of the barn and greenhouse and quickly looked away, not wanting anything to bring her spirits down again. She hugged herself and wondered if Sam suspected why she hadn't come on her own and at the same time was grateful he had come down and got her. Remembering his phone message, she turned around and said, "Well, are you going to play it or not?"

He walked over and put his arm around her shoulder. "Right this way, madam."

As Lynn entered the studio, she said, "This is more elaborate than the one over at *WKNY*."

Sam almost laughed out loud. "I don't doubt that."

He led her over to a plush chair and sat her down. As the lights dimmed, Lynn looked around the room in amazement. Suddenly her magnified image appeared on the huge screen and she had to force herself not to put her hands over her face. Eventually she regained her composure and watched through wide-open eyes. Sam kept giving her a play by play of how the music was going over and under during the ten-minute segment, and in that brief time she understood what he did for a living.

The lights went up.

"I love it! I *absolutely love it!*"

Sam had the coolly satisfied look of someone who had just hit a bull's-eye.

"Is there some way *WKNY* can use this?" she begged.

Sam feigned a disinterested attitude while he examined his finger-nails and then coyly eyed her, "Only if the star of the show properly approached me."

Lynn let out a lilting cry of delight and bounced in her chair. "Sir, consider yourself properly approached!"

He searched her face and could see he'd made her happy. "I'll give them a call." Then he stood up and offered her his hand. "Come on. Let's eat."

Lynn held his hand as they walked toward the kitchen. She waited for him to let go, but instead, in his easy way, he faced her and took her other hand also. His penetrating gaze made her blush profusely and she pulled away and went over to the counter and started preparing her salad while trying to regain her composure.

Noticing Sam getting the tray of skewers out of the fridge, Lynn followed him out onto the patio. The minute she eyed the herb garden, she exclaimed, "Oh, Sam! *How lovely.* Who planted this?"

"You're not the only member of this gang with a green thumb," he said while putting the skewers on the fire.

Lynn turned toward the setting sun and looked out over the lush fields of her farm below while Sam brought her glass and poured more wine. Together they watched the sun sink behind the horizon.

Lynn had hardly eaten anything since the food Shelly had brought Sunday afternoon, so she ate eagerly while Sam talked about the score he was composing with an understated enthusiasm she found appealing. He went on with his casual, natural table talk, mentioning he was leaving for Spain in the morning, and then about his brothers and how sad he had been that they never felt comfortable visiting his New York loft. He made excuses for his wife and said she had tried hard to make them feel welcome at first, but when she didn't make any headway, she just gave up. Lynn could tell he was hoping things would be different in Eastlake.

Sam's voice was easy to listen to: course-grained and at the same time soft and mellow. Very manly she thought.

She found his openness disarming and supposed he was like this because he came from such a large family where no one could hide anything and any hint of arrogance was immediately snuffed out by an onrush of sarcasm. Both she and Ken, as only children, had been more guarded with their thoughts.

Since Lynn finished before Sam, she self-consciously fidgeted with her spoon on the white tablecloth as she kept stealing awkward glances at him. Now that the sun had set, candlelight softened the lines on his strong face. He kept looking up at her as he ate, smiling when their eyes met. When he reached for his glass and took a drink, she recalled how warm his lips had been, and then quickly looked away so he wouldn't see her blush as the feelings she had that night poured over her.

She didn't dare make steady eye contact with him and, instead, sat quietly in the chair with her eyes fixed on the dwindling candle as the cool evening dew settled on her flesh and Sinatra crooned, *"I've got you under my skin."*

Neither of them spoke now. They had come to that moment when polite conversation would only sound hollow.

Finished eating, Sam wiped his face with his napkin, then got up and went over to Lynn. She couldn't bear to look at him as he took her hand and pulled her up. He ran his hands along her arms then gently took hold of the vest and slowly slipped it off, after which he put his arm around her waist and drew her close to him.

She had to force herself to breathe as she melted against him and felt the heat of his cheek against hers as they swayed to the music. They became still and just stood there with their arms around each other, each keenly aware of the other's body pressing against them. His warm lips brushed across her face until they found hers and then he kissed her with such a lingering, deep passion she felt faint. She opened her eyes and looked into his and saw the intense question on his face.

Lynn pressed her cheek against his, and in a faint whisper said, "Yes, Sam. I want you."

She held on to him as he picked her up and carried her upstairs.

The bedroom was dark except for the glow of the full moon through the window. He let her slowly slide down, holding her tight against his body. There was no smile on his face, just the same intensity there'd been Saturday night. As he lifted the T-shirt over her head, tiny beads of sweat covered his forehead. He looked down at her full breasts and suddenly pressed his head against hers as if in pain and whispered, "Oh, God, Lynn."

He gripped her shoulders and breathed deeply trying to bring himself to a level he could tolerate, then bent down and gently kissed her breasts. She felt his hands reach for her shorts and then slip them past her hips until they dropped to the floor.

She stood there for a moment laboring for every breath, then started to slowly unbutton his shirt. Her hands felt their way across his chest and down his muscular biceps. She opened his shirt and let her breasts touch his bare chest, then her hands searched for his zipper. All she could hear was his deep breathing as she put her hand inside. A soft sigh escaped her as she felt the firm warmth surging there.

She heard him whisper her name as if he couldn't stand it any longer, then he slowly drew back.

The room was quiet except for the sound of him undressing. When he finished, they stood for a few moments, close enough to feel the heat of each other's bodies and hear each other breathe. Finally, Lynn laid her trembling hands on his chest and slowly slid her arms around his neck feeling the firmness of his erection press against her. His mouth was demanding as they were suddenly thrown into a feverish stream of kisses.

Lynn ran the palms of her hands up and down his sinewy thighs and then slowly slid down onto the bed. She took him into her mouth and ran her tongue slowly around the tip. His fingers pressed into her shoulders as he threw his head back and softly cried out her name.

He lowered her on the bed with such a deliberateness she knew he needed to be satisfied. As she spread her legs apart she heard herself pleading, "Please, Sam."

He put his knees between her legs and whispered urgently for her to put her legs around him. Her body arched upward as he slipped himself into her, moving to some intense inner rhythm that took control of him.

She clung to him, thrilled with the excitement her sexuality had incited. With each thrust, she gave herself to him, until finally, sensing he was on the verge of coming, she let go completely and the electrifying rivulets of her passion drained her.

Sam collapsed in her arms, his head, moist with sweat, nestling in her bosom. She tenderly caressed him and ran her hand gently through his dark, soft curls. For a split second she felt sad that she could never give this man a child of his own, but forced the thought out of her mind and hated herself for marring the happiness of the moment.

As she felt the liquid trickling from her, she made a move to get up, but he held her firm. With their flesh pressed together as one, they drifted into unconsciousness.

At first, Lynn wasn't sure what had awakened her, then the melody drifted into the room again. How dark and sad she thought as she rose from the bed and went into the bathroom, which had obvious signs that Sam had already taken a shower. She finished quickly and found her robe.

Sam didn't look up at her as she came next to the piano. Every muscle in his body was operating in tandem with the music. She thought how different he was from her, capable of a wide range of strong emotions.

She felt almost serene in comparison, but the passion he'd awakened in her was taking hold again as her eyes ran down his bare chest.

He stopped playing and looked up at her as she let the robe slip to the floor. He stared straight into her eyes for a moment and then a slight shadow of a smile crossed his lips as if he realized he'd finally won her.

He went over to the tape player and slipped in Billy Holiday then lit the candles around the room with her eyes following him. There was no shyness in their movements as the man and woman began the ritual of discovery. All Sam's fears that Lynn would never be able to let go of her husband dissolved after she pulled down his sweats and started her tantalizing lovemaking.

For the next hour, they alternated between brief moments of intercourse and tender stimulation until Sam finally carried her onto the bed and made unbridled love to her.

Sam was sitting up holding Lynn in his arms as the soft gray light of early morning crept into the room. He stared ahead and fondly caressed her as he softly whispered, "God, I love you, Lynn." He kissed the top of her head. "I wish I could take you with me to Spain."

Lynn tenderly nuzzled him as she said, "And what, Sir, would you do to me there?"

He looked down at her and grinned. "For a shy little country girl, you certainly were something last night."

"Do you really love me?" she asked as she stroked the hair on his chest.

"Uh-huh."

"When did you decide that?"

He rested his head against the headboard and looked up at the ceiling. "Oh, one evening when you were playing with Jess. I watched from the window as the two of you went inside. At that moment, more than anything in the world, I wanted to be in there with you." He kissed her head and gave her a tender squeeze. "I knew then."

A faint laugh escaped from Lynn before she fell asleep in his arms. Before drifting off himself, Sam wondered if their relationship would always be like this, he easily revealing his feelings and she guarded about hers. How he wished he had heard her say, I love you.

When they awoke, Sam rushed to get ready for his flight, with Lynn as an attentive audience. Just as they were about to leave, a key sounded at the door. Lynn stepped back out of sight as Sam haltingly asked Nora to come back in an hour. Neither Lynn nor Sam were aware of Lynn's reflection in the hall mirror.

After Nora pulled away, Sam drove Lynn down the hill. She couldn't let him go as he kissed her one final time and told her he'd be back next Thursday and would try to call.

As the truck disappeared over the hill Lynn got a queer feeling in her gut, like Sam was slipping away. She shook this dark thought off and, instead, let the wonderful memories of the night swirl around in her head.

CHAPTER 21

Tall and heavy-set, Cal's son didn't resemble his dad. However, from the way he was careful not to allow his father to work too hard and easily picked up the slack, there was no question they were close.

The day was spent picking around in the debris of the collapsed barn for anything they could salvage. Four huge hand-hued beams were dragged out and put on blocks. A local builder had been asking for some but Cal said they'd dress up the new office ceiling and if Lynn didn't want to do that, his boy would take them for a family room he was building.

The bulldozer arrived around five and the volunteer firemen shortly afterward. For the most part, the firemen were farmers, but some were retired like Cal or had jobs in either Oneida or Syracuse.

Like all the volunteer fire departments in the scores of rural townships in upstate New York, the men were connected by generations of close ties. They interacted with each other in a familiar ritualistic manner Lynn noticed when she first came to live on the farm. She'd had words with Ken several times on their way home from get-togethers for she resented being blocked out of this invisible circle.

The men went about their duties and had the pile in flames by the time Shelly pulled in with Jess and her family. Exhausted from their camping trip, Shelly and her husband just dropped off Jess and pulled away with Shelly shouting she'd call in the morning.

Cal and his son left before the firemen, but once the flames had been extinguished and the rubble no more than red-hot coals, they were gone too. The bulldozer stood motionless, waiting to level everything the next day and bury any leftover debris.

Mother and son sat next to each other on the picnic bench watching the embers glow. Lynn put her arm around Jess and pulled him close. "I missed you, honey."

"I know, Mom. I missed you too."

Lynn cocked her head and raised an eyebrow the way she did when she was concerned. "I bought a great big new greenhouse and office."

Jess nodded thoughtfully for a moment and then said, "Good for you, Mom."

Lynn rested her head against his as she sighed, "I'm going to have to tell Shelly tomorrow."

They were both lost in thought as they walked toward the porch. Before going in, Lynn turned and looked up at the house on the hill.

The next morning when Shelly pulled in, Lynn was at the computer and Jess finishing breakfast.

"Here she comes, Mom!"

Lynn looked up.

"Okay, honey. You better play outside until this is all over."

Shelly tousled Jess's hair as they passed in the doorway.

"Hi, Love. Where's your Mom?"

"In here, Shelly."

Lynn was standing at the sink rinsing out the coffeepot.

At first Shelly tried hard to subdue her excitement, but in a matter of a few minutes she was revved up.

"You'll absolutely love this house I found for you. Wait 'till you see the garden!"

While Shelly extolled the benefits of the house in town, Lynn first put on some coffee, then leaned back against the sink and gazed off into space. Suddenly Shelly's crunched up brows were inches from hers.

"You're not listening!"

Shelly searched Lynn's face. "God, girl. You've got that look. Like you've just been screwed."

Lynn looked away.

Shelly screamed in delight. "You and Sam Reynolds! I knew it!"

Lynn took her by the shoulders. "Not so loud. Jess might hear."

Shelly slid into an excited whisper. "When?"

"Wednesday night, *all night*."

The two women hugged and let out muffled screams until they finally doubled over in laughter.

Since things were going a lot better than Lynn had hoped for, she casually slipped in the business about adding the insurance money to the fourteen thousand she was getting from the bank to build a bigger greenhouse. Then, for one of the first times since Lynn had known her, Shelly was speechless. She simply leaned forward and rested her chin on her hand and thought.

"Are you sure you want to do this, Lynn? You're banking everything you've got on this business." An expression of incredulity marked her face. "You really believe in this seed business, don't you, baby?"

"Yes, Shelly. I do."

"Wow. This is moving too fast for me, Lynn."

For the first time in their long relationship, Shelly seemed shaken. Then, in typical fashion, she shook it off and went on to her favorite subject: gossip. "Saturday night, Pete said he could tell Sam was really stuck on you, but that just seemed too good to be true. Sit down. I want to hear everything."

Lynn slid into a chair and stirred her coffee.

"He told me he loved me."

Shelly gave Lynn an appraising look. "What'd you tell him?"

Lynn bit her lip and didn't answer.

Shelly slammed her hand down on the table. "Good God, Lynn. You're going to blow this!"

"It's not *like* that, Shelly. If we get together, good. If not, that's okay too."

Shelly shook her head. "You're talking like a crazy person, Lynn. You've got a boy and a reputation. You know how people in this town talk. If this thing has gone this far you better get busy and land him... and fast."

The realization suddenly struck Lynn that she'd made a big mistake trying to distract Shelly from the greenhouse by telling her about Sam.

"When are you going to see him next?"

"He's in Spain and won't be back till next Thursday."

"Lynn, you've got to angle for a ring and get this guy committed right away."

"I'm not going to *angle* for anything." The words had been spoken stiffly with her back ramrod straight.

"Honey, I didn't mean to offend you. I just want this thing to work out. You and Jess deserve a break."

"I know you didn't, Shelly, but this is something that can't be rushed. We hardly know each other. I keep thinking maybe he wants kids."

"Well, what's that got to do with anything? Just because old Doc Green couldn't find out what was wrong, doesn't mean you can't have kids. If you had one, you should be able to have another."

"Believe me, Ken and I tried. Having more children is one dream I've put behind me."

Shelly tapped her long red nails on the table for a minute, then looked over at Lynn and the two burst into a fit of giggles.

Friday at three was just about the worst time to be driving into Syracuse. Lynn felt sure she'd get snarled in the five o'clock traffic on the way back. This would be the third meeting she would be having with the Farmway buyer. The whole process seemed too drawn out for getting her seeds into ten or twenty stores, but she was determined.

"Mr. Cameron," she told the receptionist.

The lobby was usually packed with salesmen waiting to see buyers, but being late on Friday afternoon, there were just a few. As she turned to take a seat, Jack Cameron came striding across the lobby. She was surprised he was greeting her with a suit jacket on. Usually she was just told, "third aisle down, fourth cubicle," only to find him busy doing paperwork in his shirtsleeves.

"Come right into the conference room, dear. Do you want coffee or a soda?"

"No. Thank you."

What's going on, she wondered as she was whisked past several small conference rooms. When the buyer opened the huge solid beech door at the end of the corridor, Lynn was taken aback. Light poured in from the wall of glass spanning one side of the room, and a handful of people in suits was clustered at the far end of a massive conference table. Even though Lynn had put on her best shift and the new T-shirt with the delicate embroidery around the neckline, she felt ill at ease.

Jack Cameron nervously ushered her toward the imposing group who stood greeting her with smiles. The merchandising manager was introduced first, then his assistant, a willowy, neatly put together woman that Lynn figured was younger than she was. The introductions also included the vice president of sales, a couple of assistants and the marketing director who she already knew through phone calls. He practically tripped over himself pulling out a chair for her.

Lynn folded her hands on the table, then noticing how rough they looked, quickly put them in her lap.

The merchandising manager was the first to speak. "Jack's told us about your little operation in Oneida County and we asked him to get you down here so we could all meet you." He waved his pudgy hand toward the others and gave her a fatherly smile. Lynn was surprised how fresh he looked so late in the day. His thick white hair was slicked back from his deeply furrowed forehead. She imagined that without the extra thirty pounds he'd be quite handsome.

He leaned way back in his chair and fanned through a binder in front of him. "Larry, our marketing director ... I understand he's had several conversations with you ... has put together a proposal that could mean quite a lot to you financially." The broad smile again, as he looked around at the faces that nodded reassuringly. "And we asked Jack to get you here so we could go over everything with you... so we're all on the same page, so to speak."

He tapped his fingers on the table, evidently concerned over not getting a response from Lynn. "I want to apologize if all of us being here makes you feel uncomfortable."

Lynn was sitting with her back ramrod straight and leaning slightly forward, her hand gently touching her chin. Her eyes, with an imperceptible squint, swept across the row of faces then rested on the merchandising manager. A slow, friendly smile was all she could rally. Somewhere deep down inside her she felt her old nemesis, her temper, starting to rear its ugly head as she felt the whole set-up was to put pressure on her. Calm down, she told herself.

He continued.

"Larry, why don't you go through your proposal."

Other than the buyer, Larry seemed to Lynn to be the only one who was nervous as he got up and brought her a binder, after which he walked over to a panel and hit a few buttons. The lights started to dim as the drapes closed and a giant screen came down at one end of the room. In moments the marketing director was walking around with a remote control bringing up slides on the screen.

"First off, we'll be the exclusive sponsor of a thirty-minute show featuring you."

Much to Lynn's amazement her image appeared on the screen with *The Farmway Garden Show* written across the bottom.

The marketing director continued. "We've already talked to two stations here and others in Binghamton, Albany and Watertown and feel confident the show will fly. Once you get off public TV, you'll see what a real audience is all about."

The next screen showed a drawing of Lynn on an antique-looking seed packet with Richardson's Herbs & Seeds above the Farmway logo, followed by a slide of a display featuring the seeds.

"As you can see, Mrs. Richardson, there will be end displays of your seeds in all our stores."

The marketing director hit some buttons on the panel and the lights went up and the screen disappeared into the ceiling.

The merchandising manager said, "Well, how do you feel about all this?"

Lynn caught her breath as he pushed a sheet of paper toward her.

"Of course, you will be remunerated well for your time and effort." He ran through the various fees they would be giving her. A monthly retainer of three thousand dollars for the first year, three-thousand-five-hundred for the second and third, and so on.

He gave her a penetrating look. "Well?"

"First of all, I have a contract with *WKNY*."

He let out a patronizing chuckle.

"Don't worry, our lawyers will take care of *that* little matter."

"Well, sir. I'd rather stay with public television. If it weren't for them I wouldn't be here right now."

"That sounds very noble, Mrs. Richardson, but frankly, the audience simply isn't there and we've got all kinds of statistics we can show you to prove it. Getting on the bigger stations will be a wonderful opportunity for you. I'm sure you can see that."

The merchandising manager's condescending tone was starting to wear on her, but Lynn kept going. "I really don't think I could supply you with enough seeds next season to stock all your stores."

The vice president of sales spoke up. "Mrs. Richardson, we're just buying *you*. We've got greenhouses and farms all over the state as well as state-of-the-art laboratories and research centers. Believe me, producing the seeds will be no problem whatsoever."

Lynn's eyes scanned the faces at the table before replying. For an instant they rested on the female merchandising assistant as if Lynn was trying to glean some knowledge from her, but the woman's unresponsive countenance made her move on. "Basically from what I gather," Lynn said thoughtfully, "you want to buy me out for three-thousand dollars a month. If I go for this, I'll end up as an employee of Farmway with no business. Right?"

"But you *would have* security," said the merchandising manager coolly. He leaned way back in his chair and fingered his pen. "Mrs. Richardson, let's talk frankly. We've researched your outlets. What you're doing right now in the dozen or so stores you've got, is peanuts. If you didn't have the mail orders that dribble in, and the paltry amount of seeds you push at the farmers' markets, your cottage industry wouldn't exist. As for that ten-minute show you've got …let's face facts, you're no Martha Stewart." His voice suddenly softened and took on a fatherly tone. "Security, dear. Isn't that what you're working for to begin with?"

Lynn felt like she was in the mouth of the monster that invented the whole "get big or get out" concept that was snuffing out small farms all over the state. She reached down and picked her purse up off the floor then looked around at everyone. "You're right, my business isn't that big and I'm no Martha Stewart, but I'm planning on expanding and I really feel that's where my security lies... not in going to work for someone else." Disappointed, her anger subsided. "I thank you anyway."

The merchandising manager spoke up. "Don't be too hasty, Mrs. Richardson." He stood up and casually walked over to the window and looked out. "We've researched this entire marketing concept, and frankly, the only reason you're here in the first place is that we feel you'll be the shortest distance between two points." He turned abruptly and gave Lynn a hard stare. "If not you, Mrs. Richardson, there's a thousand out there who will jump at this opportunity. I suggest you think this over before you do anything rash."

The vice president of sales coughed loud enough to get everyone's attention. Tapping his pen nervously, without looking up, he said, "Please remember, Mrs. Richardson, that we supply every feed store carrying your seeds with a great deal of their merchandise under an off-brand name."

The marketing director was disconcerted by the way things were going and blurted out, "We also contribute heavily to that public TV station you're on, too."

Lynn rose. She was livid. Her nostrils flared and breathing became deep. She purposely looked each person in the eye as she said, "It's easy for you to sit there and threaten me. I'm nothing but one woman all alone trying to make it while I take care of my boy. But I'll tell you something. What I'm selling, you're not going to be raising in all those greenhouses of yours... not anytime soon, that is. There's a market out there for seeds and flowers that haven't been hybridized into one final exclamation point!... flowers that give people a sense of history and wonder with their unique, individual characteristics. I know that market is out there because I hear from them every day... by phone, by mail... at the farmers' markets..."

Her voice started to crack. She stopped and took a deep breath. "Maybe you *will be able* to force me off the shelves and TV... but *I don't think so!* These aren't the kind of people to be shoved around by a bunch of bullies... and neither am I!"

She took a deep breath to calm herself, then leaned forward with both hands on the table. "I happen to be in the process of expanding my business right now with every dime I can get my hands on because I believe there's a market niche for my seeds and perennials. I've worked hard to get where I am, and I intend to succeed... with, or without Farmway."

She looked hard at the merchandising manager. "Sir, I ask *you* to think before you do anything rash. You're not going to create what my customers are looking for with nothing more than a bunch of marketing and advertising. And if you think you are, you're only kidding yourself."

She picked up her purse and walked out.

CHAPTER 22

Monday morning, the Bedesky brothers pulled the trailer hitched to their truck onto the barren spot that once was the garden center. The eighteen-wheeler that'd been following them waited on the road. They climbed down and after looking over the site started directing the huge truck in. Their take-charge attitude foretold the project would proceed rapidly.

Everything was unloaded with a crane system, and in less than an hour the truck was waved off.

Lynn, who was deeply concerned about the way things had gone at Farmway, was on the phone with Mindy. She watched the Bedeskys from the kitchen window as she and Mindy discussed the two segments that were to be filmed at the studio the next day. Lynn was annoyed that she wasn't out with Jess watching the brothers mark off the site. On top of that, Thelma and Louise were chasing Commander all over the lot and Jess kept shouting for his mother to come out. So much for making a party out of watching the greenhouse go up.

The conversation worried Lynn. Why was Mindy having her be so specific about every detail? Had Farmway already put pressure on the station? She finally asked, "What's going on? Doesn't Bob usually just direct this thing as we go along?"

There was silence on the other end.

"Mindy? Are you there?"

"Bob's not here any more and we're going to be flying by the seat of our pants until we find a replacement, so I've got to get all my ducks in line."

"Where is he?"

"Boston."

"Isn't this kind of sudden?"

"You ought to know."

"What do you mean?"

Mindy hesitated for a moment, then snapped, "Nothing."

This was the first hint of disapproval Lynn had ever sensed in Mindy's voice, and it stung.

"Mindy, let's stop right here. *What* is wrong?"

"Nobody can fault him for wanting to get ahead, but he didn't even give us twenty-four hours notice for Christ's sake."

"Certainly, you're not blaming me for *that*?"

"Well...no. But it would have been nice of you to think of us before you did this."

"Did what, for Pete's sake!"

"Had some hot-shot friend of yours get him a job."

"What are you talking about?"

"Sam Somebody. Some composer you know with a lot of network connections."

Suddenly Lynn was in another space somewhere inside her head and she couldn't hear what Mindy was saying. How could something like this happen? Especially when Farmway would be putting pressure on the station to get rid of her.

"Mindy, where did you get this garbage from?"

"From the garbage man himself."

"Let me have his number."

Lynn paced up and down the kitchen as she waited for Bob to get on the phone.

"Bob Caldwell," the voice confidently sang out.

"Just how did you land this job?"

"Hello to you too, Lynn."

"Well?"

"How does anyone get one, Sweetheart."

"Don't call me that. Just answer one question. Did Sam Reynolds get you this job?"

"I don't know what you're talking about."

"Don't hand me that crap!"

His voice suddenly sounded nervous. "Lynn, calm down for God's sake. The guy's evidently stuck on you and figured I was competition. Damn that Mindy, she promised not to say anything. If this Reynolds guy finds out, I could find myself on the street."

Lynn slammed the phone down. Jess was waving and shouting for her to come out but she was so angry she couldn't think. She felt manipulated. The whole business smelled of sneakiness and mistrust. What did Sam think? That she'd jump in bed with the first guy she met? Why did this have to happen when she was probably already in trouble with the station? The eight hundred dollars floating in every month flashed in her head and she thought she would be sick.

Then she closed her eyes and visions and sensations from their night together brought Sam's image tenderly to her as if they were one. There *had* to be an explanation. She wasn't going to panic. He was a good man. She'd put this out of her mind and he would explain everything when he came back on Thursday. Oh please, God, she said to herself, there's got to be an explanation. I can't afford to get the television station angry with me now.

Lynn's eyes shot over to the dining room table where Robin was working. Since the garden center was closed, Robin was finally getting enough uninterrupted time to put their whole operation on the computer and was so engrossed Lynn was sure she hadn't paid any attention to the conversation with Bob.

Not much happened that day except a lot of backhoeing outside and busy work in. At five, the men stopped working and started setting up their trailer while Lynn prepared chicken for a barbecue.

Robin neatly stacked the papers on the dining room table and turned off the computer. She said goodbye to Lynn as she walked through the kitchen and waved to Jess from the porch as he rode by on his bike. The heavy door of the Malibu squeaked open and she slid into the front seat.

The man in the van pulled the bandless watch from his pocket and laid it on the dash, then took an angry swipe at a mosquito. The van was stifling and he was nervous about being parked in the lane Sauterfield used to get to his cornfield. He glanced back at the watch. Five! She should be passing any minute.

From the moment Gary Snyder woke up, his whole day revolved around the six minute window when he could catch a glimpse of Robin either getting into her car at Lynn's house or out at hers.

He was careful to change his approach every day. Sometimes he timed it so he'd be coming over the hill from the east exactly at five, or from the west. Other times he'd be coming toward her house from another direction. Now that the nursery was closed, these were the only breaks from endless hours of staring at her photograph with lustful images exploding in his head. He didn't dare park on the logging road. He'd never be that lucky again.

Robin wasn't like the rest. She was sweet like the skinny little girl in the first grade who always wore panty hose and gave him things from her lunch bucket. Mostly, there was no sneer on her face like he was dirt.

That damn Lynn Richardson and her snotty boy! Putting on airs and building some goddamn big greenhouse. He couldn't stand this much longer! Then there were those goddamned dogs! Always sniffing around his place. The next time they came around he was going to get them good... like the two teenagers on the logging road.

Gary stopped breathing. His hearing became acute. Yes! The sound of the muffler on the '75 Malibu was nearing. Gary started the engine and rolled forward. But not too much forward. He didn't want her to notice him. The long black Chevy passed between the end of the corn rows like a dark shadow.

The van pulled out, careful not to raise a cloud of dust, and turned left. He slowed, giving the Chevy plenty of time to get over the hill. He'd be too noticeable if only her car and his were in the dip between Richardson Hill and the smaller rise to the south. Slowly he edged over the rise and could see the black six-cylinder up a quarter of a mile. He pressed the gas pedal just enough to get a steady acceleration. A sense that he was going to get lucky spread over him.

He gently eased up a couple of car lengths behind her and held the gas pedal steady. A noise startled him. Out of nowhere a hubcap came careening across the road. The Chevy suddenly pulled to the side. The van swerved past it. Gary's eyes shot to the rearview mirror. Don't stop! Wait until she gets out and starts walking, or better yet, tries to fix the flat!

Gary, pretending he didn't notice anything was wrong, gently sped up and continued down the road. Give her four or five minutes to get out into the open he screamed to himself. He had to gulp air to breathe. His knuckles were white from gripping the wheel, but he kept going at a steady pace until he reached Peterson Road.

He had to work fast. In minutes the commuters would be whizzing by on their way home. He took a left onto Peterson, turned around and drove back.

Robin was on her hands and knees trying to wedge the jack under the axle when she heard a vehicle pull to the side of the road. The door opened, then slammed shut and footsteps neared.

Finished lodging the jack in the right position, the girl leaned back on her heels and looked up.

The man took off his hat, laid it carefully in the trunk and said, "Let me do that for you."

Neither Trooper Mitchum nor Robin noticed the white van as it passed in the other lane.

While the chicken cooked on the grill, Lynn gave the Bedeskys a beer and a tour of her gardens. She was surprised how much the brothers knew about herbs, evidently something they learned mostly because of a need to dress up the taste of the game they caught.

"You sure do have a wide variety of thyme," one of the brothers commented.

"Before you go, I'll pot up a special planting for you."

"Yep, thyme does wonders for rabbit and venison." He bent down and plucked a seed stem of rye grass and started to pick his teeth. "A slow boil with some herbs and a little wine and you've got yourself a great dish."

The chicken, which came from a farmer down the road who raised and dressed them, was delicious. When Lynn saw how the brothers kept reaching for the warm pesto rolls, she was glad she'd made the effort.

They sat at the picnic table talking until dark when everyone got up and helped clear the table and bring everything inside. Commander followed Thelma and Louise when the brothers left. Lynn figured he was going to spend the night curled up with his two new pals, however before she turned off the lights he was scratching at the door.

After the mother and son were both in bed and the lights out, their voices drifted from their bedrooms into the upstairs hallway and hung in the darkness.

"The Bedesky brothers are nice, Mom. Aren't they?"

"Real nice, Jess."

"I can't believe we're getting a new greenhouse."

"Neither can I."

"You seem real happy, Mom."

"I am, honey."
"So am I."
"Goodnight, sweetheart."
"Goodnight."
After a moment, "Mom?"
"Yes."
"Everything seems to going real well, doesn't it?"
"Yes, sweetheart. It does."

CHAPTER 23

Tuesday saw the Bedeskys working diligently. The minute the pipes for all the plumbing and electrical were finished and the lines pulled through, all the footings were poured. The plan was to get the office built first so it could be set up while the greenhouse was being assembled.

That morning, the filming at the studio went better than expected even though Lynn and Mindy were both on tenterhooks. By the time they were finished, Mindy started to relax somewhat, but Lynn was still filled with anxiety, fearful that Farmway might start putting pressure on the studio while they were angry at her for taking away their video director. Lynn was tempted to talk with Mindy about Bob, but decided to wait until Sam told her his side of the story. On one hand, she was sure there was a plausible explanation, but on the other, after thinking through dozens of scenarios she kept coming to the same gnawing conclusion.

There was quite a stir Wednesday morning when the Bedeskys discovered Louise limping toward the trailer. The vet said she'd been shot at close range. Luckily the bullet made a clean path through the muscle tissue on the underside of her hind leg. The Bedeskys, figuring an irate farmer had shot her after going after his chickens, decided to tie both the dogs up each night.

Thursday morning, Robin came in to work on the computer and Cal stopped over and had coffee on his way into town to pick up more nails.

The new roof on his son's barn was coming along and he expected to be back at work in the nursery by the time the Bedeskys were done.

Before Cal left, Lynn pulled him aside and asked if he'd baby-sit for her that night. His eyes searched her face, and by the expression on his face, she got a creepy feeling that he knew about her and Sam. After all, they'd been so close over the years, by now he should be able to read her thoughts. How else would he have found out?

Lynn was antsy all day and could barely concentrate on figuring her seed inventory. Robin had picked up on this the minute she walked in the door and decided not to explain any of the things she was doing on the computer. She'd just forge ahead and teach everything to Lynn before she left for school. Throughout the morning they kept taking breaks, going out and sitting on the grass and watching the framing go up.

By three, the table was set for dinner, the pasta cooked, and the spaghetti sauce slowly heating on the stove. Sam's flight wasn't coming in until five and he wouldn't be there until six, but Lynn wanted to be rested and look her best when he saw her. He hadn't called except once and then only left a message on her machine that he'd call her the minute he got home so she could come on up. That was a good idea she thought. If he came to the house, the Bedeskys and Cal would only jump to conclusions. Shelly knowing what was going on was bad enough.

The plane touched down in Syracuse just after three. Those not getting off couldn't help noticing the strikingly handsome, albeit travel-weary, man as he pulled the big bundle out of the overhead storage and wrestled it off the plane. In the terminal men's room Sam caught a glimpse of himself in the mirror and was glad he'd driven his truck to the airport instead of letting Lynn drop him off. He sorely needed a shower and shave.

The chartered plane had taken an hour to get him to Madrid from the shooting site, and then he had a six-hour flight over the Atlantic. Luckily he'd been able to book an earlier flight to Syracuse and arrived a few hours sooner than expected.

In the parking lot, before he put the key in the ignition, Sam took out the ring he bought in Rome and gloated. He couldn't wait to give it to Lynn. Thank God things were finally the way they were between them. Now he could concentrate fully on all his projects. He pushed the fact that the *Men in Blue* tapes would start to arrive in three weeks to the back of his mind.

Sandini loved the melody, and the pressure was on for Sam to produce a completed score. The past six days and nights had been spent viewing rushes and taking notes so he could move ahead. Sandini wanted him in Rome in five days to view a rough cut of the film and work with his film editors. This would be a three-week stint and Sam was hoping Lynn could fly over for at least a week. How he'd longed for her each night after he dragged himself back to the hotel.

Because of the difference in time zones and the intensity with which he worked, Sam found phoning Lynn nearly impossible and was worried she might not understand. There was no day or night, nor any days of the week for that matter, when he was composing. He entered into a world of creativity that consumed him. Everyone working on the film had the same problem. He was praying Lynn would love him enough to accept this world, or at least tolerate it.

There'd only been an hour to shop at the airport but he had bought everything and anything he thought Jess and Lynn might like. He knew Jess would love the marble chess set and could picture Lynn wrapped in the lace shawl. His mind rested on an image of her with nothing on but the shawl and then he laughed out loud at himself. When would they tell Jess, he wondered? Tomorrow. We'll give him the presents and then tell him we're getting married.

Sam intended to call his lawyer the minute he got home and get the exact date the divorce would be final, probably in a week, so they could set the date that night. Even though Lynn never told him she was in love with him, he was convinced she wouldn't have responded to him the way she did unless she was. No. There'd be no problem. There'd been a bond sealed between them that night that couldn't be broken.

As he sailed over the hill and eyed the black patch of earth where the barn had stood, something told him to pull in. He slowed down and just as he was about to turn remembered how scraggly he looked. He decided to go home and shower and shave, then call Lynn to come up. This was going to be one of the most important nights of his life and he wanted everything to be perfect.

The truck skidded to a stop in front of the house. He grabbed his suitcase and started to unlock the door when it suddenly opened. Lil stood wearing a silk kimono. Sam didn't say anything, just brushed past her and dropped his suitcase in the hall. He took a deep breath and turned.

"How'd you get in here?"

"At first, your housekeeper was leery, but when I guessed the combination to your security system... twelve twelve, the same as at the loft... she let me in."

"Okay, Lil. What's this all about?"

Jess ran toward Lynn who was putting some food out for Commander.

"Mom, Sam's back!"

"Are you sure?"

"Yeah! He just went up the hill!"

Lynn held the boy close to her, and as she gazed toward the house on the hill, told him she was going to go up to see Sam and have dinner with him. Then she stepped back and said, "Honey, Cal's coming tonight to watch you. Will you promise not to tell anyone where I went?"

The boy nodded, then smiled. "I'm glad, Mom."

She put her arms around him and said, "So am I, baby."

Excited, Lynn went into the house and said to Robin, "Can you please do me a big favor and stay long enough to serve everyone dinner. Everything's all set. All you have to do is get them started at five-thirty."

"Sure."

From the questioning look on Robin's face, Lynn knew she was puzzled.

"I just need to go somewhere. Cal's coming back at six to stay with Jess."

Lynn ran upstairs, combed her hair and threw on a shift, but once outside found her truck blocked by rafters that had been temporarily laid out.

The brothers had driven off, probably into town to get supplies before the hardware store closed. Lynn's first impulse was to have Robin drive her, but she thought better of it and decided to walk.

Gigantic, billowy clouds were rolling across the sky from the north and the air was cool for that time of year. The hillside was strangely quite as Lynn walked up the road with only the sound of the stones in the gravel rubbing against each other under her feet. Then the loud buzzing of the cicadas pierced the air, making her feel apprehensive. Halfway up, she turned and looked at the farm below and for a moment felt split in two. When the image of Sam seeped into her thoughts, she swung around and kept climbing steadily toward the A-frame.

Sam was standing at the table in the front hall impatiently rubbing the back of his neck as he listened on the phone.

"The next flight to New York is at six a.m.," said the operator.

Sam booked the flight for Lil then phoned the motel where Joey had stayed. Just as he was about to shout for Lil to hurry, she came out of his bedroom and started down the staircase, her nude figure stark against the dark walls.

Sam angrily shifted his weight from one foot to the other and said impatiently, "Come on, Lil."

She ignored him and continued down the stairs with a confident smile on her face.

He tossed his head and blew out a breath in frustration.

"Lil, for God's sake, go back up and get dressed."

She came next to him and said, "Awh, come on Sam. My lawyer said we're finished as of next Tuesday."

When she slipped her arms around his neck he got a whiff of the alcohol on her breath and noticed a slight slur as she said, "I came up to this lousy god-forsaken place for one last fuck. Nobody does it like you."

Sam was repulsed, and at the same time felt a deep regret for the way this was ending. Painful memories flashed in his head. He saw her in his mind's eye in the beautiful white dress coming down the aisle, arm in arm with her father, the famous Shelby Whitely. Suddenly the outrage he felt about her showing up in his new home dissipated. Instead, tears came to his eyes as he put his arms around her and rocked her like a hurt child.

Lynn carefully brushed her hair back and straightened out her skirt before peeking in the window next to the door. The sight of a naked woman in Sam's arms struck her like lightening. Lynn staggered backward with a hand over her mouth to suppress a scream. Her heart beat in her ears. Running down the hill, she was blinded by tears and suddenly found herself sprawled over the gravel. Her knees and forearms burned but she got up and kept on running. Pain shot through her lungs as she fought to breathe. When she finally reached the lot she doubled over and threw up. Beads of blood oozed from her scraped forearms and knees as she leaned against the trailer trying to draw air into her lungs.

First Commander appeared, then Thelma and Louise, and finally Jess. His brows contorted. "What happened, Mom?"

Lynn forced a pained smile. "Nothing. I... I... fell on my way up." She feigned a laugh. "I'm so clumsy. I'll... I'll... have to cancel my dinner with Sam." She held on to the boy's shoulder for support as she limped toward the house in excruciating pain.

Sam eventually made it clear to Lil he wasn't interested, but she wasn't going without a fight. The harangue lasted for at least an hour, then Sam went upstairs, gathered her things and almost dressed her himself. Finally she was in good enough shape for him to haul her into the truck and cart her off to the motel.

On the way back to the hollow he said to hell with the shower and pulled into the farm's driveway. Lil had spoiled his plans, but once he saw Lynn he'd be okay.

He reached for the bundle of gifts and got out. But when he walked into the house everyone sitting at the table froze. Sam didn't know the two men but figured they were the ones putting up the new building. Sensing something was wrong, he dropped the bundle, eyed Jess and said, "Where is she?"

"Upstairs," the boy said solemnly.

Sam rushed through the house and raced up the steps. Finding the door to her room locked, he knocked and said, "Lynn, it's me. Open up."

The key clinked in the lock and the door swung open. Sam's face fell and he gasped for air when he saw Lynn in a rumpled nightgown, her hair askew and eyes swollen. The fury on her face startled him. He felt as if he was having a nightmare with all the women in his life suddenly turning on him.

"Why didn't you call me?" she shrieked.

She lunged forward. "Don't answer that! I can imagine why!"

Sam was taken aback as Lynn railed on him.

"That's why you had Bob moved to Boston. Isn't it? You thought I was the kind of person you are! Well, I'm not!"

Sam reached for her but she slapped him away.

"God, Lynn. I got him out of here because I love you."

"Love me? Ha! You don't trust me as far as you can throw me ... and I know why!"

Sam looked crushed for a moment but mustered a comeback.

"For Christ's sake, Lynn. I had to have you or I would have gone out of my mind. Doesn't that mean anything?"

"Not really! You may be used to getting everything you want, but I'm not used to dishing it out!" Her voice became sneering. "I trusted you. I thought you were like Ken. But you can't hold a candle to him."

As angry as she was, she stopped cold when she saw the hurt on Sam's face as his shoulders drooped and he staggered backward. Lynn slammed the door so hard she felt the room shake, then collapsed crying against it.

When Sam entered the kitchen, everyone's forks froze in mid-air. Jess came up to Sam holding his package. "You dropped this."

Sam put his hand on the boy's shoulder and said, "Those are presents for you and your mother. I'll see you after she settles down."

Walking out the door, Sam heard one of the brothers say under his breath, "I don't think so."

CHAPTER 24

The minute Gary Snyder realized the nursery was still closed, he pounded his fist on the wheel. The summer was almost over and the fact that Robin could be going back to college soon infuriated him. The sweat rolled down his face and his heart thumped in his chest. How could this have happened? It was his goddamned rotten luck again! There was no way in hell he was going to get through another Saturday without seeing Robin!

Ever since he drove by the trooper offering her assistance, he had to stop stalking her after work, fearful the police were patrolling the road that time of day.

He scanned the property. Robin's Malibu was nowhere in sight. All he could see was Lynn's truck and the one belonging to the two men building the greenhouse. His eyes became slits as he cursed Lynn Richardson. That bitch is too lazy to get her ass out and sell some plants now that she's gotten some insurance money, he mumbled angrily under his breath.

His van slowed in front of the nursery and he lowered his head to get a clear shot of the activity. The only thing appearing nearly finished was an office area. The greenhouse framing was less than half completed.

He continued up the road to Robin's house. Another goddamned disappointment! No sign of life. Just some wash hanging on the line and a bicycle lying across the corner of a sandbox. He drove by and when he got up the road about a mile impulsively hung a left onto Woodcock Road.

There was nothing but the stubble of mowed hay fields on one side and, on the other, endless rows of tall green corn, their stalks fluttering in the breeze. The valley below with its patchwork of fields started to appear on the horizon as the van climbed up the hill.

His eyes carefully scanned the scene ahead like an animal on the prowl in open country. Cortland had been like this. He remembered the thrill he got the day he rounded a curve and spotted the little girl on her bicycle with nothing else in sight. If he kept on driving on this desolate road, maybe he'd get lucky again.

By the middle of the week, Lynn's knees and arms had scabbed over, but walking was still painful so she watched the greenhouse go up mostly from the kitchen, grateful she didn't have to show up at the TV studio for another week.

The office floor was already poured and cured and a man was sheet-rocking the walls. The Bedeskys had told Lynn she could start setting up the office by the end of the week while they worked on the greenhouse. Cal would be putting up shelving on the rainy days he couldn't work on his son's barn roof.

Coffee in hand, Lynn paced the kitchen trying to push Sam out of her mind, but her throat tightened every time their lovemaking crept into her thoughts. The feeling of betrayal was burning a hole in her brain.

This had to stop. There was too much at stake to wallow in self-pity, so she decided to get up and check out the office. When the phone rang Lynn clutched the receiver for a moment then took a deep breath and picked it up.

"Hello?"

There was no reply. She knew Sam was on the other end. Salty tears streamed down her cheeks and she put her hand over the mouthpiece so he wouldn't hear her soft sobs.

"Please let me come down and talk to you. I'm leaving for Rome tomorrow for three weeks and I'll go out of my mind if we don't straighten this thing out first."

The phone was carefully placed back in the cradle. Then she rinsed her face in the sink and went outside.

The two brothers were taking a break. They sat under the shade of a big maple sipping soft drinks while Jess threw sticks for the dogs to retrieve. Lynn waved and went into the office. A man was on stilts putting a second coat of mud on the joints. The barren room smelled of plaster and was cool even with the warm breeze from the open windows. Lynn strolled around trying to get the feel of the space.

Screeching brakes and the slamming of a truck door suddenly broke the silence. Lynn's eyes met Sam's as she glanced out the window. He walked around to the front of the truck then angrily sat back against the hood with his arms folded defiantly across his chest as if he were never going to budge.

Lynn froze. The subtle sound of plaster being scraped across the ceiling stopped, making her realize the plasterer was watching. Finally, she took a deep breath, went outside with her arms folded equally as defiantly, and sauntered up to him.

"Sam Reynolds, I have nothing to say to you."

His blue eyes were piercing as the muscles in his jaw tensed and then relaxed.

"For god's sake, Lynn, I wanted to protect you. That guy's a cad."

Lynn felt like telling him what she thought of him. Talk about a cad! But aware that all work had come to a halt and all eyes including Jess's were on them, she held back.

She slowly turned and started for the house.

"I don't know how you can be so hard, woman!"

The plasterer was crouched down low enough to see what was going on through the windows and the Bedeskys had stopped work.

Lynn kept walking toward the porch.

Sam shouted, "I did it because I love you! Goddamn it!"

Frustrated, he kicked the dirt in front of him. "You're making too damn much of this! I'll be good to you ... and the boy too!"

He stood there for a moment after the screen door slammed behind her, then shook his head in disgust. His squinted eyes shot angrily from the plasterer to the Bedeskys, but when he saw Jess's sad expression, his face fell and he jumped in the truck and took off.

Less than fifteen minutes later a car pulled in. Lynn rushed to the window and saw Bob Caldwell stalking toward the house with a concerned expression on his face.

Lynn walked stiffly out the kitchen door and down the steps clutching the railing tightly. So much for pretending nothing was wrong with her knees when Sam was over. She was now paying the penalty.

Still seething from his encounter with Lynn, Sam looked through the telescope as Bob came toward her, and then put his arm around her shoulders.

Lynn shook Bob's arm off and said, "You have no business here."

"Darling, we've got to talk. Let's go in the house."

"I want you to go. *Now.*"

"Come on, Lynn. I'm an innocent victim here." He was pleading as if he honestly believed it. "I'm not to blame if this guy's got the hots for you. All I'm asking you to do is make it clear to him I didn't tell you anything, and shift the blame to Mindy."

His voice dripped with desperation, like he had just won the lottery and was trying to coax someone who had gotten their hands on his ticket to give it back.

He grabbed her arm and held her as she tried to walk away. The two Bedesky brothers put down their tools and started toward them just as Sam roared in. He flew out before the truck came to a full stop and raced toward Bob, his face red and neck veins bulging.

Bob's face reflected terror as he noticed Sam rushing toward him.

"Wait a minute, buddy. I don't know who you are, but...."

Sam grabbed him by the shirt and socked him. Bob fell back a few steps and wiped his jaw with his sleeve. But when he saw Sam come for him again he suddenly found his courage. Lynn had to cover her eyes with her hands as the sounds of smashing fists and grunts filled the air.

Just as the State Trooper pulled in, the Bedeskys and the plasterer rushed to pull Sam off. While the two antagonists were being held, the sound of their heavy breathing punctuated the air.

Dick Mitchum, who had spotted the two men fighting as he came over the hill, casually threw open the door of his trooper car, ceremoniously put on his hat, and reached for his clipboard and got out.

"Okay. Why don't we take this one at a time."

Mitchum pointed to Sam and said, "You first," and nodded toward the squad car.

Sam followed the trooper and got into the front seat.

Bob shook himself loose from the plasterer. "You all saw what happened. That attack was assault and battery for Christ's sake." He took out a handkerchief and gingerly wiped the blood off his lip. "I was just defending myself."

The group was unresponsive. The barroom-brawl-savvy Bedeskys were taking the whole thing in stride and ready to get back to work, but the plasterer seemed curious to find out what would happen next.

"Do you know who that was?" Lynn asked Bob.

The realization struck him like lightening. "Oh Christ! Not the composer!"

Bob's face was a portrait of angst.

Just as the plasterer was being drawn into the conversation, one of the Bedeskys tapped him on the shoulder, and he reluctantly went back to work.

Dick Mitchum finished the paperwork and handed Sam his driver's license and a summons, then motioned for Bob to come as Sam got into his truck and drove away. While Mitchum talked with Bob, Lynn couldn't forget the look on Sam's face as he ran out of his truck. Like he was in a life or death struggle to protect what was his. How could he be so intense about her and still be involved with another woman, she asked herself? But she had seen everything with her own eyes. Worse yet, at least two hours had passed before he came down to see her after she saw him holding the beautiful naked woman.

When Bob drove away, Dick Mitchum got out of his car and came toward Lynn who was now sitting on the porch steps with Jess.

"They both have summons to appear next month in front of Judge Harrison for disorderly conduct."

Mitchum finished jotting something on his pad, then with the pen still poised in his hand, asked, "That Reynolds fella. How long has be been around here?"

There was something about this question that put Lynn on guard.

"Since spring. He built the house up there on the hill."

"Yeah, I remember that."

Lynn looked at him intently while he jotted down more notes.

The Trooper nodded slowly and looked around.

"You've got a lot going on here." He motioned toward the Bedeskys. "Who are those two?"

"Oh. They're from the Adirondacks. They're putting up my greenhouse."

"What are their names?"

Lynn felt herself getting more and more uneasy as she gave him their names.

He looked up at the plasterer's truck. "So you've got the Sullivan Company working here too."

"Yes. The Bedeskys hired them."

"I see." He made note of that then flipped the spiral notepad closed and tucked it into his pocket. "Hopefully, we won't be having any more of this type of disturbance." He looked around. "I was just on my way into Eastlake. Remember, just call the barracks if there are any more problems."

As Mitchum pulled out of the driveway and headed into Eastlake, he picked up his radio and asked the office to run a check on Sam Reynolds.

Before Cal sat down, Lynn suspected he wasn't just dropping in for a chat, but had come on a mission. She poured them both coffee and sat down. Her eyes traced the familiar lines on his deeply wrinkled face. The thick shock of white hair was flat where his cap had been and she noticed his hands were shaking more than usual.

"You okay, Cal?"

"He took a sip and said, "Not as young as I used to be.""

"What's wrong, Cal?"

He thought for a moment, then put his cup down and took her hand in both of his. "I know you're going to hear this sooner or later and I wanted you to get it from me ... here."

"Go on."

"Well, you know Sauterfield's wife's got quite a tongue."

Lynn stopped breathing.

"By now...I guess... everyone around these parts knows about you and Sam."

Lynn closed her eyes and leaned back in her chair. How in the world had Nora found out?

"Come on, girl. Things aren't that bad." Cal let out a short chuckle. "As least not until yesterday."

Lynn's chair made a loud scraping sound against the floor as she jumped up. She nervously pushed her hair behind her ears as she paced around the room. "What are they all saying... that he... that Sam just came down to protect his territory?"

"Awh, come on, Lynn. You're not the first woman to have made a fool out of herself over a man."

"Is that what everybody thinks? That I'm some kind of fool?"

"Forget about what everybody thinks."

"That's easy for you to say, Cal. You're not a mother. How do you think Jess is going to feel when he hears the vicious gossip. And rest assured he will. Probably the first time he rides his bike down to Billy's."

"You can stop everyone's tongue from wagging by just marrying the man." Cal paused for a moment as if he was mulling something over. "You're not sweet on the one he licked, are you?"

Lynn didn't answer. She was deep in thought, staring into space though squinted eyes.

Cal knew Lynn well enough by now to know she needed time to think this through, so he got up and topped off his coffee. Finally, Lynn slid into her chair and dropped her head in the palm of her hand as she cried, "Oh, Cal! You should have been here yesterday! I can't begin to tell you!"

Cal patted her hand and gave her a knowing wink. "One of Sullivan's men painted *a pret..ty good picture* for my son last night at the Slabside Inn."

Lynn instantly imagined what must have been a raucous scene at the Slabside's bar and wanted to run out and knock the guy off his stilts.

Cal took a long swig of coffee. "Sure looks like that Reynolds fella is crazy about you." Cal was just starting to roll. "Yep, you're the talk of the town, Missy. With that TV show of yours... the greenhouse ... now this business with Sam. Hell! We've got our own little soap opera going right here in the hollow." He leaned over and gave her another big wink as he patted her hand. "I'm glad someone's around to give that Johnson band on Woodcock Road a run for their money."

As was her habit when she was in a bind, Lynn carefully brushed her hair back behind her ears, sat up straight in her chair and twisted her pursed lips as she thought.

Finally, she slapped her hands on her thighs and said, "Okay. So I'm a fallen woman. So be it!" Then in a solemn tone as she squeezed Cal's hand, "You're right. I'm glad I heard this from you, Cal. But... come hell or high water... Sam and I are history." Her life might be in turmoil, but sure as hell their broken romance was a given.

Cal knew he'd pushed her as far as he could that day.

CHAPTER 25

The young girl's eyes opened to the early morning gray seen through the curtainless trailer window above her sister's bed. She threw off the threadbare quilt exposing her tanned legs and jean shorts for she went to sleep every night fully dressed, never knowing who might be in the house. Only thirteen, yet she was wise to the ways of the world.

Even as a very small child Patsy Johnson had a sense of right and wrong. When the men who came to visit her mother in the trailer put her on their lap and fondled her, she wriggled off and ran and hid.

There were a lot of people in Oneida County like Patsy's parents, Cricket and Squeak Johnson. The only reason everyone gossiped about them so much, unlike the rest, was because Cricket called the police every time her husband beat her up. Since there wasn't a farm around that didn't have a police radio in the house or barn, these reoccurring incidents were grist for the gossip mill.

Squeak was a hard-working man but, steeped in the backwoods culture of the uneducated hill people, he believed his family should keep to themselves. By not letting his wife have a car, job or friends and insisting she stay cooped up in their trailer all day, he just made her resentful. And the only way she had to get even was to have as much fun in that trailer as she could when he was at work and the two older children, Patsy and Carol, at school.

Every once in a while, Cricket would run off with one of her regulars, only to come back to another beating and a few less teeth. This time was different, though. Everybody figured that out when she came and got the two-year-old twins.

Patsy Johnson looked over at her twelve-year-old sister lying on her back hugging her pillow with her long lanky legs hanging off the bed. The brightly colored toenails looked out of place on the kind of dirty feet you only get by running wild and barefoot for most of the summer.

By a cruel twist of fate, Patsy's sister, Carol, had been cast in her mother's image, and Patsy couldn't help wondering what was ever going to become of her.

In the bathroom, Patsy bent down and got out the Noxzema she hid under the sink and washed her face. Her mother always found the money to buy Patsy things, but she hadn't been around since the late spring when she came and took the twins away. This time Patsy was worried her father wasn't going to let her come back. Why should he? She was able to do all the cooking and cleaning now, or as much as got done.

The work she could handle. Carol was the big problem. Squeak Johnson left for work by seven and Patsy cleaned and washed until noon when Carol finally made the effort to roll out of bed to watch her soap operas. Their father wasn't getting home until after dark these days since they were loading hay almost every night at the corporate farm where he worked.

If only the girls had had some friends. There had never been any extra money for things like musical instruments or uniforms or class trips. With no car, their mother couldn't drive them anywhere or pick them up after school hours, so extra-circular activities and the friends you make at them had always been out of the girls' reach.

God, how Patsy missed the twins and wondered if they were being taken care of. They were frail little things. Preemies just like their parents. When Patsy's mother was born she was so small her cry sounded like something coming from a cricket rather than a baby. The same was true for her father. They said he didn't cry, just squeaked.

After making Carol a peanut butter and jelly sandwich for lunch, Patsy went out and weeded. Her father wasn't much for doing things around the house but kept a meticulous garden. If he had to spend his only day off weeding, they'd have hell to pay.

Patsy was grateful for the soap operas during the week because they kept Carol occupied. But she dreaded Saturdays. She had to listen to Carol's pleas to be allowed to walk down to the road so she could try to get a lift into town. She'd say she wanted to get something at the Five and Dime but they both knew there wasn't a dollar between them. Twice that summer she'd gotten away with it. If Patsy were lucky it would rain this coming Saturday and their father would be home to keep her sister under his thumb.

There was something about Carol that had always made Patsy sad. Her mother had sealed her own fate years ago, but watching her sister's personality steadily evolve into a blueprint for doom was sickening. Even as a young girl, Carol seemed sexually precocious, lip-syncing and gyrating to music on the radio. Somehow, Patsy had to keep her sister from ending up like her mother even if it were for just one day at a time.

Lynn never dreamed a toilet could make anyone so happy. The plumber asked them to stand back as he lifted the shiny white porcelain bowl and carefully squished it down on the wax. After connecting the water line, he let the tank fill and then proudly looked around at the faces encircling him as he pulled on the handle.

The standing ovation was well deserved. No more trudging to the house in the middle of a snowstorm, putting boots on and taking them off again, or letting strangers in to use the bathroom when the garden shop was open. Lynn laughed as she thought this luxury alone was worth the thirty-four thousand.

Being five weeks since the tornado they were now organized enough to open the garden shop on Saturday and enjoy two weeks of business before they shut down for the season.

There was enough stock to sell at the nursery but the farmers' markets were out of the question, so Lynn decided to give Robin Saturdays off instead of Mondays until she went back to college, and work the garden shop herself with Jess. Even though an ad had run, they weren't expecting much business, but enough to make opening worth while.

The greenhouse was pretty much completed except for the sprinkler system and the Bedeskys were planning to move their trailer out by the middle of the coming week. Cal was working full-time again, mostly building platforms and workbenches for the greenhouse.

While Lynn was busy putting final touches on the garden center, Billy came over on his bike. Jess asked if they could go to the rock piles on the edge of the hay field to hunt for garter snakes.

"Can't you leave those poor little creatures alone?"

"We won't hurt them, Mom. We just want to see if we can catch them."

As the boys raced across the field with Commander in the lead, Cal came out of the greenhouse wiping his face with a bandanna, looking more frail than usual.

Lynn shouted to him, "Come on over and sit with me for a while."

They both waved to Robin as she got into her car.

"See you Monday, honey," yelled Lynn.

"Call me if you need help tomorrow," Robin yelled back.

Lynn and Cal sat gazing at the scene in front of them with the kind of satisfaction you only get when the prize is hard fought for over a long period of time. Lynn looked around at the neat rows of perennials they'd been able to save, then the sales booth that had been retrieved from across the field after the tornado. It had a fresh coat of paint, a few repairs to the roof, and stood proud. But the new buildings looming in the background gave the place distinction, especially the office roof with the strutting horse weathervane on top of the cupola.

The sun was already starting to set, a reminder that the days were getting shorter and the summer drawing to an end.

"Can you believe how good everything turned out, Cal?"

"Yep. Those boys did one hell of a job on these here buildings."

Lynn patted him on the leg and said, "I couldn't have gotten through this without you."

"Don't forget Sam. If not for him, you'd probably of lost your seeds."

Lynn turned and looked up at the house on the hill, then gave Cal a little hug. She wondered if Sam had any idea what a faithful friend he had, and then how Cal would be affected if she told him what really happened.

"Have you heard from him? He's been gone for near three weeks now."

Instead of answering, Lynn pulled at the straps on his shoulders. "That's what I'm going to get you for Christmas! A new pair of suspenders. Red ones!"

After promising to stop by and help for a while in the morning, Cal left and Lynn went into the house to fix dinner. The boys were nowhere in sight; just screams of delight somewhere off in the distance. Good. Now she would be alone to listen to her messages.

Only one. He talked so fast she had to listen three times before getting the number down. She'd never seen that area code before and wondered who this fast-talker, Ralph Weisman, could possibly be.

She rose and went over to the huge roll-top desk, pulled out a small drawer and reached back behind for the four little tapes. Then she went back to the table that held the answering machine and sat down. She exchanged the tape and quickly skimmed over the old messages until she heard the voice that made her heart stop.

She closed her eyes tight and listened to the slightly grainy but still mellow voice.

"It's three in the morning here in Rome and I just got in. Damn, I'm tired, but I can't fall asleep for thinking about you, Lynn. From the minute I saw you in the post office, I knew you were the one."

She smiled tenderly as he excitedly went on talking about his work. She was hungry for his thoughts and her instincts told her he needed a soul mate to share them with. She was aware she needed the stimulation of his excitement and raw emotion.

Suddenly, the image of Sam holding the woman flashed across her consciousness. Oh why, Sam? Why, oh why, did you have to go and spoil everything? Even if she found forgiveness in her heart, Lynn didn't think she could ever let him touch her as long as that image burned in her brain.

She was glad he left only messages, and knew all the phone calls with no one speaking on the other end were from him. She wondered how much he must have paid to listen to the thick silence as she clutched the phone and, with her tightly eyes closed, remembered the feel of him.

The tape was carefully removed from the machine and placed with the others back in its hiding place.

Too tired to fix dinner, Lynn decided to lie on the settee in the parlor until Jess came in. The two of them could go to town for pizza later on.

When she awoke, Queenie was lying on her chest and darkness was all about her. She picked up the cat, threw aside the blanket she had no memory of putting on, and rose from the settee. Feeling her way into the kitchen, she opened the door and let the cat out.

Jess! Where's Jess! She raced up the stairs to his room, and when she saw him neatly tucked in, slumped against the wall. Commander, lying at the foot of the bed, barely looked up and then went back to sleep. What a good boy Jess was. Sure he had covered her with the blanket, she wondered if he'd had anything to eat.

Though she had been sleeping for hours, she could hardly keep her eyes open. She dropped her clothes on the floor of her bedroom and slipped on a nightgown with hardly enough energy left to hit the button on the alarm clock.

The neatly packed suitcase was open on the bed. Sam Reynolds paced around the luxury suite as he talked on the portable phone, every once in a while pushing the opulent drapes aside to glance into the busy piazza. A tall, slender man in a suit nervously checked his watch, probably waiting for someone to come out of the hotel ... or maybe for someone to arrive to take into the hotel.

When Sam heard the knock on the door, assuming the drink he ordered had arrived, he took a couple bills from his wallet on the bureau. However, when he turned around, he was surprised to see one of the assistant film editors standing in the doorway dressed in the saucy kind of chic Italian women are famous for.

Still holding the phone, Sam gave her a broad smile and listened to Sandini gush for the hundredth time how much he loved Sam's music and how *importanto* it was that he finish in time. The tray arrived and the shapely young woman slipped the bills from out of Sam's hand and gave them to the waiter, then closed the door.

Sam gave Sandini what he hoped would be a final assurance that the score would be done in time and hung up. Sam wasn't *exactly* sure why this beautiful girl was standing in his room, but he had a pretty fair idea. He looked her up and down and wouldn't have been human if he hadn't noticed the curves. He was amazed at how much better she looked in the mini-skirt than the baggy jeans and oversized sweater she always wore in the overly air-conditioned studio.

"You want a drink?" he asked.

She just smiled.

Sam had been in this kind of situation a hundred times before and could handle himself as well as the next guy, but something was radically wrong. He didn't belong in this room with this beauty. The only one for him was a million miles away and what she had was all he wanted. There was no agonizing. This was simply a fact.

He didn't have any time to waste so he took a gulp of the Manhattan and went over to her. "You're beautiful ... as well as talented. And, if I were ten years younger. Hell, a year ago I'd have taken you up on this, but... well..."

"You're crazy about someone else." The pout on her face was adorable.

Sam threw his head back and laughed out loud as he remembered the ridiculous attack on Bob. "Oh brother, you can say that again!"

Before picking up the ringing phone, he swiftly led her out the door and gave her a fatherly peck on the cheek, knowing full well the call was from Sandini. After a couple more reassurances, Sam hung up and finished packing. Not until he was in bed and darkness was all around him did the music in his head get louder. He closed his eyes, pictured Lynn and listened.

CHAPTER 26

Sam Reynolds never flew First Class. For some reason he always felt safer in the middle of the plane. He had never been much of a traveler. Vibrant days and nights in New York had more than kept his interest, they energized him. Now buckled into his seat at the start of a six-hour flight from Rome's DaVinci Airport, his mind was free to roam with no interruptions, no pressing questions to answer, or ask, for that matter.

Tomorrow was Saturday and Lynn would be at the farmers' market, but Sunday he'd see her for sure. If he woke early enough he could watch her water the plants. People would be coming if the nursery was open and she'd be in and out of the lot all day.

He didn't know if he could keep his promise to himself to totally focus on his work. This film score was bringing him to a pivotal point in his career, and he knew he had reached inside himself and arrived at a whole new plateau. This music he had created was beautiful.

All his life he had practiced discipline until it was effortless. But now, when he was reaching this all-important crossroad, his self-control seemed to be dissipating, only to be replaced by some unquenchable yearning to be one with the woman in the hollow.

Being totally immersed in his music over the past three weeks had brought him back to a place where he was in control. Yet, here he was on a plane heading straight back to that remote, peaceful landscape wrapped in an invisible cloak of turmoil.

Sam smiled to himself and thought how much his mother would have liked Lynn. She would have poked at him as she said, "go for it." How he had loved to hear her speak American slang with her thick Irish brogue.

That was going to be the trick over the coming weeks. He was definitely going to go for it, but nice and easy this time. No more fist fights or humiliating public scenes.

He slowly rubbed his beard and mulled over the calls he had made from Rome. She never hung up on him. Not once. That was *more* than just a good sign. He had even heard her breathing that Sunday afternoon as he was lying in bed with the receiver resting against his ear. The time must have been somewhere in the middle of the night at the farm and he pictured her curled up in her bed in the large room upstairs with the phone gently caressing her ear. He had wanted to tell her how much he loved her, but feared provoking her. The memory of being compared with Ken still stung. Instead, on those lonely nights when he was wound-up from an exhilarating day, he couldn't stop himself from telling his thoughts to her answering machine.

Sam glanced out the window and, seeing they were above the clouds, reached up and turned off the light. Everything that meant anything to him was now within his grasp: international success, the woman he loved. He *had* to keep focused. If he kept his emotions in check he'd get them both.

As he started to drift off, he wondered how many men around the world at that very moment were pouring their hearts out to unfeeling mechanical devices.

CHAPTER 27

There's a unique crispness in that magical moment between darkness and the first hint of sunrise. The dew has washed the grass in the meadows and the air is cool and filled with the fragrance that seems to linger in the night air. In the most undramatic way, almost like a dimmer switch slowly being turned up, light from beyond the horizon starts illuminating the landscape and the birds faithfully announce the event.

Lynn Richardson stopped for a moment, took a sweeping glance across the hollow and listened. She smiled when the red-winged blackbird let out his piercing trill causing a moment of silence to ensue. Then she remembered hearing a similar song at dawn that past spring and thinking the day would bring good luck. That's when she first saw Sam in the post office.

Her reverie was suddenly interrupted when Cal pulled into the parking lot. Without saying much, the two went about readying the garden center for the day ahead.

Lynn checked her watch. Seven.

"Cal, come on in and I'll whip up some breakfast."

"You go ahead, I'll be right in."

The smell of browning sausages had Jess down in minutes, and before long the three of them were at the table eating and cheerfully chatting about their expectations for the day.

Lynn suddenly jumped up and ran for the downstairs bathroom. Cal and Jess stood concerned at the doorway while, on her hands and knees, Lynn threw up in the toilet until she had nothing to give but dry heaves.

Cal grasped her shoulders and helped her up. "Missy, I think you should lie down for a while." He looked over at Jess. "The boy and I can handle everything at the nursery."

Lynn would have none of it. She briskly rinsed her face, straightened everything up and sat back down at the table.

The concern on Jess's face embarrassed her. She reached over and patted him on the shoulder. "Honey, your mother is going to have to get back on schedule now that the building is done. All that deli food I've been grabbing at the grocery store isn't good for us." She looked over at Cal and shook her head; "The ham I put in my sandwich yesterday must have been old or something. I'll make some fennel tea. That ought to fix me up."

Jess was being a big help so Cal left around ten. The weather was glorious but business was so-so. Mostly Lynn's faithful following wanting to congratulate her on the new buildings. Jess was happy to see his mother revel in all the attention. He laughed as she got carried away over and over again dramatically reenacting the barn falling over, each time adding some small detail that seemed to bring a satisfying reaction from her audience.

Around noon, things at the garden center being slow, Lynn let Jess ride his bike to Billy's.

The sun was hot and the breeze felt good against Jess's face as he sat back and sped down Richardson Hill toward the crossroads at Peterson Road. A van drove toward him in the other lane. When it slowed, Jess instantly recognized the man who had made him feel uneasy so many times at the nursery.

Jess started pedaling fast to get ready for when the road flattened out. Nervous about the van, he quickly glanced over his shoulder and noticed that instead of going over the crest of the hill, it turned onto the dirt road Sauterfield used to get to his fields.

Jess looked ahead. The road was deserted. Frightened, he slammed on his brakes and hurriedly carried his bike across the ditch. He quickly rolled his bike down a row of tall corn stalks until he couldn't see the road any longer.

Though the corn was a couple of feet taller than he was, Jess crouched down low and listened. Just like he thought! The van had turned around! The sound of the noisy muffler got louder, but Jess could tell the van was going slow. A mosquito buzzed around his head. He waited until the insect landed on his cheek, then carefully lifted his hand and rubbed it to a pulp. Jess held his breath as the van neared the end of the row. Sweat poured down his face and a wave of acute tension rolled over him.

Gradually the sound started to fade until there was dead silence except for the annoying buzz of a mosquito. Jess stood up and wiped his sweat-drenched face with the bottom of his T-shirt. Then he slowly made his way down the hill by weaving his way through the rows of corn until he got to the clearing where the field met Peterson Road. He carefully looked to his right and then to his left. Nothing! He quickly pulled his bike onto the road and raced toward Billy's house a couple hundred yards away.

When his friend greeted him on the front lawn, Jess wanted to tell him what happened but was afraid Billy would think he was a sissy, so he decided to keep the incident to himself.

By four-thirty things had calmed down enough so that Lynn felt comfortable about closing the garden center. Since Jess was still at Billy's, she decided to lie down and rest. Total exhaustion had set in. She'd have some yogurt with chives and dill later when Jess got home. She needed to clean out her system from all the processed food she'd been consuming since they started setting up the office. She determined not to fall into the same trap while they were filling the greenhouse with new seedlings.

At first, Sam didn't notice the flashing blue light, but as Dick Mitchum's patrol car pulled close enough behind him to be practically nosing the back of his truck, his eyes shot over to the speedometer. Seventy. Damn it! Less than five minutes from the farm! So much for getting a glimpse of Lynn before the garden shop closed. Now he'd probably have to wait until morning. He pulled to the side and reached in his back pocket for his wallet.

"Your license, Sir."

The trooper walked back to his car with the license while Sam impatiently tapped on the steering wheel with his fingers as if it were a row of piano keys. He caught a look at himself in the rear-view mirror. The white silk shirt from the expensive shop in Rome was wrinkled and his beard needed a trim.

When Dick Mitchum handed back the license along with a ticket, Sam recognized him as the one who interrupted the fight. Sam shifted his weight uncomfortably as Mitchum carefully studied the truck's interior, then gave Sam a penetrating stare.

"Been seeing a lot of you lately, Mister. You were doing seventy in a fifty-mile-an-hour zone." The trooper straightened up, and with the same kind of authoritative voice Sam had heard his brothers practice in front the mirror, said, "Slow down."

"Yes, officer."

Sam put the license back in his wallet, tucked the ticket behind the visor and pulled back on the road in hopes that Lynn might still be out.

Disappointment washed over him when he rolled over the hill and saw the deserted lot. He could also see that the boy's bike was nowhere in sight as he slowly passed.

Instead of turning right onto his road, Sam kept going, slowing down each time he passed a farmhouse until he finally spotted Cal's truck sitting next to a trailer.

Two barking dogs from the farm next door came bounding across the lot toward him as he started to knock at the trailer door. Thankfully, it swung open and Cal greeted him with a tired but friendly smile, and shushed the dogs away.

"Well, you're back! Come on in, son. Come on in."

A gently worn easy chair, obviously the place of honor in the small living room, was offered to Sam. The old man padded over to the refrigerator in his stocking feet and took out a can of beer.

"Here. This ought to cool you off."

Sam took a long swallow. After all the tepid Italian red wine, the ice-cold American beer tasted good. Cal pulled up a chair from the kitchen and sat facing Sam, clearly interested in knowing what the younger man came for.

Sam rocked slightly as he looked around the room, thoughtfully trying to come up with a way to get the conversation started. He had to get this right. He had to make this old man like him in spite of how things stood with Lynn. In his hours of watching the activity at the garden center, Sam had noted there was a special bond between the two. The only reason he dared being there right now was the distinct feeling of encouragement he'd gotten when he had asked the old man to help him with the dog. But that was a couple of months ago. Sam braced himself for the possibility of being lectured to and then thrown out.

Gripping his beer, Sam leaned forward and looked intently into the sparkling blue eyes floating in a sea of wrinkles, then glanced around the room. On the bookshelf was a picture of a kindly looking woman in a dress from the forties standing with her arm around a small boy. The room was comfortably cluttered with memorabilia of a lifetime, stuffed ducks, decoys, and tinted black and white photos that spoke of the man's past.

Nervous, Sam held the beer can so tight that he heard a small crunch. Embarrassed, he finally said, "I guess I've gone and made a fool out of myself over Lynn. I'm crazy about her... and I know she loves me too. Somehow, we've got to straighten things out." Sam ran his hand through his hair in frustration. "I think I'll lose my mind if we don't."

A slight mischievous grin rippled across the old man's face and then faded. He leaned back in his chair and folded his arms across his chest. "You don't want to do that, son. After all, the way I figure, you're going to be a father in seven and a half months."

Sam's jaw dropped. Then a broad grin appeared and he threw his head back and let out a joyous laugh. Nervously, he kept slapping his thighs with open palms as he quickly spun a series of scenarios in his head before earnestly asking, "Are you sure?"

"I've seen enough from my wife, my son's wife, and nature in general to know when a female's with child." He shook his head and grinned. "With all her smarts she can be pretty darned stupid sometimes. She thinks she's got food poisoning and them herbs of hers are going to fix everything."

Sam bit his lip and thought a while. As he rubbed his beard, he said quizzically, "She never came right out and said it, but from what I gathered, she felt she couldn't have any more."

Cal waved the comment away. "Awh, that's nonsense. She always blames herself for everything. Right after the two of them were married and she was big with Jess, Ken got kicked bad by his bull." The old man shook his head. "When they were having trouble having another one, I told Ken to get checked out but he insisted they were plenty all right in that department."

Cal leaned back confidently. "That girl's got a temper and she's proud, but once she figures out she's going to have a baby, she's going to come to her senses right soon. She's made entirely too much of this thing with you getting rid of the competition."

Cal laughed heartily while Sam looked around in embarrassment.

"I was just trying to protect her. That guy's no good."

"Awh, I knew that the minute I laid eyes on him. Struttin' around like a peacock."

The old man gave Sam a big wink. "I've been rooting for you ever since you fixed her up after Lucky was killed. I could see you'd take good care of her. After all, I'm not going to be around forever."

Sam rose and thanked Cal, then walked to the door in a semi-stupor.

"You just take this slow and easy, son, and everything's going to work out just fine. You'll see."

With dinner in the oven, Patsy Johnson decided to get out of the sweltering trailer for some fresh air. The breeze from the west was starting to pick up and the sun, now beginning to slip behind the trees on the edge of the property, would soon cast a shadow across the lot, cooling everything down.

She took the last of the wash off the line and carefully folded it in her lap as she sat on the stoop daydreaming. After washing all the sheets, remaking the beds, and scrubbing the floors, she had a moment for herself.

Her cheeks reddened as she recalled her anger at finding the hoe lying askew in the garden and Carol nowhere in sight when she took her sister a sandwich for lunch. If only it had rained, then Pa would have been there to stop her sister from going into town.

Anger turned to concern as she noticed the deepening shadows. Maybe she should walk up the road and look for Carol. By the time she got to the high point on Woodcock Road, she'd be able to see clear for about a mile. Right up to Richardson Road. Once she spotted her sister, she'd relax.

The loose gravel in their steep driveway caused Patsy to slip a few times but the coolness of the breeze rising up through the valley was pleasant. The crest of the hill and the view beyond were just a quarter of a mile from the turn onto Woodcock Road.

The asphalt made walking smoother, and quickened her pace. She perked up her ears and listened for cars coming up from behind, every once in a while looking nervously over her shoulder.

She had always been like that. The minute she left the solitude of the trailer and their private wooded lot, she felt uncomfortable. Today she was uneasier than she could ever remember. Jumpy in fact.

For all her care, she didn't hear the van coming up behind her and was startled when it passed. How reckless of Carol to go out walking alone on this deserted road! Tonight, she'd tell her father, no matter the licking they'd both get. One for Carol misbehaving and one for her not taking better care of her.

Good. The crest was just ahead. Soon she could scan the road for Carol. Suddenly the van was coming at her from the other direction. Patsy's eyes fixed on the man inside and the queer expression on his paunchy face frightened her. She broke into a run. The brakes screeched and she could hear the door open and heavy clomping behind her.

She fought to get over the crest of the hill, just moments away. Suddenly, her sneaker pulled off and, lightening fast, she flew across the pavement into a ditch. She scrambled up the embankment only to see the oversized soiled sneakers planted in front of her face. Her eyes followed the panting figure upward, resting on the huge flabby face. She sprang up and started to run but he had her in his arms in seconds.

No amount of scratching or kicking stopped him from running with her to the van. He flung the rusted door open and threw her into the darkness. She kept slamming the palms of her hands along the walls hysterically searching for a way out when the sound of a chain being fixed on the door made her freeze.

Other than the distinct odor of burnt food, the trailer was immaculate. Trooper Mitchum pulled out a chair and sat down.

"Do you want a beer?" Squeak Johnson asked.

"No, thanks." Past eleven and his shift almost over, he'd soon be having a long cold one with his wife.

"When did you notice she was missing?" Mitchum asked.

"When I got home, my other daughter, Carol, came runnin' at me. Let's see. I punched out at ten-thirty... ten minutes to get home. I'd say around then."

"Do you think Cricket may have come and got her?"

"Nah. She called here last night from Texas wanting me to send her money. I felt like telling her to piss off, but I'm worried about the twins. I'm planning on sending something Monday."

"Where's your other daughter now?"

Squeak looked toward the back of the trailer and yelled, "Carol. You come out here!"

Unlike the father, the girl was distraught. From the puffiness of her eyes, Mitchum knew she'd been crying and suspected she had something to cry about.

He wrote down her name and age, then asked her to tell him when she noticed her sister was gone.

"I don't know. I was watching TV all day. When I smelled the dinner burning I yelled for her but she wasn't there."

"What time was this?"

"I don't know!"

The trooper glanced up at the father. "Tell me Carol. What were you watching on TV?"

"I don't know. I don't remember!"

Squeak grabbed his daughter by the shoulders and yelled, "You better start remembering or I'll beat the tar out of you!"

Mitchum rose, all six feet the essence of authority. "That'll be enough, Squeak. Why don't you step outside and let me conduct this investigation."

All eyes were on Squeak as he angrily left the trailer slamming the door behind him. Mitchum turned to Carol. "Your father's not showing it, but he's very concerned about Patsy. Come on, Carol. We both know you know more about this than you're telling."

"I don't! I swear I don't!"

"Carol, you want us to find your sister, don't you?"

The girl covered her face with her hands. "He'll kill me. He'll kill me if he finds out!"

"Finds out what, Carol?"

"I went into town." Her head fell back and her face contorted as she cried out loud.

Mitchum put down his pen and slowly looked around the neat trailer fearing this story wasn't going to end well. He let the girl cry for a minute and then said, "Carol, if you want your sister back, you're going to have to help us. Your father's not going to kill you. I promise you that."

The girl stopped crying, reached for a washcloth from the stack of clean laundry and blew her nose.

"When did you go into town?"

"Before lunch."

"What did you do there?"

"I went down to the park at the lake."

"Did anyone see you?"

"Yes. I hung out with a bunch of kids all day. That is, until everyone had to go home for dinner. Then I started walking the five miles back."

"When did you get home?"

"Late. Maybe six. Maybe later." She started to sob again. "I don't know!"

"Okay. That's all right. What happened when you got home?"

"Smoke was coming out of the kitchen and the meatloaf was burning so I threw it on the lawn."

"Is that when you realized Patsy wasn't here?"

She nodded.

"Has Patsy ever been missing before?"

"No. She sticks to this house like glue. She doesn't even like going to school even though she gets good grades."

"Has anyone been coming to see you? Hanging around the house?"

"No. Nobody comes up here. Not even my mother anymore."

"Do you have a dog?"

"No. And our cat took off after my mother left."

"Carol, have you noticed anything strange whatsoever?"

The sobs started up again. "Something's happened to her. I know something's happened to her."

"What makes you think that, Carol?"

Through the sobs Mitchum made out, "Her shoe. I found her shoe."

Mitchum's voice became stern. "Carol, stop this and tell me about the shoe."

The girl blew her nose again, then rose from the chair and went over to the couch. She knelt down, retrieved a sneaker from underneath and brought it over to Mitchum.

"On my way back I found this on the road."

Mitchum took the sneaker from the girl's shaking hand and read the initials, P.J., boldly written on the inside heel.

"Patsy put them there. Last year someone stole her sneakers from her locker and Pa wouldn't get her a new pair and she was in trouble with the gym teacher all semester."

Mitchum talked with the girl for a few more minutes then went outside. He was convinced Patsy had been abducted. The second one counting little Marylou Cramer from Cortland. Same M.O. A child disappearing on a lonely country road. Was this a serial child molester striking for the second time, he wondered?

Squeak, who was smoking nervously as he paced, took on an eerie look every time the blue light from the patrol car landed on him as it flashed around the lot. The voices coming over the radio drowned out the sounds of the night.

Before he continued with Squeak, Mitchum radioed for help. Investigators from B.C.I. would be on the scene within the hour. Dogs would be coming too. Carol would have to show them where the shoe was found and the area searched that night. Everyone would have to be carefully interviewed again, for the police knew all too well that facts get hazy and jumbled by the next morning.

Mitchum would have to ask Squeak to go back in the trailer with him. He had to get the details down before the investigators got there. Her height, weight, eye and hair color. They'd need pictures also. But before he did, he was going to ask the dispatcher at their Oneida barracks to phone his wife and tell her he'd be late. Hell, what a Saturday this had turned out to be.

CHAPTER 28

One can always tell when it's Sunday morning in Eastlake. The exclusive shops along Main Street are closed and the streets deserted; any cars that do pass by are usually carrying well-dressed passengers on their way to church. Even the town cop, Charlie Sanderson, sleeps in instead of lying in wait on a side street for the unfortunate out-of-towners who don't take notice of the reduced speed limit as they spill into town on the old Cherry Valley Turnpike, now U.S. Route 20.

The road was originally an Iroquois path that evolved into a trail for early settlers, then a plank road, and by the 1800's stretched from Albany to Syracuse with stagecoach stops in all the small towns in between. Now by-passed by the New York State Thruway, the road was used mainly by commuters and tourists. All summer they sallied up and down the highway that runs through wide, hilly expanses of green dotted by farms. Every ten miles or so lies a picturesque village with fewer than a couple hundred inhabitants.

Lynn could see the tall white spire of the Presbyterian Church on Main Street above the green canopy of maples and Douglas fir on the horizon. The approach into town was lined with Victorian homes, their gingerbread-like porches silently guarded by the cats weary from the night's hunt, waiting patiently for their owners to waken.

This was Lynn's favorite time to do her grocery shopping at the twenty-four-hour IGA that Cal jokingly told her stood for "I Gyp 'em

All." The store was mostly deserted except for the local college kids home for the summer who were busy replacing the depleted stock and readying the store for the onslaught of the after-church crowd.

Lynn took out her list and systematically proceeded down each aisle. Before going to the checkout she decided to get some donuts, the last sin before she officially put her diet on the straight and narrow.

Reaching for a cruller, she was overcome by nausea. She quickly wheeled the cart to the checkout. As the teenager rang her up, she fought off a sickening sensation that she was turning green.

Frightened, was the best way to describe how she felt as she headed for home. She kept dismissing the obvious, too disastrous to consider. She and Ken had tried for years. But she'd been so tired lately. She racked her brain for the date of her last period, but with the storm and all the construction, everything was a blur.

By the time she reached the Sauterfield farm, the realization that she was pregnant had sunk in like a heavy rock. She ran her hands over her breasts and could feel they were engorged.

She had to fight off all the demons shouting in her head. Of all the times for this to happen? Farmway's threats were haunting her night and day, the monthly mortgage payments had already started, and all the money was spent!

Maybe she should drive right up to Sam's place and just have it out with him. This was his responsibility as well as hers. She'd make him promise to be true to her and they'd get married and that would be that.

She wasn't that stupid! There was no way her temperament would allow her to play the long-suffering wife. Every time he went out of town she'd be tormented with jealousy until her suspicions drove her out of her mind. No. What kind of life would that be for Jess and this new child?

A shiver ran up her spine as she realized that within the past half-hour she'd become totally committed to the soul growing inside her. There was no question she'd die to protect it.

Deep in thought, she was almost on top of the roadblock before she came to a stop. She gazed absent-mindedly out of her open window onto Sauterfield's pasture as she waited for the trooper to finish with the car in front of her. Two Holsteins were grazing near the fence and the sharp smell of fresh manure occasionally mingled with the cool morning air.

The car in front moved on and the trooper approached. "License and registration please." As Lynn riffled through her purse he asked, "Did you drive on this road anytime yesterday?"

"No, officer. What's wrong?"

"One of the Johnson girls is missing. Where do you live?"

"Just up the road. I'm Lynn Richardson."

"Did you see anything suspicious or out of the ordinary yesterday around five."

The burned meatloaf had helped the police pinpoint six as the approximate time the girl left the trailer.

"No. As a matter of fact, I was in the house by then."

He handed her back her ID, slapped the side of her truck and waved her on with, "If you think of anything, give us a call."

Lynn spotted a neighbor sitting in a truck in the other lane waiting her turn to be questioned. "One of the Johnson girls is missing," Lynn told her after she pulled up next to her.

The woman nodded thoughtfully. "Well, with the way that family has carried on over the years, something was bound to happen sooner or later."

Lynn nodded sadly, then pulled away. A wave of depression washed over her as she climbed Richardson Hill. She thought back to Saturday. No, there'd been nothing.

When Sam awoke on Sunday, he realized this was the first time he'd actually felt at home since moving to Eastlake. After chugging down an Alka-Seltzer, he went over to the window and carefully scanned the hollow through the telescope, not missing a detail as he searched for Lynn and the boy.

Probably having breakfast. They'll be out soon.

The new greenhouse sat comfortably on the land, he thought. The heirloom garden was fading. Mostly just roses. The distant wetlands covered with Joe Pyeweed created a pink halo behind the greenhouse.

A smile spread across Sam Reynold's face as he was suddenly seized with patriarchal pride. Part of him was growing inside her. Tears welled up in his eyes and music played in his head as he felt somehow changed. He had always wanted to be a father, but somewhere along the line the dream had faded. This was like a gift he didn't deserve and the only way he was going to earn the privilege was to be the best father a child could have.

Then his thoughts shifted to Lynn. Cal was right, as soon as she realized she was going to have his child, she'd come around.

Hell, he'd give her a week. Then they'd have no choice but to sit down and work things out. With the baby coming she'd just have to get past this thing with Bob.

Today he'd go through his mail and tomorrow he'd plunge into work. He was glad he had spent a couple of hours on the phone with Ralph and Wally Saturday after he got to the house. That was now out of the way.

There were a million notes in his briefcase that had to be organized before he even dreamed about pulling together the final score. Then there were the *Men in Blue* tape that would arrive in a few days. No problem. That could be completed in a day and a half if he worked non-stop.

He took his mind off his work for a moment and wondered if the child would be musical. His laugh echoed in the room as he vigorously rubbed his hands together. Things were definitely looking up.

Gary Snyder had figured nine in the morning on a Sunday was early enough to get in and out of town for gas without anyone getting a good look at him. The scratches were covered with some makeup he found in the medicine cabinet but they couldn't stand close scrutiny. He'd pump ten dollars worth and drop the bill on the counter when the attendant was busy, mumble something, then leave. A ploy he'd used successfully before.

When the van started down Richardson Hill toward town he could see the roadblock way off in the distance. His heart thumped in his throat. He quickly glanced in the rear-view mirror. Nothing. One suspicious move and he was done for. The van slowly rolled onto the dirt road Sauterfield used to get to his rented fields. Ever so carefully he pulled out again and went back over the hill.

He held his breath and kept his eyes glued to the rear-view mirror; terrified a trooper might notice he was dodging the checkpoint. When he headed back down into the hollow and the roadblock faded from the mirror, fear grabbed him like a viper striking at prey.

He eyed Lynn Richardson watering her plants and wanted to pull in and pound the hell out of her. No. I can't let the troopers get me. There's no way they're ever going to lock me up again.

As he turned onto Swamp School Road, he spotted a trooper car flash by on Richardson Road in his rearview mirror. Things were closing in fast. Suddenly afraid he'd never get out of Lenox Township alive, he decided when he reached the house he would run the van into the ravine behind the old barn so no one would suspect he was there.

That goddamn Lynn Richardson caused this! After Cortland, he was never going to kill again. The voices stopped on Saturdays when he got close to Robin, but that cheap Richardson bitch had ruined everything trying to save herself a buck on labor. That's okay. She'd get hers soon enough. Just like the little slut that scratched up his face.

CHAPTER 29

Trooper Mitchum and Special Investigator Atkins shook hands and sat down. The room was sparse with nothing but a legal pad on Atkins' desk.

"Dick, you want a cup of Java?"

"No. I'm all coffeed out."

Only seven a.m., Mitchum had been on the road since five and had already tossed down three cups.

Atkins pushed the legal pad aside and asked wearily, "You got any new leads?" Like all the rest of the Troop D squad, Atkins hadn't had much sleep since Saturday night.

"Not much. How about the rest of the guys?"

"Remember, we're talkin' the hill country of Oneida County. We've got so damn many suspects it isn't funny. Right now we're interviewing every parolee, anyone with a sex offense, or anyone who thinks they might have seen something. The father's story checks out. So does the sister's. The mother's in Texas with the same guy she's been running with on and off for the past ten years. Other than that..." Atkins shook his head.

"Looks more and more like Cortland every day," Mitchum observed.

"Tell me."

"I'll put my money on the girl being abducted by someone who just chanced by. This kid never strayed away from the house. From the crest of Woodcock Hill you can see a lot of Richardson Road and it's likely Patsy went to look for her sister. From the skid marks near where the shoe was found I see her running, putting up a struggle and then..."

Mitchum stopped himself from further speculation since that wasn't his place, but he couldn't help thinking of all the horrible things that could be happening to Patsy Johnson. He looked at the investigator from bloodshot eyes hoping to hear something positive.

"We're going to expand the ground search tomorrow. We've got more dogs coming and another fifty or so troopers from downstate. That ought to cover all the ravines and wooded areas, then we're back to scratching for leads."

Mitchum nodded and stood up. "Maybe the investigators will come back with something tonight. I've got to shove off. I'm following up on two transients that work with the father. That's all I've got right now."

On his way out, Mitchum passed a couple of troopers coming in but didn't take the time to chat, just nodded hello. Troop D's Bureau of Criminal Investigation was calling in a lot of the investigators for personal interviews this morning instead of holding their usual team meeting. Already four days since the girl was missing, they still had nothing concrete to go on. The trail was only going to grow colder.

That morning Mitchum had gone to the farm where Squeak worked and interviewed two of the drifters temporarily hired to help with the haying and morning cleanup. They were the typical shifty-eyed outsiders that tripped into town every summer. By the way they responded to his questioning, Mitchum had no doubts they'd had run-ins with the law before. But without vehicles, they weren't good candidates for this crime. However, their alibis would have to be checked out before they had a chance to skip. He could still bring them in for questioning this afternoon. Once buckled up, Mitchum sped out and headed for the flophouse in downtown Oneida.

The thin face of the thirteen-year-old wouldn't budge from Dick Mitchum's mind. He'd gotten to know Patsy from all the times he'd been dispatched to the Johnson's. There was a decency about her that he respected. The last time Squeak beat up Crickett, Patsy had quietly made a pot of coffee and put a cup in front of him. He remembered her soothing the twins and gently wiping their tears as the mother screamed profanities from her grotesquely swollen mouth.

What kind of a chance does a kid have coming from that background? But in spite of everything she had going against her, there was a grace about her.

Who could have snatched her off the road? Mitchum couldn't get past a gnawing fear that she was somewhere out there needing help. He regretted the fact that there was no huge team grinding out posters and pleading for Patsy on TV like there'd been for the missing little girl in Cortland. Just the B.C.I. doing what they could. Dick Mitchum felt a commitment deeper than any he'd ever experienced. Patsy's plight seemed to him the very reason he was a New York State Trooper.

After checking out the alibis of the two transients, he was going to follow up on a hunch. The girl disappeared from Cortland right after that hothead across from the Richardson farm appeared on the scene. Coincidentally, Patsy disappeared the same day Sam Reynolds came back from Italy.

The search he had run on Reynolds after the fight revealed nothing, so he was going to nose around a little more before asking B.C.I. to bring him in for questioning. He'd drop by and chat with Nora Sauterfield whom he heard was doing Reynolds' cleaning.

By noon, Mitchum was knocking on the Sauterfield door.

Nora was a large woman whose closely cropped hair and habit of dressing in jeans and flannel shirts gave her a manly look. She'd come to the Sauterfield farm as a hired hand twenty-some years earlier and gossip had circulated that she did a lot more for Sauterfield than milk his cows. He finally married her three years ago, and ever since he made an honest woman of her, she'd become holier-than-thou.

The delight on her face the minute she saw Mitchum told him he was in for a long-winded rehash of the town dirt.

She took her sweet time pouring him coffee and settling in. A king-sized menthol was lit, then she took a deep drag, blew the smoke out slowly and said with a confident grin, "You want to know what's going on around here, don't you?"

"We're just looking for any clues that might help us find the Johnson girl."

"That slut of a mother of hers has been messin' around for years. That's the first place you should look, if you ask me."

Mitchum scanned the kitchen. She'd been canning and the jars were stacked on the counter. He decided to get right to the point, otherwise he'd be listening to a lot of hot air for the next half-hour.

"I understand you do the cleaning for Sam Reynolds up on the hill."

An eyebrow shot up. By the expression on her face and the way her eyes had turned to slits, Mitchum could tell her imagination was in overdrive.

"Have you noticed anything out of the ordinary there?"

Mitchum was slightly taken aback by her wild-eyed look as she spit out, "Sex!"

He reached for the spiral pad in his shirt pocket, laid it on the table, then got out his pen. Finally, they were getting somewhere. "What specifically are you talking about?"

She leaned forward and asked. "Just where do you want me to start?"

Mitchum was beginning to get impatient.

"Mrs. Sauterfield, could we please have the facts."

She didn't pick up on his annoyance or, more likely, just dismissed it and continued with the dramatics. She was on center stage and intended to take full advantage of her position.

"Nudes all over the place. Statues, wall pictures. No wonder he does it so much."

"Does what?"

"First he was with that prissy Lynn Richardson. Well, I'll tell you. She's got no right to be prissy any more. I made sure the whole town knows what *she's* been up to."

Mitchum stared at her over his glasses as she took a drag of her cigarette and flicked the ashes in the tray.

"Then there was the blond," she added maliciously. "She said she couldn't find her key. She knew him all right; she even told me the combination to the security system, so I let her in."

After listening to her for another five minutes hoping for some shred of a lead, Mitchum finally got out. He radioed in to headquarters as he pulled onto the road and started for the Richardson farm.

"Joyce, patch me through to Captain Atkins."

"Atkins."

"Mitchum here. I'd like to bring in a Sam Reynolds for questioning. Voluntarily, of course."

"What do you have on him?"

"Nothing but an active love life right now. But both girls turned up missing when he came back into town."

"Okay. Let us know if you're bringing him in."

"Can you send another car? I'll wait in the parking lot of Richardson's Nursery on Richardson Road."

"We'll send someone from the Morrisville station."

Five minutes later, Mitchum waved to Robin who came from the greenhouse when she heard the squad car pull in. Once he zipped his window down and told her he was just waiting for someone, she went back inside.

The patrol car from Morrisville arrived in a matter of minutes. Mitchum gave the trooper a run-down and the two cars proceeded up Sam's driveway while Cal and Robin watched from the greenhouse.

Music could be heard but no one answered the doorbell. Just as Mitchum was going to take a look around, the door opened. Sam, who had been working on *The Men In Blue* score non-stop since the day before, looked bemused and somewhat annoyed.

"What is it, officer?"

"Can we come in?"

"Of course."

Sound blared from the studio and the troopers could see action on the huge video screen. Sam leaned against a hall table and casually folded his arms and crossed his feet at the ankles. "What can I do for you gentlemen?"

"We're investigating the disappearance of the Johnson girl."

Sam looked less relaxed as he readjusted his arms and pursed his lips.

"We're talking to all the people who might have seen her on Saturday."

Sam was now stroking his beard and looking thoughtful.

Mitchum got out his notebook and pen and asked. "Where did you go after I gave you the ticket?"

"As a matter of fact, I drove over to Cal Wilkinson's place and had a beer with him."

"How long were you there?"

Sam slowly blew out his breath. "I don't know exactly. Twenty minutes. A half-hour maybe."

"Then what'd you do?"

"Came home."

"Did anyone see you here?"

"Wait a minute officer. What's this all about?"

"We just want to ask you to come down to the barracks and make a statement. This is purely voluntary."

Sam ran his fingers through his hair and took a deep breath. "Just a minute."

He picked up the phone on the table and dialed. After a moment he said, "Can I please speak to Chief Reynolds?" He turned his back to the troopers and drummed on the table with his fingers as he waited.

"Sean, it's Sam. Yeah... Yeah.... Sean, I need your help. There are two New York State Troopers here and they want me to go with them to make a statement." There was a pause. "A girl's missing... I don't know. Let me ask."

He turned to Mitchum. "Who'd you say was missing?"

"The Johnson girl. She lives on Woodcock Road."

"Where's that?"

"About a mile and a half from here."

Sam's attention went back to the phone. "Did you hear any of that?"

Sam kept nodding his head. "Uh-huh, uh-huh. Okay. Okay." Then he looked at Mitchum and asked, "What barracks?"

"Troop D in Oneida."

"Did you get that, Sean." Sam listened for a moment then thanked his brother and hung up.

He turned to face the troopers.

"Okay. I'll be happy to cooperate with you in any way I can. But first I've got to take care of my equipment."

While Sam was in the studio the two troopers glanced around. The trooper from Morrisville nudged Mitchum, then nodded toward the Jackson Pollock. "What the heck is that supposed to be?"

Mitchum ignored him. He was too busy eyeballing the telescope.

"Okay, gentlemen. I'm good to go."

"Mind if I take a look out of that?" Mitchum asked as he pointed to the telescope.

"Sure. Go ahead."

Mitchum was careful not to move the telescope's position as he looked in. There in the lens was Cal and Robin peering out from the greenhouse toward him.

As the two patrol cars made their way down the hill, Lynn came into the greenhouse and noticed Cal and Robin staring at the road.

"What's the big deal?" she sang out.

"Lynn, come over here quick and take a look at this," Cal said.

The tone of his voice made Lynn move swiftly. When Mitchum's patrol car turned onto Richardson Road right in front of them, Sam was in the back seat. Before Lynn could say a word, the office phone rang and she ran to get it.

"Hello."

"Hello. This is Ralph Weisman of Weisman Productions in New York."

"Oh yes. I got your message. I'm sorry I didn't get back to you ... things have been a little..."

He interrupted her with, "I've been taking a tape of your show around to some of the networks and stations and I think I've got some interest."

"Where did you get a tape of my show?"

"A friend. Sam Reynolds."

Lynn stopped breathing. Instead of listening to Ralph's pitch, she searched feverishly for reasons why Sam would be in the back seat of the patrol car.

"So what do you think?"

"Think? About what?"

"I just told you. You need to sign a contract with me."

"I'm sorry. I wasn't listening. Where did you say we would do the taping?"

"Boston."

"I don't know. I'm kinda overwhelmed."

"Okay. Let me overnight you a proposal along with a contract. Everything's all spelled out. After you've had a chance to look at it, give me a call and I'll walk you through the whole deal. I'll throw in a copy for your lawyer to look at. But we can't sit on this. The station's hot on this deal today, but who knows about tomorrow."

Lynn was in a daze as she gave Ralph the address. Lawyer? She didn't have a lawyer. She'd give the contract to Mindy after Tuesday's shoot and get her advice. Right now her only concern was Sam.

Ralph leaned back in his swivel chair, propped his feet up on his desk, and fell deep in thought as he tapped his pen on the palm of his hand. The last place he figured he'd get his big break was from some nature girl in the boondocks. But he knew this was the chance he'd been waiting for the minute the *Home and Garden* network went ballistic over the tape. God, that woman made an impression on them. Sam's music intro didn't do any harm either.

He'd overnight the package for Saturday delivery, give her the weekend to take a look at it and then fly up on Monday and massage the whole deal until the contract was signed.

Mitchum asked Sam to wait in an interrogation room, and after a few minutes came back with Atkins and another Senior Investigator.

"Thank you for coming in to talk with us on a voluntary basis," Atkins said. "We're interviewing as many people as we can to draw a clear picture of the Johnson girl's movements on Saturday."

Atkins looked Sam over. He appeared tired but totally at ease.

"Do you know the Johnson girl?"

"I don't think so."

"Have you ever driven on Woodcock Road?"

"No."

Sam was sitting casually with his chin resting on his fist.

"Mr. Reynolds, can you please tell us what you did from Saturday morning until Sunday afternoon."

"My plane got in around three on Saturday. I drove home and, as you probably know, got a speeding ticket just outside of town. Then I went to see Cal Wilkinson and went home. Actually, I haven't left the house since then."

"Approximately what time did you leave Cal Wilkinson's?"

Sam wrinkled his brow and thought for a moment. "Five, five-thirty. Somewhere around there."

"What did you do when you got home?"

"Nothing much. Since I'd been in Italy for three weeks I spent two or three hours on the phone with a few of my associates. Then I went to bed. We're about four or five hours behind here and I was bushed."

"Have you ever driven through or near the city of Cortland?"

Sam suppressed a smile as he asked, "Where's Cortland?"

"South of here, off Route 81."

"I don't think I've ever been on Route 81. I go back and forth to New York on the Thruway when I don't fly."

Atkins stood up and offered Sam his hand. "Thank you, Sir, for coming in and giving us this information. We'll let you know if we need anything else."

Sam tossed his hands and said, "That's it?"

"Yes, we'll have Trooper McBride give you a lift back."

When the door closed behind Sam, Atkins was quick to answer the question on Mitchum's face.

"Dick, we'll have Judge Black sign for us to get at his phone records and see what that tells us, but I don't think we've got anything here. This guy didn't show any reluctance to assist us, and ... before you pulled in, I got a call from Albany. Reynold's brother is chief of detectives for New York's seventeenth precinct, and well known in police circles. In fact, all four of Reynold's brothers are connected, in one way or another, to the New York City Police Department."

Atkins leaned against the wall and fumbled with the change in his pocket as he said, "And as a point of interest, he does all the musical background for the *Men in Blue*."

"You're kidding!" said the senior investigator excitedly.

Mitchum's mind wandered as the two investigators kicked around the possibility that there might someday be a series on the New York State Troopers. After all, weren't the Texas Rangers being glorified every night on TV? Perhaps he'd been wrong to suspect Reynolds, but thinking back to the house on the hill, why the telescope? Reynolds was hardly observing nature.

After shaking off the depressing thought of what might have happened to the missing girl, Sam glanced at his watch as the patrol car headed toward Eastlake. The good news was he could get back to work in ten minutes. He'd be finished with *Men in Blue* before the night was over and have Fed Ex pick up the tape before noon the next day.

Sam's thoughts were interrupted.

"So, you do all the music for *Men in Blue*?" asked the trooper.

Sam thought for a second and smiled to himself. Sean must have called the barracks.

"Yeah. In fact I'm doing next week's show right now."

"That must be interesting work."

"There are moments." Mostly the money he thought to himself with a good bit of cynicism.

"That must be some studio you've got." There was a pause. "My boy really loves that show. He's musical too."

"Why don't you bring him up some time and I'll show you both around."

"Gosh! That would be great! Sure you wouldn't mind?"

"No, I'd like to."

The trooper was silent, obviously thinking about the big announcement he'd make once he got home. As they turned onto Richardson Road the trooper observed, "Too bad that Sauterfield woman is such a busybody."

Sam turned to him. "What do you mean?"

"She's told everyone in the township about you and the Richardson woman." He laughed a short laugh. "And that fight you had with another one of her boyfriends hit the headlines too."

Like a shot out of a cannon, Sam's anger rose. His fingers drummed feverishly on his knees.

"I guess old Nora must have given Mitchum an earful. I got the call to come over right after he left her."

Sam felt his cheeks redden. He had to hold his temper. How in the hell did Nora find out about him and Lynn? Then he recalled her coming to the door that morning. She must have seen something. He closed his eyes tightly, then tenderly pictured Lynn and felt he would explode. Being a suspect in the disappearance of a child had really bothered him, but nowhere near as much as the besmirching of Lynn's reputation.

Damn it! He had only made matters worse by going after Bob. Then he wondered if she knew about all the gossip. She was so damn proud, something like this would really hurt her. The sooner they married the better.

Lynn couldn't concentrate on potting and neither could Cal.

"Cal, let's go out and watch for the troopers to bring Sam back." She checked the time. "They've been gone almost two hours." There was no point in hiding her concern; Cal would know what she was thinking.

"Let's give 'em another half hour, then I'll call the station," Cal replied.

Lynn paced the lot straining to focus on the crest of the hill, when like a mirage, the patrol car appeared on the horizon.

"There, there, girl. They're bringing him back. We had nothing to worry about."

Lynn fixed on the car, and as it neared, zeroed in on Sam. Their intense eye contact was only broken when the car turned abruptly and disappeared in a cloud of dust.

"Missy, why don't you go in and lie down. You look as pale as a ghost."

"Good idea, Cal."

She wearily started for the house, then stopped and turned. "Cal, when Shelly brings Jess back, ask her to come upstairs."

Lynn awoke with Shelly sitting at the edge of her bed.

"Hi, baby," spoke Shelly.

Lynn stiffly sat up, fluffed up her pillow and rested against the head-board. "Has Cal gone yet?"

"He left a few minutes ago."

Shelly gave Lynn a long, hard look. "You look bushed."

"Well, Shelly, I'm a lot more than bushed. I'm pregnant."

Shelly slowly rose and went over to the window and looked out blankly while Lynn stared ahead at the wallpaper with the bouquets of lilacs, tears streaming down her cheeks. A warm breeze made the lace curtains flutter and from somewhere off in the distance came the vibrating sound of the katydids.

"Boy, this has been one hell of a summer," Shelly said. She paced slowly around the room with her arms folded, then gently shushed the cat off the rocker and collapsed. Finally, she said, "You're just going to have to swallow that damn pride of yours and marry the guy."

There was no emotion in Lynn's voice as she said, "I can't."

"What do you mean, you can't!"

"I didn't tell you everything, Shelly." Lynn reached over and pulled a couple tissues from the box on the bed table and dabbed at the tears streaming down. "He'll marry me all right, it just won't last. I'll be jumping from the frying pan into the fire."

"What on earth are you talking about! The guy's loaded! He's hand-some, talented...*and let us not forget*...the father of your child."

"Remember the day I hurt my knees? That was when Sam came back from Spain. Well, I fell running from his house. God, Shelly, I was the happiest person in the world when I walked up there. But when I saw him through the window caressing this beautiful nude blond, my heart broke." She cried softly in the quiet room. "He didn't come down to see me for over two hours. Next to Ken's accident, I don't think anything's ever tore me up like that."

The sound of Shelly's rocking stopped. "Okay. So he's a pig. Honey, I'm telling you, you're in no position to be picky." She paused for a moment. ".... unless you want to get an ...."

"No! Never! Never!" screamed Lynn. "And the worst thing is, I'm worried about Sam, Shelly. I mean really worried. There's been so much talk about him ... and me ... and now that little Johnson girl's missing." She started to cry again but quickly got hold of herself. "The troopers took Sam in for questioning this morning. Oh, Shelly, he would never hurt anyone. I feel like this hollow's been bad for him. Maybe, he just doesn't belong here."

Lynn fell into uncontrollable sobs as Shelly rocked her in her arms.

Jess tiptoed down the stairs, careful not to step on the one that creaked. He went outside and got on his bike and started up the hill to the A-frame. Sweat poured down his face but he steadfastly kept pedaling until he reached the house. Then he got off, hit the kickstand and started for the door. Before he rang, he wiped his face, first with one sleeve, and then the other, then his sweaty hands on his shorts. No answer. He rang again, only this time much longer.

The door suddenly opened. Sam studied the boy. From the way he stood, feet apart and set solid on the ground, and the way he had folded his arms high across his chest, Sam knew the boy had come on an earnest mission.

"Jess?"

In his most manly voice, the boy replied, "Why'd you do it, Sam?"

Sam's face broke into a twisted expression of questioning. "What are you talking about?"

"You know. The naked lady."

"What on earth are you talking about, son?"

"You broke my mother's heart. She saw everything."

Sam got down on one knee and clutched Jess's arms. "What did she see, son?"

Jess pointed to the window next to the door. "Through there. She saw you holding the naked lady when she came up to see you."

Sam stood up and pulled the boy to him while he threw his head back and laughed to the skies.

He happily tousled Jess's hair and said, "Son, I didn't do anything wrong. This whole thing has been a big misunderstanding!" He looked Jess straight in the eyes. "You've got to believe me. I love your mother and would never do anything to hurt her. Or you either." He quickly lifted Jess's bike into the back of his truck and swung open the passenger door. "Hop in! We're going to straighten this thing out once and for all!"

Shelly was standing at the kitchen window sipping tea when she spotted the trail of dust barreling down the hill. Something told her things were coming to a head. She glanced over at Lynn who was silently crying as she sat holding her head in her hands with her back to the door.

"Brace yourself, Lynn. I think Sam's on his way."

"Don't let him in. I'll die if he sees me like this."

"Honey, you've got to listen to him. In your condition, you're on a roller coaster of mood swings right now. Just sit back and give this a chance."

Sam and Jess flew out of the truck and raced up the porch steps and into the kitchen. They both paused when they saw Lynn's stooped shoulders. The kitchen was dark now that the sun was on the other side of the house, and the only sound came from the clock in the parlor.

"Go away, Sam Reynolds!" sounded pathetically from Lynn who hadn't lifted her head from her hands.

Sam stepped forward. "Lynn, you've got to listen to me!"

"I said, go!"

"Lynn, I'm so sorry all this happened. You never deserved this. That woman you saw at my house was my ex-wife. She means nothing to me! Nora Sauterfield let her in, and it took everything I had to get rid of her.

Christ! I had to fight with her for nearly two hours! You must have looked in as I was trying to get her to go up and get dressed."

Lynn gripped the table as if she were going to push herself away.

Sam, in utter frustration, ran his hands through his hair. "I'm sorry about Bob. Especially the fight. I made a complete fool of myself ... "

Shelly moved toward Jess. "Come on, honey. Let's leave them alone."

"No!" Lynn shouted. Then she sat erect, laid her hands flat on the table and said in a voice straining to sound normal. "Sam, I want you to leave now."

Sam's pained eyes jumped from Shelly to Jess, pleading for help.

Then the silence was broken by Lynn's casually spoken words. "Tomorrow we're closing the garden center down for the season. Come for dinner Sunday at two."

Sam couldn't restrain himself. His head fell back as he laughed joyously. He started for Lynn, but Shelly stopped him and whispered in his ear, "She's been crying and doesn't want you to see her like this. She's got a big day ahead of her tomorrow. Give the lady 'til Sunday."

Sam flashed a playful grin at Shelly and put his arm around Jess's shoulder and started for the door. Before he left, he paused for a moment and without turning, said, "I love you, Lynn."

Looking out from the kitchen window, Shelly watched Sam hug Jess before he got into the truck, then carefully, so Lynn wouldn't notice, wiped the tears from her eyes.

CHAPTER 30

Cal got out of his truck early Saturday morning and waved to Lynn who was watering the heirloom garden. Out of the corner of her eye, Lynn saw Jess rush up to him, and from the way Cal patted Jess on the back and then strolled toward her with an arm around the boy's shoulder, she knew Jess had told him what had happened.

"Well, gal, when's the wedding?"

"Yeah, Mom! When are we getting married! Where are we going to live?"

"Wait a minute everyone! He hasn't asked me yet." Lynn brushed her hair back behind her ears, cocked her head and raised an eyebrow as a slow smile spread across her face. "But I'm sure he will tomorrow when he's over for dinner."

They all laughed heartily as they fell into doing chores.

Lynn, who was now watering the plants in the garden center, yelled over to Cal. "And the very first thing I'm going to do once we're married is fire that Nora Sauterfield."

"Oh, girl, he's already *done* that!"

Lynn slapped her hand on her thigh. "Let me guess. Your son heard it last night at the Slabside!"

They all laughed again.

"If it weren't for the Slabside, we wouldn't know what in tarnation is goin' on around here," Cal said.

The smile lingered on Lynn's face as she gave the plants one final spraying, every once in a while wistfully looking up at the house on the hill. Where *would* they live, she wondered?

Finished setting up the booth and dragging out the seed stand, Cal came up to Lynn. "Why don't you let me take the boy tomorrow so the two of you can be alone. My son's having a little 'do' at the farm and Jess'll have a good time. He can spend the night with me."

Lynn thought for a moment. "That's not a bad idea, Cal. My ad says we're closing today at two. That'll give me enough time to clean the house and figure out what I'm going to cook tomorrow. I'll do the shopping early in the morning and you can pick Jess up after lunch."

"Now don't you be overdoing everything, Missy."

Lynn squinted as she tried to read the expression on Cal's face. "You know about the baby, don't you?"

Cal's eyes sparkled.

She looked at him intensely for a moment and finally asked, "What about Sam?"

"I never saw a man happier."

Their embrace was automatic. "Cal, I never really knew my dad, and you're the closest thing to a father I've ever had. I love you."

He patted her on the head. "Girl, I love you like my own daughter."

Lynn excitedly pulled away. "Will you give me away when Sam and I get married?"

"I'll be proud."

Robin had already left for college, so Lynn, Cal and Jess had to handle the last day of business without her. After the turbulent summer and the prospect of filling the greenhouse with thousands of seedlings in the coming months, they were relieved to see the season end.

Business was surprisingly brisk all morning with bargain hunters scooping up the last of the battered plants, on sale for a dollar. Returning from loading up a customer's station wagon, Cal stopped for a moment and watched Lynn ring someone up, and smiled. She noticed his gaze and smiled back.

Jess came up next to Cal. "Her heart sure don't look broken any more." He tugged on his T-shirt and looked down in embarrassment. "We were wrong about Sam. I'll never doubt him again. He's going to be a great dad."

Cal looked down at Jess. "Do you want me to take you over to Billy's for a while? Things are slowing down. I think that'd be okay with your mom."

"No, that's all right. I think I'll just hang around."

"You okay, boy?"

"Yeah."

As they spoke, Dick Mitchum's unmarked car drove by.

Like repeating strokes of lightning, horrible visions of bloodied body parts flashed through Gary Snyder's head and he leaned over and puked. Before long the troopers would be swarming all over the place, and no matter how much he cleaned the saw blade, they'd still find bits of blood and bone. No, he was just going to leave this one in the shed wrapped in an old piece of carpet he found in the upstairs hall.

He wasn't coming back. This he knew. They were never going to lock him up again and let those same horrible things happen. Painful memories of that dark, ugly shed with those filthy drunks made him puke again. The screams from the girls mixed with those of the little boy those years ago and he put his hands over his ears to make them stop.

He would never have killed this time if it hadn't been for that witch! Now he was going to be on the run again. He slowly rubbed his skinning knife back and forth on the stone, every few minutes nervously glancing up at the kitchen clock. Time to go. He carefully slipped the knife into the sheath bucked to his belt, picked up the Montana license plates and started for the woods in back.

He knew her routine by heart. The nursery closed at five and dinner was served almost on the dot at six. The dog was the only thing he worried about. The mutt hadn't allowed him to come nearer than the clearing at the meadow behind the barn. But he still had been able to catch sight of the Richardsons at night walking around the kitchen or the bedrooms upstairs. Sometimes he'd watch them eat on the picnic table. He was relieved the two builders had left and taken their damn dogs with them. That shot he had landed on the one when they were sniffing too close to the mound behind the shed must have kept them away from the property after that.

The sun was just beginning to set as he started for the path leading to the woods. Two mallards suddenly flew up from the brush and made him jump. Their honking resonated throughout the woods as they flew in the direction of the Richardson farm. Brambles tore at his pants and arms. Already, dew was starting to form on the ground and the early evening vapors were merging with his rancid sweat.

A dark desire pushed him forward through the thicket as he thought about Lynn Richardson. He wasn't just going to kill her. First he was going to show her who was boss. She'd beg, all right. Just like he begged her not to let them take him into the shed when he was a boy. She *had* to be punished for letting those horrible things happen to him.

He'd slash the dog's throat straight off once he got close to him. If he were on his chain he'd have to rush the house. Gary stopped for a moment. Good, a strong breeze from the west. Maybe the dog wouldn't pick up his scent until he was upon him. Once he reached the meadow, he'd hunker down low and run across to the high corn in their garden.

He wouldn't do the boy until after he was done with Lynn. Just tie him up first and make him watch. The way the little snot stared at him last Saturday had made him worry all week that he might have told the police about him.

There had to be some money in the house. When he finished, he'd fill her truck with gas from the farm pump, change the license plates, scarf up as much food as he could and take off. The roadblocks would be down by now, but he'd better make his way to Rt. 81 before the trooper crews went out to start netting the drunk drivers. No matter! They wouldn't be looking for Lynn's truck until Sunday morning at the earliest, and by then he'd be in the Blue Ridge Mountains with Montana license plates.

Lynn finished drying the last plate while Jess spread out some newspapers on the table and brought out the model airplane he had been working on. Lynn studied the boy and just as she was about to speak the honking of the two mallards distracted her. Lynn looked out and saw them winging their way across the sky.

"They'll be going south before long," she said. "I'll miss them." She turned to Jess. "How about you, sweetheart?"

"Oh, sure, Mom."

Lynn thought about the mallards. Just about the time they would be going, she'd be starting a new life with Sam. How different would things be when the ducks returned in the spring? There'd be a new baby, the greenhouse would be full of luscious plants, and Jess would have a father.

She wondered what being married to Sam would be like and blushed at the thought. She put the plate in the cupboard, got out her French cookbook and went over and sat down across from Jess.

"You want me to drive you over to Billy's for a while?"

"No. That's okay, Mom."

"You didn't eat much tonight, honey."

Jess kept working on his model.

"You're not worried about Sam and me getting together are you, babe?"

Jess carefully snapped a piece of the plane out of the sheet of balsam and laid it on the newspaper.

"No, Mom. Marrying Sam is a good thing. You need somebody... and I need a dad."

"Then what's wrong, honey?"

"Billy says Patsy's dead."

"Nobody knows that for sure. Maybe she's just run away."

Jess looked up at his mother with an uncharacteristically grim expression on his face and said, "I don't think so, Mom."

Lynn propped her head up with her hand and pursed her lips. There was something Jess wasn't telling her. By nature, the boy rarely talked about things he was still mulling over. He'd think them through, and when he came to a conclusion, make a statement of fact. Usually Lynn let him work things out for himself, but something told her this time he needed help.

"What makes you think she hasn't run away?"

Jess tossed his head slightly and snapped out another piece.

"Oh, I don't know."

Lynn leaned back in her chair and tapped her hands on her lap as she thought, and then in a serious voice said, "Jess, is there something about Patsy's disappearance you're not telling me?"

All of a sudden Jess's face contorted. "That's just it! I don't know!"

Lynn was alarmed. She reached forward and squeezed his hand. "Tell me, Jess! What's happened?"

"I didn't want to tell you before ... because I was ... I didn't want everyone to think I was a sissy!"

"I'd never think you were a sissy, son. Calm down and tell your mother what you know."

"Will I have to tell the troopers too?"

"It all depends, Jess. First, you've got to tell me."

Jess examined the skeleton of the model as he spoke.

"Last Saturday when I was bicycling to Billy's..." He put the model down and folded his arms across his chest. "... I saw the guy in the beat-up van again. Mom, I've seen him hanging around Robin a lot and he scares me."

Lynn was dismayed. Jess had had this bottled up inside him for most of the summer and she hadn't even noticed!

"Like I said, I was bicycling down to Billy's just before we closed, and as I was cruising down the other side of the hill, I saw him coming toward me."

Jess got excited.

"There's something about the look on his face that scares me. So when I saw him turn onto Sauterfield's dirt road, I ran with my bike and hid in the cornfield!"

Jess's cheeks were flushed and eyes wide-open.

"Mom, he turned around and I just knew he was looking for me. I could hear he was going real slow."

Jess wiped his face with his hands. "Geez, Mom. Am I in trouble because I didn't tell you? The troopers were over at Billy's house asking questions and I wanted to say something then, but I thought everyone would think I was silly."

The boy looked in his mother's eyes. "But I don't think so any more."

"Jess, would you be able to recognize this man or his van if you saw it again?"

"Oh yeah! I'll never forget that mean face of his."

Jess looked pleadingly up at his mother. "What are we going to do?"

Lynn slowly blew out her breath and nervously tapped her hands on her lap.

"We're going to have to call Trooper Mitchum and you're going to have to tell him what happened."

Someone at the barracks picked up on the second ring.

"Troop D."

"Hello. This is Lynn Richardson on Richardson Road in Lenox Township. Is Trooper Mitchum there?"

"He just left on a call to the Oneida Reservation. Can anyone else help you?"

Lynn looked over at Jess and decided to wait until she could talk to Mitchum since the boy was already familiar with him.

"No, but can you please have him call me as soon as he can?"

The operator took her name, address and phone number and hung up.

Jess bent down and petted Commander who was sitting attentively with his mouth open, eyes darting from Jess to the table scraps.

Noticing the dog and wanting to keep occupied until they heard from the trooper, Lynn said, "Let's feed Commander and then go for a short walk. Dick Mitchum just left on a call so he won't be getting back to us for a while."

The coolness in the air made Lynn hug herself as she watched Jess feed the dog. She put her hand on the boy's shoulder and said, "Come on, honey. Let's take a look at the garden." Suddenly, the horrible afternoon when Ken was killed and all her dreams were destroyed flashed in her head and made her shiver. "The garden's not going to last too much longer," she said somberly.

Lynn looked up at the house on the hill, ran her hand across her stomach and wished Sam was with them. She'd call and ask him to come down when they got back to the house.

Commander, who just finished eating, came charging toward them. The boy crouched down and vigorously massaged behind the dog's ears while his mother looked on. Suddenly Commander's muscles tightened. His upper lip quivered above bared teeth as he emitted a threatening, guttural sound.

Lynn was shocked to see a figure in the tall corn at the edge of the garden.

Jess jumped up and pointed. "That's him, Mom!"

Without taking her eyes off the man, Lynn grabbed Jess and started toward the house. She was struck with fear when he started after them. Instinctively, the mother and son ran.

"Hurry, Jess!"

Maybe they could get to the barn and latch the door! When the heavy breathing at their backs seemed to disappear, Lynn quickly glanced back and saw the man trying to kick Commander off his leg.

"Jess! The barn!"

Once inside, terror struck her when she saw a stack of plywood leaning against the door! The loft! She pointed to the steps. "Get up there!" Her heart was beating hard in her throat as she watched Jess's bare legs scamper up ahead of her. She was so close behind him his heels pounded against her. Suddenly a hand clutched her ankle. She held onto the steps and tried to pull her foot loose. A huge arm grabbed her around the waist.

She turned and screamed at the ugly sneering face inches away. Commander leapt onto the man's back and tore into him. When the arm released Lynn to struggle with the dog, she franticly scrambled up the stairs, thrust herself into the loft and slammed down the trap door. Feverishly, she grabbed bales of hay and started piling them on. Jess kept throwing bales down from the stack as he climbed to the top until there was a jumbled pile at least four feet deep.

A blood-curdling yelp from Commander made them freeze. All became quiet except for the sound of their heavy breathing. Loud thumping at the trap door made Lynn scream. Then she covered her mouth with both hands, her wide-open eyes glued to the bouncing pile of hay bales. The pounding stopped. Lynn looked up at Jess. His face was red and sweaty, eyes like saucers. Neither of them dared move.

The ladder! He could lean it against the barn and come after them through one of the two doors on either side of the loft! Lynn checked to make sure the long two-by-fours that sat in brackets across each door were braced against the sides. Then with trembling legs she made her way to the stack of bales and collapsed. Jess knelt next to her, sickening fear on his face.

Lynn hugged him and pulled him close. His body was hot and she could feel his heart thump. Then she thought of the child in her womb and another shock wave of fear washed over her. Somehow she had to save both of them. She felt herself sway, then forced herself to take long, slow breaths.

Everything was quiet below. Lynn listened intently but could only hear the ringing in her ears. When the screen door on the porch slammed, Jess scampered over the bales and peeked through a crack in the plank siding.

"I think he's in the house, Mom!"

They were both still for a while. Should they make a run for it now? No! That was insane! He could come out any minute and catch them in the doorway!

"Mom, here he comes! No! He's going to the truck. I think he's leaving!"

Hope jumped into Lynn's mind as she heard the truck start.

"No! He stopped at the pump! He's just filling up the tank!"

Lynn shut her eyes tight, bit her lip in disappointment and held back the urge to cry.

Moments seemed like hours.

"He's coming back, Mom!"

"Come over here with me, Jess!" she whispered urgently.

Lynn picked up the sound of the man moving around below. She carefully crawled to where the floor was bare and pressed an eye to a knothole. Nothing! Just the cluttered floor below. Suddenly his balding head passed underneath and her heart started pounding again.

What was he looking for! Maybe she should open the loft door that faced the road and scream for help. That wouldn't do. No one would hear and the barn was too far back behind the greenhouse for anyone to

notice them. He could find the ladder, pry off some siding with a crow-
bar and come after them.

Is this what happened to Patsy Johnson last Saturday? The fine-
boned girl wouldn't have stood a chance against this animal. Thank
God for Commander! She blocked the thought of what must have happened to him from her mind.

When Lynn's cheek accidentally brushed against the floor, hay dust
fell through the knothole. In seconds Gary was looking straight up at
her with a chilling smile on his face. Lynn sprang to her knees and
crawled over to Jess. The two hugged each other tightly as noises below
continued and Lynn racked her brain for a way out.

All became still again. What on earth was he doing? Soon darkness
would fall. The light from the setting sun, shining through the cracks in
the plank siding, painted bright orange stripes on the barn wall. The
hay dust that was suspended in its rays momentarily mesmerized Lynn.
Just moments ago, she had everything. Now, everything she had was
threatened. In a daze, she ran her hand down the boy's face and thought
about the child in her womb that she had yearned for for years. She
closed her eyes tightly. Why hadn't she told Sam she loved him?

She was suddenly jarred out of her trance.

"Mom! What's that!"

The distinct odor of kerosene filled the air.

The two flinched as they heard the thumping against the trapdoor
beneath them.

"Come down or I'll burn you alive."

Lynn's body started vibrating. She dug her fingers into Jess's shoulders and whispered through her dry, tight throat, "You've got to make a
run for it!" She pointed to the loft door facing the road. "Sneak over
there. I'll go to the other door and start making noises; then I'll take the
brace off. Watch for my signal, then quietly open your door." She
pointed to the rope hanging from the rafter. "Then let yourself down on
that rope."

She looked into the trusting eyes and batted back tears as she said, "Jess, the minute you hit the ground you've got to run like the wind. If you see anyone on the road, flag them down; otherwise get up to Sam's as fast as you can. And, whatever you do... no matter what... don't look back. Just keep running."

Tears were welling up in the boy's eyes. Lynn gently brushed back the wet hair from his sweaty forehead. "Your mother loves you with her whole heart and I've always been proud of you. Never forget that, Jess."

Tears streamed down his face.

"Baby, I want you to do something for me." She cradled his face in her hands. "Tell Sam I love him."

The shout startled them.

"I'm going to count to ten...and if you're not down here... I'm going to burn you out!"

Lynn jumped up and motioned Jess toward the loft door.

"One!"

Lynn's legs were strong again as she stomped toward the door facing the back of the farm. Fear had been replaced with determination. Jess *had* to survive.

"Two!"

She lifted the board from its saddle making as much noise as she could while looking over her shoulder at Jess who was carefully taking the board from the other door. Thank God Cal had nailed the door underneath Jess shut after the greenhouse went up. If the man heard Jess, he'd have to come out from the door below her, and by then Jess would be able to outrun him.

Lynn motioned for Jess to start as she swung her door open with enough force to hit the side of the barn with a bang.

"What are you doing on our property," Lynn screamed. "You get out of here! Right this moment!" She was desperate to grab the man's attention while Jess let himself down.

A pathetic whimper came from near the driveway. Commander! He's still alive! He must have been trying to go for help.

The man slowly backed out of the door underneath, straining to look upward. He was holding a kerosene can. As he eyed Lynn, a nasty grin slowly traveled across his face.

"See this?" He waved the can, and then with his other hand brandished a lighter. "You two better come down or I'm gonna torch you!"

"You do and there'll be people swarming all over this place in minutes!"

"There ain't gonna be people swarming around here in minutes, you lying bitch!" He tossed his head toward her truck. "Besides, I've already got your keys, gas and a pile of dough out of the desk. The minute this thing goes up, I'm out of here. They won't find what's left of you 'til morning."

She had to buy time! Jess must be across the road by now. She caught sight of a pitchfork leaning against the wall next to the casing. What good would it do her? If she threw it at him, he'd just deflect it with his hand or step back.

"Why are you doing this?" she shouted. "We never did you any harm!"

When Lynn saw the rage in his eyes, she knew what was coming next.

"No harm! You let them do those things to me in the shed, you cowardly bitch! I begged you to not let them take me in there! But no! You were just saving your own ass! You trashy bitch, you made me kill all those girls, and now you're going to get yours!"

Lynn's hair stood up on the back of her neck at the chilling realization that the man standing only a few feet beneath her flicking his Bic was out of his mind.

There was no way Sam and Jess would make it down in time. In seconds the new life inside her could be ended. Tears streaked down her sweaty flushed face as she realized the only way to save the baby's life was to hurt the demented hulk who was now wildly splashing kerosene against the barn.

Sweat poured down Lynn's back as she nervously fumbled for the pitchfork. She pushed the horror of impaling a man to the back of her mind and focused on survival. Then she braced herself.

Jess was making the final turn on the hill but his frenetic pace had slowed as he tried desperately to suck air into his burning lungs. The sight of Sam's truck recharged him and he willed himself to breathe as he pushed painfully up the final stretch. Blaring music thumped on the other side of the door as he pressed the bell. At the same time, he banged his fist violently against the door.

When the door flew open, Sam's face contorted at the sight of the clearly panicked child.

"My mother! You've got to help her!"

Sam ran with the boy to the truck and took off down the hill shouting, "What's wrong, son?"

Jess pounded on the dash. "Hurry! He's going to kill her! She's upstairs in the barn."

The truck slid off the road at the turn, but Sam pressed the pedal even harder as he swung back on. Suddenly, they heard a muffled explosion and a huge balloon-like flame engulfed the barn. Jess cried, "Oh my God! Please, God. No!"

By the time the truck skidded to a stop the fire was roaring, with flames shooting up a hundred feet. Jess jumped out and ran toward the barn but Sam caught him and buried the boy's head in his chest. Jess, crying uncontrollably, managed to pour out, "Oh, Sam. She said she loved you."

Sam solemnly led the boy back to his truck, then started for the barn. He was going to find the man who did this and kill him with his bare hands.

As he walked to where the barn faced the back of the farm his heart skipped a beat. Two figures were lying on the grass. He shouted for Jess as he ran toward them. At the same time a patrol car, sirens blaring, pulled in.

Sam found Lynn lying motionless on the ground. Another still figure lay nearby. A pitchfork embedded in his chest stuck upright in the air.

Sam quickly swooped Lynn up and ran from the intense heat and laid her down on the grass next to the house.

"I'll call an ambulance," said Dick Mitchum over Sam's shoulder.

Sam, who was cradling Lynn in his arms, caught Jess with one arm as he flew to his mother's side. They both looked down at Lynn as she opened her eyes.

"Where's Commander?"

Sam threw his head back and laughed almost insanely.

"Mom! You're all right!"

Lynn tried to sit up, but wearily fell back down again.

"Do you hurt anywhere?" questioned Sam.

"I don't think so. I broke my fall when I jumped on top of him." She looked over at the roaring blaze. "We've got to find Commander. I know he's out here somewhere."

"Don't worry, we'll find him. Right now I've got to get you upstairs."

Sam lifted Lynn up and carried her into the house and up the stairs. He carefully laid her on the bed and sat down next to her. The dancing flames cast ghostly shadows on the walls but a strong breeze blew the smoke away from the house. The lawn was quickly becoming a scene of feverish activity with fire trucks and ambulances arriving along with a battery of patrol cars.

Sam reached over and turned on the light next to the bed and looked down at Lynn. Overwhelmed with tenderness, he took her in his arms and began to sob. She put her arms around him and said, "I love you, Sam Reynolds."

Sam gently laid her down and went into the bathroom and rinsed his face, after which he came back in and tenderly wiped hers with a damp cloth. She lay there motionless as he wiped each arm in an effort to remove the kerosene.

Barely resting his hand on her stomach, he said, "Do you want me to call a doctor?"

"No. Just hold me."

They both looked up as a trooper appeared in the doorway.

"We'd like to talk with Mrs. Richardson, if at all possible."

Before Sam could speak, Lynn said, "I'll be all right." She squeezed Sam's hand. "Go down and look after Jess."

Sam stood up, went over to the investigator and said in a soft, calm voice, "Try to make this as short as possible. She's pregnant."

The investigator shook his head and whispered, "Boy this thing was a shame. Is she going to be okay?"

Sam told him he thought so, but there was a shadow of concern on his face.

"Don't worry, I'll make this short. There're only a couple of questions we need answered tonight."

Sam went downstairs and found Jess being interviewed by an investigator with Cal standing next to him.

Sam went over to the window and looked upon the grim scene. The body, lying on a stretcher and encased in a bag, was being lifted into an ambulance while a trooper was trying to clear a path for the vehicle. The flames were almost out and two fire trucks loaded with smoke-smudged volunteers were pulling onto the road and heading back to Morrisville. Cal could be overheard telling the investigator, "That's enough. We've got to get this lad to bed."

Sam eyed a somber-looking Dick Mitchum coming through the kitchen doorway.

Mitchum took off his hat and placed it on the counter, then ran his hand through his hair. "This was a pretty close call for Mrs. Richardson and her boy." He glanced out the window. "The body has been identified as that of Gary Snyder who lives just behind here on the Mile Strip Road." His voice sounded somewhat controlled as he looked Sam hard in the eyes. "I just heard over the radio they found what they think is the body of the Johnson girl in his shed. Someone's gone to get the father for a positive I.D."

They both watched Cal shepherd Jess out of the room saying, "Don't you worry about Commander, son. My boy's taken him to the vet. I don't think there's anything seriously wrong. They'll put that leg in a cast, give him some stitches and he should come along just fine."

"He's a hero, Cal."

"So are you, son."

Mitchum looked at Sam. "I'm glad things turned out as well as they did for the Richardsons." He shook his head. "I've been driving up and down these back roads, even on my off hours, looking for *anything* that would give me a lead. I must have passed the old Snyder place a hundred times. There was no vehicle, no activity. I thought it was deserted." He took his hat off the counter and put it on. He started to say something, but evidently had second thoughts.

He looked around the room and then at Sam. "Well, I guess the firemen have everything pretty much under control. Everyone should be clearing out of here soon." He offered his hand and the two men shook.

After the trooper who'd been interviewing Lynn came down, Sam went upstairs and found Cal just finishing getting Jess out of the shower and into bed.

"I'll go and take care of everything downstairs, Sam. I'll stay the night and sleep on the couch."

After tucking Jess in, Sam tousled the boy's hair and said, "You did good, son. I'm proud of you."

As Sam turned to leave the room the sight of Lynn in the hall startled him.

"I've got to have a shower and get this kerosene off. My skin's burning."

"Are you sure that won't be too much of a strain?"

She nodded.

Sam helped her undress and then sat her down on a nearby stool as he got his clothes off. He helped her into the shower and gently washed her hair. She let the warm spray splash on her face while Sam tenderly scrubbed her. Once out, he reached for a towel and wiped her off, then sat her down again and dried her hair, after which he carried her into the bedroom.

"Where's your nightgown?"

Lynn's eyes pointed to a drawer. Sam helped her get one on, then pulled aside the blankets. After being tucked in, with heavy eyelids blinking, Lynn said, "Turn off the lights and come to sleep."

The huge bed with its massive headboard creaked as Sam got in. The cool pillow felt good as he reached for Lynn who instantly clung to him as if her life depended on his protection. He put his arm around her and gently stroked her head until her breathing became fainter and fainter and the iron grip slowly melted away.

The night fog that had settled on the earth and mingled with the smoke seeped in through the open window. The sound of the downstairs door being locked drifted in, then the light from the kitchen vanished and all became dark. Every once in a while a loud crack exploded from one of the old hand-hewed barn beams, now red-hot chunks glowing on the blackened pile outside.

CHAPTER 31

Lynn mixed some peat moss with the dirt at the bottom of the hole, then carefully pressed in four daffodil bulbs and covered them over. She sat back on her haunches and looked at the greenhouse at the bottom of the hill. The year and a half since the Bedeskys had been there seemed like a lifetime away.

Lynn's eyes roamed the horizon to the spot where the old horse barn had stood. She forced the memory of those hideous last moments out of her mind, then reached over and gently petted Commander who was lying next to her.

The woods were ablaze with fall color and the sweet smell of fallen leaves scented the air.

She got up and put her two pails and the shovel in the wheelbarrow and rolled it down exactly five paces. Instead of digging a new hole, she leaned against the shovel and remembered that summer. A lot of the things Cal had said to her now seemed like he was trying to tell her he was dying. She had been so disappointed he didn't live to see the baby. In the spring she planted a row of rosemary around the gravesite and tended it herself knowing that his son would be too busy with the farm to do so.

Her syndicated show would have meant more to her if only Cal had lived to share in the glory. Then she thought about Ken and his parents, Emma and Cale, and knew they'd all be proud of her and the way she kept the farm. Even though her legal name was now Lynn Richardson-Reynolds, the business would always be known as Richardson's Herbs and Seeds and she was certain Jess would follow in her footsteps, keeping the Richardson name on the farm.

She almost laughed out loud when she thought of Ralph Weisman and what the success of her show meant to him. By now, she had finally warmed up to the man. Every time she came back from Boston, Sam and Jess looked forward to her good-hearted imitation of his latest impresario affectation.

Commander flopped down with a humph and the hole was dug. Rubber wheels on gravel sounded behind Lynn and she turned and saw Jess coming down the hill with the stroller. Waving, she shouted, "Hi, sweetheart," then got down on her knees and prepared the ground for another planting.

In minutes Jess was standing next to her. Little Elizabeth reached up to him and he picked her up and held her in his arms. How different the two looked. Jess was almost eleven now and looking more and more like Ken with the Richardson's trademark blond hair and gray-blue eyes.

The baby stared down at her mother and sucked on her teething ring. Her eyes were blue too, but deep and dark like her father's and her head crowned with a sea of the same black curls.

"Dad said he'd be quitting in an hour." Jess laughed. "He said for me to tell you he was *real* hungry."

Lynn finished covering the bulbs, stood up and brushed off her jeans.

"I guess that means I better get the dinner going."

Her hands were too dirty to touch the baby, so she just nuzzled her. Elizabeth tapped her with the gooey teething ring and they all laughed.

Jess squeezed his sister and said, "Mom, you should have seen her with dad. She was standing in her walker, watching the screen and rocking to the music."

Lynn shook her head and smiled. She didn't know if the child's affinity for music was hereditary or just the result of spending so much time listening to her father play the piano. Because of Lynn's work at the nursery and her syndicated show, from the time the child was born her father took her up to his studio every day and cared for her while he composed.

Ever since the success of the Sandini film, Sam had more than enough of the kind of work he really wanted, eventually giving up the *Men in Blue* serial.

Instead of finding the care of his daughter a chore, Sam seemed to relish it. Every time he needed a break or time to have the music settle in his head he would play with her. Once Lynn walked in and found him dancing joyously around the room with Elizabeth; and just like her father, the child threw back her head and laughed.

Lynn tossed everything into the wheelbarrow while Jess put the baby back in her stroller. Then they started down the hill toward the farmhouse with Commander at their side.

Just before they crossed the road, Lynn turned and looked at the house on the hill, then the small mounds of dirt that lined the driveway.

"Next spring the daffodils will be beautiful, Jess."

The boy stood with his mother and studied the landscape.

"Mom, you know what I was thinking?"

"No, honey. What?"

"A hundred years from now, when none of us are around any more, will they still be there?"

"Sure, honey. In big, beautiful clumps."

"Do you think anyone will wonder who planted them?"

"Yes, sweetheart. I do."